A Comedy of Erinn

To Lauren —
Our adventures
continue!

Love,
Celie

KENSINGTON BOOKS are published by

Kensington Publishing Corp.
119 West 40th Street
New York, NY 10018

All Kensington titles, imprints, and distributed lines are available at special quantity discounts for bulk purchases for sales promotion, premiums, fund-raising, and educational or institutional use.

Special book excerpts or customized printings can also be created to fit specific needs. For details, write or phone the office of the Kensington Special Sales Manager: Kensington Publishing Corp., 119 West 40th Street, New York, NY 10018. Attn. Special Sales Department. Phone: 1-800-221-2647.

First Electronic Edition: September 2013
eISBN-13: 978-1-60183-124-8
eISBN-10: 1-60183-124-2

First Print Edition: September 2013
ISBN-13: 978-1-60183-125-5
ISBN-10: 1-60183-125-0

Printed in the United States of America

To my mother-in-law, Fionna
Who never, never, never gave up

Acknowledgments

A job in cable TV does give a person lots of ideas for a book.

Robb Weller and Gary Grossman, thank you for years of employment, understanding, and the chance to be part of Weller-Grossman Productions. Alessandra Ascoli, Laura Chambers, Sergio Coronado, Geoff Coyle, Jolene Dodson, Lisa Ely, Michelle Hobird, Christine Jagolino, Peter Karlin, Cassie Lambert, Monica Lloyd, Jane Manfolk, Kelly Mooney, Renato Moore, Clare O'Donohue, Lorelei Plotczyk, Steve Rice, Gilmore Rizzo, Riley Ray Robbins, Jill Roozenboom, Stephanie Rose, Suzie Segal, Dave Shikiar, Lisa Sichi, Jorge Suarez, George Sylak, Duane Tudahl, Andrew Wollman,—the list goes on—thanks to all of you for rocking my world and for just being so damn entertaining.

To Tara Sandler, Jennifer Davidson, Drew Hallmann, Robbie White, and my new cohorts at Pietown Productions, thanks for keeping the adventure going.

To my friend and mentor, Jodi Thomas, who guided me so lovingly into this series, a huge thank-you, and to Jodi's Pioneers, who cheered me on. There were many days when I wrote just so I wouldn't disappoint you.

To Jim Lara, who lived through many versions of this story over the years—you are a treasure.

Thanks, Mom, for withholding your judgment on everything but my writing—you have always been my first and bravest editor. To my agent, Sharon Bowers, and my editor, Martin Biro; it's still a thrill to just type your names. Thank you always.

To my brilliant family, both by blood and by marriage; I am grateful to be part of such a tribe. And finally, to my husband, Billy—I hope to be the person you see when you look at me through that lens of yours.

CHAPTER 1

Erinn Elizabeth Wolf leaned on the fence that kept visitors from sliding down the bluff into the ocean. She glowered at the young couple snuggling on *her* bench—in *her* park. The young man and woman occasionally looked at the water, but spent most of their time sinking into each other's eyes.

The sun was just dipping into the water. The world was suddenly filled with coral, russet, violet, periwinkle, and cornflower. Erinn was getting impatient, very impatient. She decided to take matters into her own hands.

She joined the couple on the bench. Nudging the young woman aside with her hip, she heaved her oversized bag onto the bench and hunkered down.

"Look at that sunset," Erinn heard the young woman sigh softly. "God's masterpiece."

Erinn snorted.

"God wouldn't have a prayer creating a sunset like that," she said. "This is a masterpiece only city smog could produce."

The couple ignored her. It was obvious Erinn was going to have to crank up the annoyance factor. She studied the couple. Gauging that they were liberal arts students from one of the local universities, Erinn formulated a plan. With a quick prayer, asking forgiveness from her beloved Democratic Party, Erinn said, "Since he's now out of office, I think Dick Cheney is really coming into his own, don't you?"

The couple left their spot on the bench—he frowning, she beaming with politically correct good will.

That's one way to get your bench back.

Erinn glanced at the rapidly advancing sunset and realized she had not a moment to spare. She reached into her bag and pulled out a battered, hand-held video camera. She quickly and expertly adjusted her settings and started panning steadily over the horizon. She was getting pretty good at her camera work—if she did say so herself.

The view at Palisades Park in Santa Monica, California, was the billion-dollar vista featured in movies since cinema's golden era. Although Erinn had lived in Santa Monica for nine years, she never got used to the incredible beauty the park offered.

Whenever Erinn was shooting, she was nimble—and confident in her movements. But as soon as she shut the camera off, a transformation took place. She suddenly appeared heavier and slower, as if gravity had taken hold of her—as if she were rooted to the earth. When the sun had gone, Erinn stowed her camera and made her way home. She didn't walk far, as she was the owner of another masterpiece—one of the few remaining Victorian houses on Santa Monica's main drag.

While Erinn would never be mistaken for the stuff of fairy tales, the courtyard of her house looked like something out of *Beauty and the Beast*. The old climbing roses that crawled up the lacy wooden pillars also disguised layers of peeling paint on the porch. An uneven walkway curled quaintly toward the side yard.

She retrieved a large silver key from a keychain that looked like a medieval jailer's and fitted it into the front door lock. The door squeaked open, and Erinn was home.

She shrugged off her coat, hung it on an old-fashioned hall tree, and carefully put her camera aside. She caught a glimpse of herself in the mirror and rearranged a few bobby pins, hoping to control her wild, coarse hair. Even with her hair pulled back in a severe ponytail, corkscrew tendrils tended to escape. Her hair was still mostly pepper, but now with a sprinkling of salt. Erinn had made no attempt to halt the aging process, which she knew was practically a sacrilege in Southern California—but she stood firm against useless vanity. Even so, without the weight of the camera bag on her shoulders, hints of the graceful young woman she used to be were still evident in her posture and the way she moved. Almost miraculously she had remained an extremely attractive woman.

Not that she cared.

Not that anybody cared.

The doorbell rang. She peered out. A man in ripped jeans, a tight T-shirt, and carrying a skateboard was trying to open the gate. Erinn instinctively stepped out of sight, but kept her eye on the man. He managed to get the latch open and headed up Erinn's path. He marched up to the porch and knocked.

It suddenly occurred to Erinn that this must be someone who wanted to rent the guesthouse.

"Damn it, Suzanna," she cursed under her breath.

Her younger sister, Suzanna, was worried that Erinn would lose the house if she didn't generate some income. She had placed a rental ad on craigslist without Erinn's knowledge or consent. Erinn balked when she heard about it, but promised her sister she'd keep an open mind and at least meet with a few people.

The man, in wraparound sunglasses, knocked on the door again.

She yanked open the heavy wood-beamed door.

"Hey there, how you doing?" asked the young man, as he removed his glasses. He put out his hand by way of introduction. "Craigslist."

He had the casual gait of a man—Erinn would put him at about twenty-eight—at ease with himself. He was also extremely well built, with biceps peeking out from under the sleeve of his snug T-shirt.

"That's an interesting mode of transportation," Erinn said, indicating the skateboard.

"Yeah," he said. "It's a pain in the ass sometimes, but it's a real chick magnet."

"Pardon?"

"The babes really go for a guy on a skateboard."

"*I* don't."

"Well, you're not a . . ."

He propped his skateboard against the house and stepped inside, without invitation. Erinn followed him. He walked around, whistling appreciatively.

"Wow, this place is awesome," he said.

He walked into the living room and started to pull open the curtains.

"Dude! You have an ocean view . . . why do you have the curtains shut?"

"If you must know, I like to keep to myself. I like the privacy," Erinn said. "Besides, I find Southern Californians vastly overestimate sunshine."

"Well, it's a cool place anyway," he said as Erinn closed the curtains. He squinted in the darkness. "You could do a spread in *Better Caves and Gardens*."

The cat rubbed against the young man's legs.

"Sweet! I love animals," he said, scooping up the cat. "Whoa! This is one fat cat!"

Erinn reached out and patted the cat, a large, flat-faced, silver point Himalayan.

"His name is Caro," she said.

"Hello, Car-ro," he said, pronouncing two *r*'s.

"It's pronounced with one *r*," Erinn said. "Car-o. It's Italian for 'dear one.' "

"Isn't that what I said?"

"No . . . you said '*Car*-ro' . . . that's Spanish for 'truck.' "

"Well, no offense, dude, but Truck's a much better name for this guy," said the young man as he put the cat down and headed toward the kitchen.

Erinn kept her face impassive. This boy was not winning her over. "And my name, in case you're interested, is Erinn."

"Wow, nice kitchen, Er . . . Do you mind if I call you 'Er'?"

"Massively," said Erinn.

"What about Rinn? Or Rin Tin Tin?"

Does he want the guesthouse or did he just come here to insult me?

"Why would you call me Rin Tin Tin?"

"Just shortening the process, dude. That's how nicknames are made. You start out with something that makes sense, like Rinn, and pretty soon you're Rin Tin Tin. It's totally random."

"I didn't catch *your* name," Erinn said.

"Jude . . . Raphael."

Common ground at last.

"Ah!" she said. "As in the artist!"

"As in the turtle," Jude said. "Hey, let's go check out my guesthouse!"

He stood and followed a stormy Erinn into the backyard.

If love could have kept the place up, Erinn would have had no worries. But like everything else about the Wolf residence, the yard was looking a little down-at-the-heels. The one-room guesthouse was nestled in a patch of large fig trees. It was a miniature Victorian, complete with a tiny porch and hanging swing. Its bright red door stood out from the greenish tone of the rest of the exterior, and its window boxes overflowed with geraniums.

"This is it," she said, trying to hide the pride she felt in the place.

Jude stood back and looked the building over.

"Huh."

Erinn turned on him.

"Is there a problem?" she asked.

"Nah," he said. "I'm just not really big on these gingerbready kind of places, ya know? They're kinda gay."

"Gay?"

"I mean . . . not in a bad way. Like . . . not even in a gay way, you know?"

"Shall we go inside?" asked Erinn, since she hadn't the faintest idea.

She clicked on the light but didn't step inside. Her eyes scanned the room lovingly. Jude stood on the porch, looking in over Erinn's head. The room had an open floor plan, and every inch of space counted. A small kitchen was fitted into one corner and a bathroom was tucked discreetly into another. There was a wrought-iron daybed that functioned as a seating area as well as a bed and a tiny, mosaic-tiled café table and chair set. Even in this small space, there was an entire wall of bookcases. Erinn turned to Jude.

"Is this gay as well?" she asked as she walked into the room, Jude at her heels.

"Hey! If you're gay, I don't care. Really," Jude said. "I'm, personally, not gay. I'm, you know, metro/hetero. But whatever floats your boat, I say."

"Thank you. I was so worried it might be offensive to you somehow, if I were gay."

"Whatever, Erinn. I mean . . . gay is as gay does, right?"

"Well, obviously, that's true," Erinn said. "But I don't do as gay does, because I'm not gay."

"Whoa . . . you know that old saying . . . something about . . . you're protesting a shitload."

"Are you perhaps thinking of 'The lady doth protest too much?' from *Hamlet*?"

"Moving on, Erinn," Jude said. "Your sexuality isn't the only thing in the world, right? There's food, the beach, the theater . . ."

Erinn winced and walked around the room, trying to ignore the cretin who was taking up much too much space—and oxygen—in her little sanctuary. She started opening blinds to make the room seem somehow bigger.

"I don't go to the theater," Erinn said.

"What do you mean?" asked Jude, trying out the daybed. "Erinn Elizabeth Wolf, the famous New York playwright, doesn't go to the theater? That's crazy!"

Erinn almost choked, she was so surprised by this comment. Any use of her full name by someone other than her mother usually meant she was being recognized. Jude had his back to her and was studying a line of books in the bookcase. He turned to look at her.

"Did you realize your initials are E.E.W.? EEEEEEwwwwwwww."

Erinn tried to ignore Jude's inept attempt at winning her over with a nickname. But she definitely wasn't finished with the conversation.

"You . . . you've heard of me?" she asked.

"Sure. I was a theater major. You're in the history books."

Erinn tried—and failed—to hide her dismay. She was surprised to hear that, at forty-three, she was already considered a relic and consigned to history. She tried not to let on that Jude had delivered a verbal slap.

"Not the *history* books, exactly . . . but . . ." he said.

"But . . . like . . . you know," offered Erinn, who could see he did not mean to hurt her feelings.

"Well, yeah."

Erinn sat down at the mosaic table. Jude continued to look around the room and stopped to admire a photograph. It was a close-up of a wrinkled old man playing checkers.

"This is cool," Jude said.

Erinn studied the picture, lost in thought, remembering the first time she saw Oscar sitting in the little park across from her loft in Manhattan. He was always so focused on his game. That was nearly twenty years ago . . . by now, he was probably dead, or just another lost New York memory.

"I took that years ago," she said.

"You took that? Awesome."

Erinn warmed to the praise.

"Well, I've always been interested in the visual arts. I'm actually learning how to shoot an HD camera and I'm thinking of trying my hand at editing, too. I like to keep up on those sort of things."

"Hmmm," Jude said. "That's pretty cool for somebody . . . uh . . . not totally young . . . to be into that stuff."

"Let's talk about you, shall we?" Erinn asked as her good will ebbed away.

"Sure," said Jude, grabbing the chair opposite her. "Well, let's see . . . I'm in the business . . . television mostly. I mean, in this town, isn't everybody?"

Erinn looked at Jude thoughtfully. What could Suzanna have possibly been thinking? She'd been hoping to rent to a fellow artist, but everyone who applied seemed to be from *television.* Erinn realized that her mind had wandered, and she tried to tune back in to whatever it was Jude might be saying.

". . . but, you know, until I can produce my own work, I pick up assignments wherever I can."

Erinn watched Jude as he picked up the rental agreement on the table.

"Well, I don't think you really need to read that just yet. . . ." she said, trying to grab the document that would have damned her to her own personal hell should he sign it.

Jude picked up a pen from the table. Erinn watched in silence as he lost interest in the document and started doing curls with the pen, watching his bicep rise and fall with the motion. He was mesmerized. Erinn coughed, hoping to get his attention. Jude looked up and smiled sheepishly.

"I read that you should work out whenever—and wherever—you can," he said.

"Oh? You read that?"

Jude laughed. "Well, I downloaded a workout video to my iPod so I could listen to it while I was skateboarding. Same thing."

Erinn arched an eyebrow. Jude suddenly looked up at her.

"What about Tin Lizzy? That would be an awesome nickname for you!"

"You know, Jude, I'm not sure this is going to work out."

He looked up. "Oh? Why not?"

"Well," Erinn faltered. "I just think that, if two people live in such close proximity to each other, there should be some symbiosis . . . if you get my drift."

Jude looked at Erinn for a minute, then smiled.

"Oh, you mean 'cause I'm in such good shape," he said. "Don't worry about that. I can help you get rid of that spare tire in no time."

"No, no, no," Erinn said. "I appreciate your offer. Although I wasn't aware I *had* a spare tire."

"Oh, big-time."

"It was more along the lines of, well, I don't feel we're . . . intellectually compatible."

Jude frowned.

"I'm not smart enough to rent your *guesthouse*?"

He held up the rental agreement and waved it in her face.

"Is there an I.Q. test attached to this?" he asked.

Erinn stood up so fast she knocked the chair over, and stormed out of the guesthouse. Jude sprinted after her, and Erinn wheeled on him.

"I'm sorry, Jude, but clearly this isn't going to work."

"Tell me about it. You think you're some sort of god because you wrote one important play a hundred years ago? Nobody can even make a joke around you? I'm out of here."

"I assume you can see yourself out?"

"If I can find my way around your huge ego, yeah," Jude replied, as he walked toward the main house. He stepped over the cat, which was sunbathing on the walkway.

"See ya around, Truck."

Apparently, Jude had not succeeded in giving *her* a nickname, but poor Caro did not escape unscathed.

Erinn went back into the kitchen, stung by Jude's comments. To distract herself, she decided to make a pot of soup. She pulled out her large stockpot, added some homemade chicken stock, and started scrubbing tubers in a fury. *Who does he think he is, talking to me that way?* she thought. *I dodged a bullet with that one.*

The phone rang. Erinn wiped off her hands and reached for the cordless, hesitating just long enough to grab her half-moon glasses, and checked the caller I.D.

It was Suzanna.

Erinn put the phone down without answering it. She took off her glasses and returned to her soup.

CHAPTER 2

Erinn made sure the front door was securely bolted for the night and walked into her living room. She flipped on the light and admired the heavy, dark furnishings.

Sunshine, for God's sake. She bristled as she thought back to that half-wit Jude's reaction to this thoughtful, peaceful room.

She sat down at her computer—a twenty-four-inch behemoth that looked out of place on a highly polished clawfoot desk. She settled in to pay a few bills online. Caro pounced upon her, eager for attention. Erinn opened her eyes and scratched him thoughtfully.

"The bills won't pay themselves, Caro," she said, as she held the cat up and looked into his green, unblinking eyes.

With a sigh she went upstairs and changed into her men's striped pajamas, brushed her teeth dutifully for two minutes, and headed back downstairs to the kitchen. One of Erinn's little rebellions was that she brushed her teeth before she had her late-night hot chocolate.

Caro padded softly down the steps behind her.

Erinn's kitchen, like every room in the house, was a monument to a more gracious era. The room was square, and the cabinetry was white with glass window inserts, so all the contents were proudly on display. A KitchenAid mixer, a Cuisinart, a Deni electric pressure cooker, a Vibiemme Domobar espresso machine: all had a place in the Wolf kitchen. If times were tough, they weren't always.

As Erinn stirred her cocoa, she heard a key jangling at the back door. She grabbed another mug and smiled slightly as she started another serving of hot chocolate. The key continued its clanking, grinding medley for several seconds. Finally, the back door swung open.

"Hi, Erinn. I was in the neighborhood . . . ," offered a voice from the door. "Can I come in?"

"Don't let the cat—" called Erinn as Suzanna wrestled with the key still jammed in the lock.

Caro scooted out the door.

"—out," Erinn finished.

Suzanna flung herself into the room, laden with bags from Mommies and Babies, Jellybeans in a Jar, and Naturally Natural Yarn. Suzanna was seven months' pregnant and was taking to the experience like Mother Nature to spring.

"I can give you a new key," Erinn said.

"That's OK. This way you hear me coming," Suzanna said. "I don't want to scare you."

She set her new purchases on the table and dumped out several maternity outfits and skeins of orange, brown, and lime-green yarn. Erinn picked up the yarn and examined it—could this be for the *baby*?

"It's not your lack of skill with a lock that scares me," Erinn said.

Suzanna was in her midthirties. She had recently married Eric, the object of her desire since high school. Suzanna owned the Rollicking Bun Tea Shoppe and Book Nook: Home of the Epic Scone on the other side of town.

"I thought orange and green were safe for either sex," Suzanna said.

She and Eric had decided that they didn't want to know the gender of their baby beforehand.

Erinn watched as Suzanna continued to unload her bags.

"God! I love shopping," said Suzanna.

"You were shopping? At this hour?"

"Erinn, it's eight-thirty. People shop at eight-thirty."

Suzanna tossed a small box to her sister, who caught it clumsily.

"I bought you a lipstick!" she said. "Try it! It will look great with your . . . pajamas."

Ever since Suzanna had gotten married, she'd been obsessed with

Erinn's single status. She was on a one-woman campaign to get Erinn out in the world.

Suzanna and Erinn had not been close as children. Erinn was nearly ten years older, and had moved to New York City when Suzanna was still young. Since moving to Santa Monica, the siblings had gotten closer, and as she examined the lipstick, Erinn doubted the wisdom of this. She eyed the waxy red tube with suspicion.

Suzanna snatched it back. She grabbed her sister's mouth and forced it into a pucker. "Don't move. . . ."

Suzanna finished the application, whipped out a mirror from her purse, and handed it to her sister. Erinn inspected her new lips.

"If one is a sheepdog, why try to look like a Pekingese?" she asked as she returned the mirror.

"Well, Scooby-Doo, you could do with a little lift, that's all. Don't you remember when people used to say you looked like Valerie Bertinelli?"

Erinn nodded, trying not to gag on the waxy taste of the lipstick.

"Well, since she's been on Jenny Craig . . . not so much."

"And one lipstick will do for me what a year on Jenny Craig did for Valerie? I think not."

"Baby steps, big sister. Baby steps."

Erinn was grateful for her sister's concern, but missed the days when Suzanna was in awe of her and treated her with respect instead of with incessant camaraderie. While her sister reloaded her bags, Erinn covertly wiped off her new lipstick and took a hefty sip of cocoa.

"Well?" Suzanna asked.

"Well what?"

"Did you find a tenant for the guesthouse?"

"No, I did not," Erinn said. "And I have to say, I think neither Craig nor his list is the way to go."

"You aren't trying."

"It's my guesthouse, Suzanna. I don't have to try. They do."

"Well, keep looking."

"Let's change the subject, shall we?"

Erinn had pulled out her big sister voice, which wasn't really fair. She knew Suzanna would cave in.

"OK," Suzanna said. "How's the new play?"

Erinn got up and went into the living room. Suzanna had started casting yarn onto a set of large circular needles and had to scoot after her sister to catch up.

"How long have you been practicing that casual delivery?" Erinn asked.

"Uh . . . all week, if you must know," Suzanna said, following closely at her sister's heels.

Erinn thumped down on the sofa and put a pillow over her head.

"Erinn, come on! I'm worried about you. You stay holed up in here day after day, not talking to anybody. . . ."

"That is not true," Erinn said from under the pillow. "I had a very interesting conversation with a nice couple I met in the park just this afternoon."

Suzanna sat next to Erinn. She pulled the pillow off her sister's head and tossed it aside. Erinn noticed the corners of the pillow were a little frayed. *But, hey, get in line.*

"Listen, I'm not just talking to you as a sister," Suzanna said. "Mimi was in the shop yesterday, and she said you've been avoiding her."

Mimi was Erinn's agent.

"She shouldn't be discussing my business with you!"

"She's worried about you. She says she needs something to sell."

"And what if I don't have anything right now? She'll drop me?"

"How should I know? Hey, we forgot our cocoa," Suzanna said.

"I'll get it," Erinn said.

Erinn headed back to the kitchen. She tested the temperature by dipping her little finger into the cocoa. She put the cups in the microwave to reheat. While she watched the cups go around and around, she suddenly noticed how quiet it was. Leaving the cocoa to its carousel ride, she dashed frantically back into the living room, but she was too late. Suzanna was staring intently at the computer screen.

Erinn tried to block the screen and said, "It's not ready!"

"Just a peek!"

"No! It's still rough."

"I'll make allowances."

Erinn couldn't budge her sister. Suzanna countered every move like a prizefighter—years of sisterly combat had her trained—and the two women stared at the screen.

MRS. FURST

John, you may be the president, and this might be the White House, but it's still our home . . . where the buffalo roam and the deer and the antelope play.

Erinn turned off the monitor and started to pace.

"It's hopeless," she said. "I'm hopeless."

"It's not that bad," Suzanna said. "It's very patriotic."

"Do you think Mimi will like it?"

"Oh, who cares if she likes it? She's an agent . . . she only cares ten percent," Suzanna said as Erinn chewed on a thumbnail. "I, on the other hand, am your sister. So I care one hundred and ten percent."

Erinn turned, midpace, and stared at her sister.

"That's a good line," she said, going back to the computer. "That's a very good line. I bet I can use that."

Suzanna smiled wanly. She started to twist her hair nervously as Erinn's fingers blazed over the keyboard.

"Sorry, Suzanna, you need to go. I need to write!" Erinn said without looking up. "Could you let yourself out? And let the cat in?"

"Sure," Suzanna said, kissing Erinn's hair. "Good night."

Erinn glanced up as her sister waddled away in the muted light of the living room. She saw the little girl who used to look up to her. *How did it come to this?* Erinn wondered, as she stared back at the computer screen.

How did it ever come to this?

CHAPTER 3

It was Wednesday, and Wednesday was Erinn's favorite day.

She wandered down 3rd Street, passing all the high-end stores, her enormous messenger bag slung over her shoulder. Try as she might, she was not able to bypass the Apple Store, a Pleasure Island for anyone with a taste for the latest electronics. Telling herself she would only stop in for a minute, Erinn entered the store to check out the computers and new software.

She stared at a computerized sign overhead that announced YOUR GENIUS IS HERE TO HELP. Scanning the store, her eyes briefly met those of Steven, who quickly looked away. Erinn understood that the poor man found her questions annoying, since she would spend hours trying out new programs and never buy anything. She knew that when her ship came in—again—she would make it up to him with massive amounts of purchasing. But there was no point trying to explain that. For now, he would just have to suffer. Erinn went up and tapped him on the shoulder. He smiled thinly.

"Hello, Ms. Wolf. On your way to the farmers' market?"

"It's Wednesday, isn't it?"

"Is there anything I can help you with today?"

"Yes. I read online that a new version of Final Cut Pro just came out. I've been thinking of learning how to edit."

Steven pointed to an empty computer station.

"We just installed it," he said. "Go take it for a test drive."

Erinn headed over to the computer, but indicated that Steven should follow her.

Knitting her brow, she tried to navigate the system, but to no avail. She turned to Steven for help. He pulled up footage of a motorcycle careening wildly around California mountains.

"Here," Steven said. "Let's try editing this commercial. It will give you a sense of what you can do."

Erinn had no desire—or any intention—of editing a motorcycle commercial.

"Steven, I don't think this is going to help me."

He looked at her and blinked.

"No, Ms. Wolf, I don't think this will help you, either."

She wondered if Steven wanted to get rid of her. She knew she could be difficult. But it seemed insane to her that the geniuses had decided that, in order to get a grasp of the editing system, she should be working on a motorcycle commercial. She had no use for this sort of . . . *commercial* . . . editing. Just the sound of the word set her teeth on edge. She wanted to learn to edit the way she wanted to edit! Or at least, the way she thought she might want to edit, once she understood how it all worked.

"This is all about postproduction, Ms. Wolf," Steven said. "Maybe you should be worrying about scripting before you tackle this."

Was he actually telling her that she should be writing? Who did he think he was—her sister? Well, he thought he was a genius, of course. He'd been told he was a genius. *Genius* was on his badge after *Hi, My Name Is Steven.*

Erinn tipped her half-moon glasses down, studying Steven as he looked at the computer screen. She could not read him. Her genius was a sphinx.

"If I'm going to start making my own films, I need to have a complete vision," Erinn said.

Steven cleared his throat.

"If you're going to make a film, I think you should concentrate on your script. Especially if you don't want to learn editing the way we teach it."

Erinn hesitated, then said, "I'm having trouble with my script right now."

"Well, then, you don't need to worry about editing at all."

Erinn left the Apple Store, demoralized, but changed her mind about one thing. Steven really was a genius.

Her mood lifted as she approached the farmers' market, which was her every-Wednesday destination. The Santa Monica Farmers' Market offered fresh produce, flowers, and, incongruently, soap, to the locals at a fraction of the cost of the supermarkets. Erinn looked around the thriving market—even in December, fruits and vegetables were laid out in full force.

That's one thing I have to give Los Angeles, she thought. *No outdoor farmers' markets on 42nd Street in winter.*

She pulled out her little expandable pull-cart and unfolded a coolie hat, both of which she had stored in her messenger bag. She started loading up on yams, multicolored fingerling potatoes, carrots, and green beans. She eyed the pale yellow and pink orchids, which reared over the heads of the shoppers in an explosion of floral majesty, but she didn't buy one. Erinn remembered a time when she thought nothing of tossing two or three heavily laden moth orchids into her cart, but those days were gone. She chided herself: *On hold, not gone*.

Thinking about money—or the lack thereof—always got her down. And, of course, as her bank account diminished, her sister's nagging had escalated from gentle to volcanic. Erinn recalled all the strange creatures craigslist had sent her way over the last few weeks. Was it her fault that everyone was impossible to deal with?

"What was wrong with Bunny?" Suzanna had asked about a possible tenant. "She was a writer! You would have had tons to talk about!"

"She communicates with the spirit world," said Erinn.

"At least she communicates with somebody," said Suzanna.

"She told me my spirit guide was Dorothy Parker."

"You could do worse."

"Very true. As a matter of fact, if you recall, I have often been compared to Dorothy Parker."

"That's great, Erinn. But don't forget," said Suzanna, stroking her pregnant belly, "Dorothy Parker died a lonely old woman."

Deep in thought over her sister's words, Erinn frowned at the display of red and purple carrots. She absentmindedly held a large arrow-shaped Italian cauliflower to the sun. She loved the way the sun backlit the vegetable—you could see every detail outlined perfectly. Erinn could study the Italian cauliflower for hours—some would say it was an Italian broccoli, but she knew better. The florets grew in a spiral, one after another, according to a rhythm called the Fibonacci series, which was the origin of all aesthetic harmony according to Renaissance artists. Erinn marveled that proof of this medieval concept was sitting right in her hand.

"Excuse me, madam," said a deep, heavily accented voice behind her. "If you are not interested in that particular romanesco, would you allow me to purchase it?"

Erinn realized her mind had wandered. How long had she been standing in front of this vegetable stand? She turned to apologize to the man behind her.

"Mi scusi, signore," Erinn said. *"Stavo sognando ad occhi aperti."*

Erinn almost stumbled on her words—she was hoping she had said, "I was daydreaming"—as she turned around and took in the gorgeous man smiling at her.

"How did you know that I was Italian?" he asked.

Erinn felt her face getting hot. She had always had a weakness for smoldering Italian good looks, but this man, with his liquid mercury eyes, was almost impossibly handsome.

"I . . . I . . . you said . . . only Italians call this a romanesco. Most Americans don't even know what it is!"

Out of practice conversing with attractive men in any language, Erinn looked down at her feet.

"Ahh . . . you are so ripe you are ready to burst."

Erinn froze, then looked up, relieved to see the man had picked up a pear and was holding it up to the sun for inspection.

"Gorgeous, no?" he asked. "But you must have it; I will choose another."

He held the fruit out to Erinn.

"Oh, no," she said, pushing it back toward him. "Please. It's yours."

The man, with his thick head of graying hair, put out his well-manicured hand. "*Grazie.* My name is Massimo Minecozzi."

"Erinn Wolf."

"Piacere."

Erinn smiled and went about her business choosing fruits and vegetables. While she was studying the spaghetti squash, Massimo nodded good-bye and headed into the crowd. Erinn paid for her purchases quickly and tried to keep him in her sights. She followed him to the berry stand.

"So we meet again," said Massimo when he caught Erinn's eye.

He had purchased several cartons of raspberries and was packing them gently into a well-designed grocery cart.

"You must be a big fan of raspberries," Erinn said, trying to seem interested in some blueberries.

Massimo shrugged. "The berries . . . they speak to me."

Erinn picked up a three-pack of assorted berries and indicated that she was ready to pay for them. Before the vendor could reach for her money, Massimo lifted the carton of the berries out of her hands.

"The blackberries are bruised," he said. "Let me choose."

Massimo looked over the berries with an expert eye. Erinn was not one to sit on her tuffet while a man took the reins, but this man appeared to be some kind of berry expert. Massimo didn't seem to find a carton to his liking, and instead created his own three-pack. He bowed slightly as he handed it to her.

"These are *perfetto*," he said.

"Grazie, signore," Erinn said.

"How is it that you speak Italian?"

Erinn hesitated. She hadn't spoken Italian in years and she was nearly breathless from the emotions that were bobbing to the surface—the bitter fighting with the sweet.

"I have loved many, many things about Italy. Especially the language."

"You speak it well."

"*No, signore, ma grazie. Il mio Italiano è orribille, ma amo parlarlo.*"

Massimo seemed to be studying her, which made Erinn extremely nervous. She never had gotten the hang of the Italian male's undivided attention. She turned back to the vendor and waited for her change.

"May I buy you a cup of coffee?" Massimo waited patiently for her to pocket her coins. "The espresso here is very good."

Erinn felt heat rising up her neck—she was well out of her depth and she knew it. But she, too, had always found the coffee delicious at this local farmers' market, so she followed him to the espresso bar. Erinn had often wondered if it was only in prestigious, pretentious Santa Monica that there was a coffee bar settled snugly among the summer squash and the tangelos. But, in the scheme of things, good coffee was good coffee—why question it? Today, Erinn was grateful for the coffee bar for many reasons.

They sat in what she hoped was companionable silence instead of in the acute awkwardness she felt. Finally, Erinn found her voice.

"How long have you been in America?" she asked.

"Just two years. And those years I live in New York City. I am an actor, and people, they tell me I must come to Los Angeles. And so!"

Erinn was of the opinion that real actors belonged solely in New York. Serious artists, New York; vapid stars, Los Angeles. But he was here now, and it wouldn't really help for Erinn to tell him he'd made a terrible mistake, so she kept it to herself.

"What films did you make in New York? Anything I would know?"

"I was not a success in New York. In Italy, yes. But here, no. I am in Los Angeles to try something new." He smiled at Erinn. "Whatever that may be."

Massimo told Erinn that he found Los Angeles, as a whole, very confusing.

"It is so big," he said. "I still look for a place to live, but I am not happy with what I see. I want to live in the vicinity of the water, but I cannot afford to live in the vicinity of the water. I have only some money. While I wait for success, I serve a restaurant."

"Do you mean, you are a waiter?"

Massimo looked offended.

"I am a chef! At Bella Bella."

Erinn had never heard of Bella Bella but nodded enthusiastically. She had obviously wounded his pride by calling him a waiter. She remembered how carefully you needed to phrase things around artistic Italians. It was all coming back to her. Erinn looked at him. She was not one to jump into anything at this stage of her life, but it seemed as if destiny had not only taken her hand but slapped her across the cheek.

"You should come home with me," she said.

"But I hardly know you."

Erinn, horrified at the implication, tried to clarify. Massimo laughed an easy laugh, and Erinn relaxed. She could tell he was just teasing.

"I have a guesthouse for rent."

"To me?" asked Massimo, beautiful brown eyes growing wide.

"Well, let's go see," said Erinn.

The two chatted amicably as they strolled up Ocean Avenue. Massimo, deeming Erinn's cart unworthy, had loaded her purchases into his own and he pulled it along as they walked. He told Erinn about his life in Italy, how interesting he found America, and his change of heart toward California wines.

"When I first am to America," he said, "I refuse to drink the California wine. But now . . . I think the California wine is very good. Sometime."

"It's interesting that you should mention California wine. . . ."

Erinn warmed to the subject of California wines. Although she was born in New York, her parents had moved to Napa Valley when she was nine—a year before Suzanna was born. Although she moved back to New York City as a college student and didn't return to California for almost twenty years, a large part of her heart remained in Napa.

Massimo, who seemed to have a short attention span, pointed out a large white Spanish Revival building called the Sovereign Hotel.

"That is made by the woman who made Hearst Castle," said Massimo.

Erinn smiled. She remembered when she, along with half of Santa Monica, was under the impression that the building was designed by a firebrand named Julia Morgan, the woman who designed Hearst Castle. Erinn loved the fact that the famed woman architect in the 1920s and 1930s was given such a huge commission in an era where women were not really taken seriously in "manly" arts such as architecture.

The smallest bit of research on Erinn's part, however, dug up the fact that Morgan had designed the Marion Davies Estate on Pacific Coast Highway, not the Sovereign Hotel. Currently, the Davies Estate was in the midst of being "repurposed"—a newly invented verb, as far as Erinn could tell—to make way for a public bath club. Not that

that took anything away from Julia Morgan. She had still designed a fantastic building. But Erinn had been giving the cold shoulder to the Sovereign ever since.

They were well past the building by the time Erinn had finished her Julia Morgan story, and Massimo appeared lost in thought.

"I particularly think California makes a pretty pinot noir," he said.

Before Erinn realized it, they were at her front gate. Massimo looked at the house.

"This is beautiful, Erinn," he said. "A beautiful, beautiful house."

Erinn swelled with pride as she led Massimo around the side of the house into the backyard.

"This is a dream!" Massimo said as he entered the snug little guesthouse. "I will take it!"

Erinn picked up a pen and the blank rental agreement from the little café table. She started to hand it to Massimo as Caro entered majestically through the front door. He let out a meow as he stared at the man in front of him. Massimo smiled and picked up the cat.

"This is Caro," Erinn said.

"Hello, dear one," Massimo crooned at the cat. *"Parla Italiano?"*

Erinn took Caro in her arms as she handed the rental agreement to Massimo. He furrowed his brows as he looked at it, shaking a pair of reading spectacles out of his pocket. He studied the document and then looked at her.

"My English . . . she is . . ."

As a writer, Erinn had learned many lessons, including this: Don't complicate a perfect story with details. He was new to the city—what references could he have? She could tell that Massimo and she were kindred spirits; there was no need for a rental agreement. Taking heed, she took back the rental application and slid it into her pocket.

"Meraviglioso," said Erinn. "It's yours."

CHAPTER 4

Like most artists, Erinn was in her element when she sat back and observed the world around her. Sitting at her favorite spot at her sister's tea shop, where she was to meet her agent, she found that her new video camera (the one she bought with Massimo's deposit) was somewhat of a hindrance when it came to people watching. The folks who strolled up and down Main Street either glowered, turned away, or waved at her. She stowed her new Panasonic high-definition camera in her bag, frustrated that she was not invisible to passersby. Besides, it was too exhausting keeping one eye on the door. If Suzanna saw this camera, she'd be hysterical. Erinn wasn't sure how many more times she could pull out her big sister voice and have it be effective.

She pulled a notepad and pen from her bag. Stationery never garnered any attention. She could observe to her heart's content. Humankind's foibles were on parade . . . and all for her entertainment, it seemed. She watched as a middle-aged couple skated by, tentatively, on Rollerblades. Both were wearing padded knee pads, elbow and wrist guards, and bulbous helmets, which distorted their shapes to the point where they looked like a pair of Michelin Tire men on a skate date.

Erinn turned her attention to a man-on-the-street interview that was taking place nearby. Movie equipment on every other corner was a little annoyance Santa Monicans had learned to live with. Erinn actually embraced it. She learned a lot about equipment from the camera and audio guys, who were always willing to talk shop. The camera operator signaled that the crew should take a break, and he walked by, carrying a gorgeous high-definition camera with a long camera microphone attached.

"Nice camera," Erinn said.

"Thanks," he said. "I noticed you checking it out. Are you in the business?"

Erinn almost blushed. "What makes you say that?"

"Well, Zach Braff is doing our interview, and you didn't even notice. You just kept looking at the camera."

"Well, you have the biggest camera mike I've ever seen."

"Lady, you sure know how to talk to guys!"

Mercifully, the man went into the bookstore. She was embarrassed that she had made such an obvious faux pas. And she wondered . . . who was Zach Braff?

Erinn looked at her watch. She had been savoring the news about Massimo for days and couldn't wait to tell Suzanna. She sipped her tea, perched on an incredibly uncomfortable chair at an outdoor table. Just before Eric and Suzanna had gotten married, there had been a substantial earthquake in the area. The insurance money afforded them the opportunity to add an outdoor patio to the establishment, which brought in a whole new group of customers. She pulled out the camera's owner's manual to pass the time.

Suzanna came through the double doors and wagged a teapot—the international signal for "More hot water?"—at Erinn. Erinn shook her head and went back to reading.

Instinct made her look up as her agent, Mimi, arrived, twenty minutes late, as usual. With her ear glued to her cell phone, Mimi navigated the narrow aisle of tea drinkers and tried not to bump anyone with her yoga mat or computer case. As Mimi acknowledged Erinn with a wave of her free little finger, she continued to harangue the person on the other end of the phone. When she finally hung up, she seemed less than cheerful.

"I am sick to death of everything," said Mimi.

"What kind of attitude is that for someone coming from yoga?" asked Erinn.

Mimi shrugged and sucked down some water.

"That was Jonah," Mimi said, pointing to her phone. Jonah was the head honcho agent from the New York branch of her agency. "He says hi."

"Hello back," Erinn said, trying to sound California Casual. "Anything new with him?"

"No," Mimi said tersely.

"How's New York?" Erinn asked. She was jealous that Jonah still got to call New York home.

"It's fine. I'm sure New York is fine."

"So . . . anything new with you?" Erinn asked.

"No. Nothing is new with me," Mimi said. "Everyone hates me. Business as usual."

"Mimi, you're an agent. People are supposed to hate you."

Mimi shrugged again. Normally, when her agent was in a foul humor, Erinn just ignored her, but Erinn was too happy to let her agent's mood ruin her day. OK, so she didn't have a job. And, if you wanted to be a stickler, her script was not going at all well. But, she had a tenant and a new camera. Life was good.

Suzanna came out on the porch, carrying Mimi's usual: two slices of unbuttered toast, black tea, and a sliced banana.

Erinn flipped over the camera's owner's manual, hoping Suzanna didn't see it.

"Hey, Suzanna," Mimi said. "How are things?"

"Great," Suzanna said. "My doctor says my uterus is two and a half inches under my belly button."

Erinn dropped her spoon dramatically.

Is this breakfast conversation?

"Sounds about right," Mimi said, who had twin preschoolers, Dori and Dora.

Suzanna owned the shop for years before she and Eric had gotten married. Suzanna had been the overseer, while Eric managed the Book Nook, and another friend of theirs from high school, Fernando Cruz, had managed the tea shop. Fernando left to open a B and B on Vashon Island near Seattle just about the time of the earthquake, and Suzanna had taken over his managerial duties. Sometimes her chatting got the better of her and service could be slow—especially with uterus stories flying around the room.

Truth be told, while Erinn loved the tea shop, the Book Nook was of much more interest to her. As annoying and horrific as she found the pregnancy details, and as much as she loathed hearing everyone nattering about Suzanna's "baby bump," her sister's life had always appealed to Erinn's sense of story. Although friends since high school, Suzanna and Eric had only recently confessed their undying passion for each other. There was a whirlwind wedding—and now there was going to be a whirlwind baby. She was happy that Suzanna and Eric were adding another interesting chapter.

A customer at a nearby table signaled that he needed a refill, and Suzanna went back to work.

Erinn watched as Mimi fished an organic, non-caloric sweetener out of her bag and added a few oily drops to her tea. Mimi's phone rang again and she stabbed wildly at the volume key.

"Did I just witness Mimi Adams shutting off her phone?" Erinn asked.

"Don't worry . . . it's on vibrate."

Erinn's good humor vanished as she noticed her agent was still not smiling. Instead, eyes downcast, Mimi sipped her coffee and twirled her hair around her finger. Erinn's stomach plunged.

"You have bad news."

"I do not!"

"You do! You're twisting your hair, and you always twist your hair when you've got bad news."

As a writer, Erinn prided herself on noticing—and remembering—people's tics and quirks. Mimi twisted her hair when she had bad news. Suzanna bit her lower lip when she was upset. Their mother scratched her left cheek with her index finger when she was stretching the truth. Erinn took it all in—a student of human nature. For all the good it did her.

Mimi stopped twisting her hair and clutched the table. Erinn waited. Mimi's knuckles turned white, but she was at a loss. She started twisting her hair again.

"Oh God, oh God!" Erinn said. "Your agency is dumping me, aren't they? That's what you were talking to Jonah about!"

Mimi sighed.

"Every time I'm not dancing on tabletops, you think you're being dumped," Mimi said.

Erinn exhaled. "OK, so I'm not being dumped."

"Well, actually, you are."

"Oh my God! Why is this happening?"

"What do you mean, 'Why is this happening?' You know why!"

"After all these years?"

"It wasn't up to me," Mimi said. "I did everything I could. You've run out of material, and I've run out of excuses. Face it, Erinn, you haven't generated any buzz in years. "

"I haven't generated any *buzz*?" Erinn asked. "What happens now? I get stripped of my wings and sent to the depths of the hive?"

"I told you everybody hates me."

"Oh, I forgot, Mimi, this is about you."

Erinn's radar told her that her agent was ready to have a good, long, defensive battle—after all, they were friends as well as business associates—but then Mimi seemed to have a change of heart—and personality. Erinn knew these signs well . . . there must be an Important Industry Person nearby. An Amazonian blond woman approached them, brimming with Southern California good health. Mimi was suddenly all smiles.

"One word out of you, Erinn, and you'll never work again, I swear," Mimi whispered through her veneered smile.

". . . And that would be different . . . how?"

The blonde grabbed Mimi and kissed both her cheeks. The two women shrieked as if it had been years since they'd laid eyes on each other, although Erinn was show biz savvy enough to know that this woman was Cary Caldwell, queen of reality TV production, and that Cary and Mimi had gone to a fashion show in Beverly Hills just three days prior.

"This is my client . . . uh . . . friend, Erinn," Mimi said. "Erinn, Cary Caldwell. Cary produces *American Icon*, *Dancing with the D-Listers,* and . . . oh, wow, Cary . . . what else?"

"*Isn't That Weird*?" Cary offered.

"Isn't what weird?" Erinn asked.

Mimi's smile was frozen on her lips, but she managed to speak through clenched teeth.

"The TV show . . . *Isn't That Weird?*" said Mimi. "The show where they eat spaghetti with their feet."

"Really?" Erinn asked. Catching Mimi's eye, she attempted to make the best of it and turned her steady gaze toward Cary. "You must be very proud."

At Mimi's insistence, Cary joined them for herbal tea. She sat crossing and re-crossing her impossibly long legs while catching up with Mimi. Erinn went back to people watching when Mimi suddenly squeezed her wrist. In their early days together at power meetings, that squeeze meant "earth to Erinn" and translated in leaner times into "Pay attention, God damn it."

"Cary was just saying how much she enjoyed your plays . . . back in the day."

"Really?" Erinn asked, genuinely startled whenever someone remembered her work.

"Oh yes," Cary said. "Especially *The Family of Mann.* I saw it many times with my mother. We loved it!"

"Well," Erinn said. "It can't compare with *Isn't That Weird?*"

Mimi glared at her, but, in her determined agent's way, she tried to keep the focus on Erinn's accomplishments.

"Oh, I remember the reviews," said Mimi. " 'Erinn Elizabeth Wolf tugs at your heartstrings and brings tears to your eyes.' It was quite a time!"

"And now here I am, having tea with the woman who tugged at a million heartstrings and brought tears to a million eyes," said Cary.

"Two million eyes, actually," said Erinn absently. "Unless you're assuming that *The Family of Mann* played to one-eyed audiences exclusively."

Mimi looked ready to kill, but Cary laughed and slapped Erinn on the knee. Suzanna came by with a fresh pot of tea, which Mimi and Cary accepted. *No swift deliverance from this torment,* thought Erinn. As Suzanna turned to leave, she knocked Erinn's manual off the table.

"I guess I'm getting clumsy already," she said.

Cary stooped to retrieve the manual before Erinn could stop her.

"Oh, the Panasonic 3CCD MHC150," said Cary. "Great camera."

"I just got it," said Erinn, daring her sister to say anything.

Suzanna's mouth dropped open as Erinn pulled the new camera out of her bag, but Erinn carefully ignored her. She lovingly handed the camera to Cary, who studied it.

"I want to start making my own films," Erinn said, keeping the conversation going. "Writing, directing, shooting."

Cary nodded. "That's a very good idea. Tough, though. I mean, it's very different from theater, isn't it?"

Since Erinn hadn't actually written, directed, or shot a movie, she just nodded back and hoped she looked sage.

"This is the camera I use on all my shows," said Cary. "And you can handle this thing?"

Erinn said nothing, but tried to look confident as Cary handed her back the camera. Suzanna was making Erinn nervous as she still stood over them. Mercifully for Erinn, Suzanna was pulled away by another customer wanting to know why the shop no longer carried Pomegranate Madagascar tea.

That should keep her busy for a while.

"Erinn, what are you doing these days?" Cary continued.

Erinn looked to Mimi for approval, but could only read *Don't blow it* in her agent's eyes.

"This and that . . ."

"Look," said Cary. "I'm producing a new show called *BATTLE ready!* for the History Network. My crew will be traveling around the country, shooting reenactments."

"All over the country?" asked Erinn. "Revolutionary War . . . Civil War in the East and South. Spanish conflicts in Texas. What else? We've got a pretty short history in the United States."

Cary beamed. "Erinn, you would be great! You've already cut to our number-one problem. We just don't have enough material to flesh out a season."

"She is so good. . . ." said Mimi.

"We're sort of playing it by ear," said Cary. "Right now, we're thinking about adding some local gang wars in Los Angeles. You know, keep it fresh. Contemporary."

"I don't think the point of history is keeping it fresh. Or contemporary," said Erinn. "That's why it's history."

Mimi looked green as Cary took a last sip of tea and stood up.

"Well," she said, looking at Erinn, "we're always open to suggestions."

Erinn held her breath, fearing she had blown this opportunity. If she had, Mimi would never forgive her. But Cary smiled at her.

"So, you up for a producer gig? We pay crap, the hours are brutal, and we'll beat the shit out of your camera."

"It's perfect," Mimi added.

"We run a tight ship. We send out four people—two teams—at a time and you support each other. I think you'd be a powerful addition. We don't have many women shooters. You up for it?"

"She is!" said Mimi.

"Good," said Cary, as she handed Erinn a business card. "See you Monday. I'll introduce you to your partner."

Cary left. Mimi and Erinn sat in silence, not daring to look at each other.

"Too bad your agency is dumping me," Erinn said. "That would have been an easy ten percent."

"Oh, no you don't," Mimi said. "I brokered that deal. You're still my client whether you like it or not."

Erinn looked up and saw that Mimi was smiling. She kissed Erinn on the cheek and stood up.

"I've got to go pick up the Double Ds at preschool. Gotta run. I'll send the contract over to the house."

Erinn tried to process the events. She had a tenant, had narrowly dodged being dropped from her agency—and now that she had a job, her sister couldn't say one damn word about her new camera.

As soon as Suzanna saw that Erinn was alone, she came over and tried to climb up on the high stool Mimi had vacated. The pregnancy made the trip awkward, and Suzanna resigned herself to standing opposite her sister.

"Did you hear any of that?" Erinn said.

"No, I was busy," Suzanna said. "But I noticed you seem to have a new camera."

"I do. And it was *very* expensive." Erinn knew she shouldn't tease her sister, but she couldn't help herself.

Eric came out to the patio and waved to Erinn. He came over and hoisted Suzanna onto the stool, making sure she was secure before he let go.

"Hey, Erinn," Eric said. "I ordered that book on the Silk Road for you."

"*The Silk Road, Two Thousand Years in the Heart of Asia*?"

"The very one."

"Not *Empires of the Silk Road: A History of Central Eurasia from the Bronze Age to the Present*?"

"Never."

Erinn always thought Eric had an unusual sense of humor and could never tell when he was joking. Eric gave his wife's wild, curly hair a few affectionate strokes and retreated to the bookstore.

"Well?" Erinn asked. "Don't you want to know what's new with me?"

"I'm pregnant," Suzanna said.

"Uh . . . that's what's new with *you*," Erinn said. "I asked if you wanted to know what was new with *me*?"

"I just mean, I'm pregnant. Please don't torture me."

"Well, when you put it that way . . . I'll tell you what's new with me. I got a job!"

"Oh, thank goodness!" Suzanna said. "I thought Mimi might be letting you go."

"Oh, no, no, no," Erinn said. "She just wanted to introduce me to my new boss, Cary Caldwell."

"From *Isn't that Weird?* Wow, I'm impressed."

"And there's more. I rented the guesthouse! To a man I met at the farmers' market. We started talking, and the next thing you know, I had a tenant."

"Wow!" Suzanna said. "I . . . I . . . I'm stunned!"

"And I found him myself," Erinn said. "No need for you or the infinite wisdom of craigslist."

"Tell me about him."

"Well, you'll be happy to know he's a filmmaker. He's a serious actor—God knows what he's doing in Los Angeles. Between projects, he's a chef. Very serious about food. He's . . . of a certain age . . . and is stimulating company. He's . . . foreign."

Suzanna distractedly rummaged through her pockets, but stopped mid-rummage. She looked coolly at her sister.

"How . . . foreign . . . is he?"

"He's Italian."

"Italian?" Suzanna said, smacking the table. "Are you kidding?"

"No, I'm not."

"Do you . . ." Suzanna said haltingly. "Do you think . . . you're ready for another Italian?"

"You haven't even met him, and you've decided you don't like him. Suzanna, that is unfair."

"I haven't decided I don't like him. *That's* unfair." Suzanna reached out and put her hand on top of Erinn's. Erinn tried not to pull her hand away, but she was never comfortable being handled by people. She didn't even like massages.

"I just think you should use some judgment," Suzanna continued. "You can't arbitrarily love all Italian men."

"I don't love *all* Italian men, just selected ones. Besides, having Massimo around will help me keep up with the language."

"Oh! For all those trips to Italy you plan on taking in the near future?"

"I refuse to discuss this further. You said get a tenant and I got a tenant."

"OK. Fine. But if I may make one small suggestion—save the money."

CHAPTER 5

Erinn balanced a small vase of flowers in one hand and carried a *Welcome to the Neighborhood* card in the other. She unlocked the guesthouse and artfully arranged her offerings on the small café table just inside the door. Massimo was moving in today, but she would be at Apple Pie Entertainment, starting her new job. Opening the curtains to let in the morning sunlight, Erinn caught a glimpse of herself in the mirror. She squeezed the new tumble of curls on the top of her head and tried not to smile. Maybe the tides were turning.

Don't get ahead of yourself.

Erinn locked the guesthouse and was returning to the house to grab the last of her camera gear—with the prospect of this unlikely new life as a producer and camera operator, Erinn had bought every accessory available for her Panasonic over the weekend—when she saw Massimo pull up in front of the house. Her self-confidence of a moment before came crashing down.

"*Ciao,* Massimo," Erinn said as Massimo came to meet her in the driveway. "Wow, you're getting an early start!"

"Sì, bella," Massimo said, grabbing a leather suitcase from the passenger seat. "Our new life is waiting! I will put this suitcase in the little house and we will get espresso, no?"

"No!" Erinn tried not to sound rattled as Massimo stopped in the walkway and looked at her in surprise.

"No? But, *bella . . .*"

Erinn ushered him down the path, busying herself with unlocking the door for him.

"I have to go to work. I start a new job today."

She swung the door open and Massimo walked in with his suitcase. He saw the bouquet of flowers on the table. Erinn was mortified. Trying to focus on anything but Massimo, she shut the curtains she had just opened. She realized how dark the room was and snapped on the light. When she turned back around, Massimo was smiling down at the *Welcome to the Neighborhood* card.

Why can't I leave well enough alone?

She met Massimo's eyes, but couldn't hold them.

"I . . . I'd better get going," she said.

Massimo grabbed her hand as she walked to the door. He kissed it and continued to hold it to his chest until she looked up at him again.

"I am very happy," he said. "I will remind you of everything you love about Italy."

You already have.

As Erinn drove into Burbank in her 1994 Honda wagon, her new cell phone, a gift from Mimi, rang. Erinn was not used to having a cell phone and she almost swerved into traffic at the sound. Taking her life in her hands, she stuck the earpiece in her ear and answered it.

"I can't talk, I'm driving."

"It's an acquired skill. Get used to it," Mimi said.

"I'm hanging up," Erinn said.

"I don't understand how you can be practically a savant with all other technology, but can't operate a cell phone."

"Other technology doesn't involve other people."

"Erinn, you're part of cable TV now. You've got to accept other people."

Erinn snorted and pulled the earpiece from the side of her head. She tossed it on the seat as she crested the mountains that separated the beach from the San Fernando Valley, practicing the mantra Suzanna wrote for her after the meeting with Cary.

"I will not alienate my fellow workers. I will not alienate my fellow workers."

She tried to stay focused on her mantra, which, she had to admit, sounded a little clumsy to her trained ear. Erinn admitted that, in the past, she had perhaps alienated a co-worker or two, but, whoever it was that found him- or herself alienated—had undoubtedly deserved it. Erinn found her pulse quickening as she took umbrage with the unfairness of her manta.

She turned on the car radio . . . deciding to face her new comrades mantra-free.

Erinn found her destination with little difficulty—a blessing, given that she rarely ventured into this part of Los Angeles County. A huge sign on the building read APPLE PIE ENTERTAINMENT—*Go APE!* Erinn pulled into the designated parking structure. *Business must be good,* she thought, as she drove up two ramps in order to find a space. She got out of the car and adjusted her clothing. Having no idea how she should present herself, she had asked her agent what to wear.

"When you work in TV, there are two kinds of people," Mimi had said. "There are staff people and there are production people. Staff people dress as if they are getting ready to take over the studio. . . ."

"I'm production, right?"

"Right," said Mimi. "Production people dress as if they're going to paint the studio."

Although that description pretty much summed up Erinn's wardrobe, she did think she should clean up for the first day and was now wearing black dress pants and a white sweater. At Mimi's insistence, Suzanna had dragged Erinn to a hairdresser and the sisters fought about covering the gray in Erinn's hair and about its length.

"Mimi says nobody has gray hair in show business," Suzanna said.

"I'll be a trendsetter."

"You'll be Gramma."

They compromised. Erinn had the gray "highlighted," but she kept the length. The last thing she wanted to worry about on her first location shoot was having to figure out how to use a blow-dryer. The hairdresser arranged Erinn's hair in a tousled updo, which seemed to satisfy them all.

As she looked around the office, Erinn saw immediately that she was overdressed, as assorted soon-to-be co-workers poured into Apple Pie Entertainment wearing cargo shorts, sloppy T-shirts, and flip-flops. As Erinn rode the elevator to the fifth floor, laden down with her camera gear, she also noticed that everyone else was young. Very young. Very, very young. Under thirty young.

The elevator door opened, and Erinn was jostled by all the busy television people getting ready to start their day. Cary walked by as Erinn arrived in the lobby and snared her.

"Wow, look at all that gear," said Cary. "Let me get a P.A. to help you with that."

Learning the terms of the television world was like learning a foreign language, thought Erinn as she recalled that a P.A. was a "production assistant." For all her prowess with the camera, Erinn really had not had to learn anything related to other people until now.

Cary led Erinn down a hallway as a wraith of a girl, introduced as LeeLee, came to help her with the gear. Being separated from her camera was not part of Erinn's plan, but she had promised her sister and her agent that she would, as Mimi put it, "be breezy," at least the first day. She watched as LeeLee struggled with the camera equipment. (Erinn was reminded of her earlier traveling days and watching guiltily as prepubescent boys in Morocco strained under the weight of her luggage. It hadn't taken her long to rethink her packing habits.)

"It's very enlightened of Apple Pie to hire women camera operators and P.A.s," Erinn said *breezily*, trying to keep an eye on her gear.

"Yeah," Cary said. "Well, don't kid yourself, Erinn. We still work cheaper than the guys."

Cary gave Erinn a perfunctory tour of the company as they threaded their way through bull pens and low-walled cubicles. Each desk had an occupant who seemed to be either on the phone or lost in his or her own iPod world.

"We do all kinds of production here. Lifestyle programming, reality, food, travel, history. It's exciting, but it's hard to know what the programming flavor of the month will be," Cary said.

"Well, at least with history, your story is already written."

"True," Cary said. "The challenge is making sure we've always got our facts straight. We're TV people, not historians, and the network suits get really nervous if our information isn't exactly right. Not that I blame them, but I always feel like I'm defending my dissertation when I have a history gig."

Rounding a corner, Erinn was startled by the sight of row after row of people whom Erinn recognized—by their intensity—as editors.

She waited respectfully as Cary stopped to watch one of the editors. A sign over his cubicle read ADAM.

Adam wore enormous headphones and his hands flew over the keyboard and mouse, making adjustments to the video on the monitor. Cary and Erinn watched in silence for a minute, focusing on the black-and-white war footage on the screen.

"We have a great library of stock footage here," Cary said in a low voice, so as not to disturb Adam. "It helps fill in the blanks when we can't afford to re-create everything with actors."

Cary put her hand on Adam's shoulder. He took his earphones off and smiled at her.

"Hey, Cary," he said. "I'm almost done."

Cary introduced Adam to Erinn. They chatted a moment about how editing had changed over the years . . . although Adam was so young he really had only heard tales of darkened edit bays. Erinn, making a mental note to stop talking about the good old days, quickly changed the subject and turned her attention to the monitor.

"What are you working on?"

"A piece about World War One," he said.

Erinn laughed.

Cary and Adam turned to her.

"Is . . . something funny?" Cary asked.

"I guess this is something to do to the new kid . . . not that I'm a kid . . . just to make sure I know my history, right?"

Cary and Adam shot each other a quick look. Erinn continued to beam.

"As if I wouldn't notice those soldiers were wearing World War Two uniforms!"

Adam and Cary turned back toward the screen and stared at it for several seconds.

"Adam, go back to the library and get the right stock footage, please," Cary said.

Adam, looking slightly green, nodded, and Cary steered Erinn down the hall.

"Thanks, Erinn," she said. "You just saved our ass."

"Asses," Erinn said, forgetting her mantra for a moment. Then, to redeem herself, she added breezily, "Or 'our collective ass' . . . that would work, too."

They arrived at a large conference room, already swarming with people. Production people, Erinn decided, given their attire. Cary turned to Erinn as they headed into the room.

"Since you're new to this, I'm going to team you up with one of our most seasoned directors."

Cary took Erinn by the elbow and steered her over to the coffee—a cardboard box from Starbucks, surrounded by little plastic tubs of cream, scattered packets of sugar, and a rainbow of sweeteners. Erinn thought fleetingly of Massimo and how he would have probably cried at the sight. A man in the ubiquitous cargo shorts and duct-taped sandals was pouring himself a cup. Cary tapped him on the shoulder.

"There you are!" Cary said. "I want you to meet our newest producer."

The man turned around and stared at Erinn.

"Erinn Elizabeth Wolf," continued Cary, "this is Jude Raphael. Jude . . . Erinn'll be your camera op and field producer."

Jude looked at her, his face unreadable. He took a sip of coffee.

"Erinn Wolf," he said. "Who says God doesn't have a sense of humor?"

Cary looked surprised.

"Oh, do you two know each other?" she asked.

"Not really," Erinn said. "He almost rented my guesthouse, but found it too gay."

"I almost rented her guesthouse, but found the company . . . I mean, the place . . . claustrophobic," Jude said. "How's Truck?"

"He's well, thanks," Erinn said. "I'm sure he thinks of you often."

"What can I say . . . I have a way with cats."

As auspicious beginnings go, this was one for the books, Erinn thought. Perhaps she would one day look back and laugh. Or, even better, look back and write.

Cary rapped on the large mahogany conference table that dominated the room. The cargo-pants brigade started making its way to the table and, mercifully, Erinn was spared any further interaction.

Cary took a spot at one end of the table, a stack of papers to her right. Cary's easy, casual demeanor seemed to have been replaced by a no-nonsense attitude. Erinn glanced quickly around. She hoped she could sit as far away from Jude as possible, but the seat next to his was the only available space.

"Hey, everybody," Cary began. "Well, we've finally staffed our last team member. People, this is Erinn Elizabeth Wolf. She'll be field producing with you guys and Jude."

Erinn inclined her head in greeting. She hoped she signaled the confidence that she sorely lacked. She was actually terrified of being at this table. She hadn't been in a setting with this many people in years. Her social skills, while never her strong suit, were so rusty it would take a wrench to release them. She nodded woodenly.

If the Queen of England had a nod instead of a wave, this would be it.

"Let's go around the room and introduce ourselves," Cary said. "Most of you know each other, but let's give Erinn a fighting chance to catch up."

The next few minutes were a whirlwind of first names and impressions. The shoot they were going on apparently was going to have three field producers-slash-camera people and one director. She already knew that Jude was the director, and she tried to focus on each producer as he was introduced.

Carlos had thick black hair and he wore his cool like a refrigerator. His piercing black eyes gave him a menacing look . . . until he smiled. Carlos had a smile that lit up the room. He was attractive, charming, and appeared to know it.

Cary introduced another producer. He was as handsome as a 1940s' movie star. Erinn noticed he was wearing a tiny rainbow pin.

"I'm Gilroi Rose. It's spelled G-I-L-R-O-I," the man said to Erinn. "But it's pronounced Gil-*whah* . . . not Gil-*roy*."

Erinn lifted an eyebrow. She tried not to show her annoyance.

"I know how to pronounce *roi*," she said. "It's French, for king."

The slight hum of distraction that buzzed through the room suddenly came to a standstill. Everyone in the room was staring at her. Erinn realized she was already distancing herself from the group and she needed to recover quickly.

"It's like the old English name St. John. On paper, it's 'Saint' and 'John' but we all know that it's pronounced 'Sin-gin.' "

"What the hell is she talking about?" she heard Carlos whisper to Gilroi.

"I don't know." Gilroi, who was looking right at Erinn, winked. He was talking to Carlos, but he made sure Erinn could hear him. "But I adore her."

Erinn let out a sigh of relief. Well, she had at least one person on her side. Erinn stole a quick look at Jude, who was doing his maddening arm curls and staring at the table. Cary interrupted Erinn's tallying of friends or foes.

"Well, Erinn, you're the writer, so I guess I can rely on you to introduce yourself without any help," said Cary.

Erinn cleared her throat. "I'm Erinn Elizabeth Wolf. But, please, call me Erinn."

"Or Tin Lizzy," said Jude.

Erinn felt her face start to flush, as laughter erupted around the table.

"Jude . . . seriously, enough with the nicknames."

"Don't listen to him. He always tries to give people the lamest nicknames imaginable. . . . He keeps trying to get people to call me 'Gil.' "

Erinn made a mental note that Gilroi should always be called Gilroi.

"He's also tried to saddle me with Gil-Wah-Wah . . . Gil Roy Rogers . . ."

"Gil Roy Rogers? That's as bad as Rin Tin Tin."

"Rin Tin Tin! From Erinn he got Rin Tin Tin? That's a stretch," said Carlos, joining the conversation.

Erinn raised her eyebrows and nodded, happy to have allies against the demon nicknamer.

"You just have to ignore him," Gilroi said.

"Does that work?" Erinn asked, looking right at Jude.

Maddeningly, Jude seemed to bask in the attention. He just grinned at her.

"Darling . . . it's him against us," Gilroi said. "I don't know about you, but I will *not* answer to Gil-Wah-Wah. Just be strong."

Erinn felt immediately better and she plowed ahead. She addressed everyone at the table.

"My background is in theater . . . New York theater."

"Are you one of those people who thinks everything is better in New York?" asked Carlos.

"No!"

"No?" asked Jude, the corners of his mouth tugging into a smirk.

"Well . . . some things. The culture. The atmosphere. The food."

"What's left?" asked Gilroi.

Erinn looked around the room and realized she had gone down the wrong path. She was so used to commiserating with New York expatriates, she'd forgotten how to converse with Los Angelenos.

"The light. Los Angeles has very good light."

This seemed to do the trick, and Erinn relaxed. Leave it to TV people to appreciate good light.

"OK," Cary said. "Let's get down to business. As you all know, we're going to start shooting *BATTLEready!* on the East Coast. Everybody ready to revisit the Revolutionary War?"

Erinn tilted toward Gilroi, having practiced her first line of casual banter.

"I guess we're taking American wars in order then."

Gilroi whispered back, "Nah. We're starting with Philadelphia because HBO just finished a series about the Revolution and we can get a bunch of props on the cheap."

Erinn nodded, cringing at the low-budgetness of it all.

"And we have an actor who looks like George Washington. He's about a hundred years old—seriously, he's gotta be forty-five—and will work for nothing."

Erinn's lips tightened in sympathy. Imagine being a middle-aged thespian and the most that could be said about your professional accomplishments was that you bore a faint resemblance to a man who lived over two hundred years ago. Erinn looked around the room at all the young faces. She felt awkward among them.

Cary stood up and started distributing packets.

Erinn opened hers and studied a map of a section of the East Coast . . . the map centered on Pennsylvania, but also included New Jersey, New York, and Maryland.

"We are going to concentrate on Pennsylvania. We've managed to get a release that covers a good number of the historic parks. Most of the parks have lots of replicas of uniforms and weapons, so even if the HBO connection falls through, we won't be behind the eight ball."

"What about extra crew?" asked Carlos.

"Since when have we ever gotten extra crew?" Gilroi said.

"Shouldn't be a problem," Cary said, ignoring Gilroi. "All the parks now have their own information centers. They usually show short films featuring local reenactors shooting muskets and cannons at each other. Where there are reenactors, there is crew. We can pick up extra people where we need them."

Erinn continued to thumb through her packet, which was divided into three sections: Washington Crosses the Delaware, the Battle of Brandywine, and Valley Forge.

"Let's go over the pitch," Cary said. "You know the drill. You'll work together, but each producer will spearhead a battle. Carlos, you'll have Washington's crossing; Gilroi, the Brandywine; and Erinn, you'll handle Valley Forge."

Erinn flipped to the section on Valley Forge, but caught Cary's eye.

"Let's start with Washington Crosses the Delaware, shall we?" Cary said.

Erinn, chastised, turned back to the crossing. She quietly read through the description of the piece. It was a well-written page describing how a dispirited George Washington and his men crossed the Delaware River on Christmas Day in order to carry out a surprise attack on the Hessian outposts on the New Jersey side of the river. The famous Emanuel Leutze painting of the crossing was photocopied at the bottom of the page, which Erinn thought was a nice touch.

"Any thoughts?" Cary asked.

"Our cameras won't stand up to this kind of cold," Carlos said. "Remember when we were shooting on Lake Erie and the camera froze?"

The group erupted in glee as they one-upped each other with frozen camera stories. Jude laughingly added his own tale of woe. He was videotaping an ice-skater on a frozen creek and the two of them suddenly crashed through the ice. Jude managed to keep his camera arm out of the water. He made sure the producer had a firm grasp on the camera before they helped the skater out of the water.

"Chivalry is dead," Cary said.

"No . . . just frozen," Jude said.

"I'm serious, you guys," Carlos said, stabbing at the historic depiction on the packet. "Look at this painting of the crossing. It's the same time of year as *now* . . . and there were frickin' icebergs, man."

Erinn let out a small squeak, but it was clearly audible. The group turned to her.

She felt the color rising on her neck, but knew she was up to the task ahead.

"That painting is full of artistic licenses," she said.

Everyone stared at the picture and Erinn continued.

"The crossing took place at night in the pouring rain, not during the day with dramatic lighting. And Washington sure as hell wouldn't have been standing up. Who stands up in a rowboat? And as for the icebergs, they were modeled on the solid sheets of ice that form and break up in the artist's native Germany . . . the Rhine River, specifically. There aren't icebergs in Pennsylvania."

Erinn finished speaking. The group continued to look at the painting. No one looked at her. She felt her face flush, as she watched her new co-workers absorbing her words. Well, these kids did seem interested in learning, she thought.

Suddenly, a dull, snoring sound broke the silence.

It was Jude.

Everyone in the room busted up laughing. Cary gave Erinn a quick sympathetic look and tried to quiet the group.

"Let's not worry about frozen cameras or icebergs," Cary said. "I'm sure your equipment will do just fine."

"Yeah . . . I'll bet George Washington told his men the same thing," Carlos said.

Cary moved the meeting onward. She introduced the section on the Battle of Brandywine, a very straightforward battle—albeit one won by the British.

"We're shooting a battle won by the enemy?" Jude asked. "How incredibly politically correct of us."

Everyone at the table snickered.

OK, how are we ever going to do a documentary series when everything is a joke with these guys?

"It says that this battle took place at a spot called Chadds Ford," Gilroi said. "Sounds kind of remote."

"Wouldn't know," said Cary.

"Chadds Ford is beautiful," Erinn said, eager to have something positive to add.

"Frankly, my dear, I don't give a damn," Gilroi said.

"It's got wonderful history—not just the Revolutionary War, but the Pennsylvania Dutch settled not far from there. The whole area is quaint," Erinn said.

"I don't do quaint," Gilroi said.

"You'll do quaint and you'll like it," said Jude.

Everyone laughed.

"Chadds Ford. I don't even know what a 'ford' is!" Gilroi said.

"It's the place in a creek where it's shallow enough to cross," Erinn said.

"They should have changed the name before the British got there," Jude said, and the room erupted in laughter again.

Cary, who impressed Erinn with her cool demeanor (she never seemed to notice all the snide sidebars), went over the details of the battle with the team. This segment, according to Cary, was the most dicey, production-wise. The "British" were going to burn a reconstructed village, and the footage had to be captured in one take.

"No mistakes, people," Cary warned. "We had to fight like hell to get this approved."

"Do we have the right fire permits this time?" asked Carlos, apparently an old hand at shooting burning villages.

"We're still working on that," Cary said, "but you know the drill. It's better to beg forgiveness than permission."

Erinn felt herself getting nervous as the group turned to Valley Forge. She was already thinking of it as *her* Valley Forge.

The packet described the horrors experienced by the Continental army as they froze and starved through the winter of 1777–1778. Erinn finished reading and looked around as the teams nodded and conferred among themselves. The guys seemed to have such easy camaraderie, and she tried to think of something to say to Jude. She glanced over at him, but he was still reading, so she left it alone. There were going to be many long days of trying to think of things to say, she feared.

Cary asked if there were comments. Erinn cleared her throat, and everyone at the table turned to her. Erinn noticed that Jude slumped in his chair, folded his arms, and waited.

"Well, I do have one question," Erinn said. "This series is about famous battles, right?"

"Right," Cary said.

"Well, there was never a battle at Valley Forge. They just . . . waited . . . at Valley Forge."

A dispirited hush hung over the room. Everyone stared at the pitch as if looking for some sort of answer.

"Dude. The series is called *BATTLEready!"* Jude said. "Couldn't you say that they were getting *ready* for *battle* at Valley Forge? You know, cover it with a voice-over at the top of the piece?"

Erinn could feel Jude looking at her, his triumph almost palpable. She slowly turned to face him. She might have been out of the workplace for a while, but she knew a challenge when she saw one. *BATTLEready!* seemed to be the perfect production for them, she thought.

CHAPTER 6

Driving home from her first day of work, Erinn mulled over her new job. On the plus side: an interesting topic, travel, getting to use her camera equipment, and, as much as she hated to admit it, a steady paycheck. She furtively glanced down at the large envelope perched on her front seat. It appeared to beg for attention, with its hideous bright-yellow-and-green graphics. Apple Pie's insignia, a demented-looking monkey, swung across the envelope, a toothy smile on his face. Erinn could only wonder how a graphic artist had managed to sell this loathsome design to a production company, but, much like the six hundred, hers was not to reason why. The packet was the human resources welcome brochure from Apple Pie Entertainment. It promised a dizzying array of benefits, from health care to inclusion in their 401k. In her New York days, Erinn had watched cocaine-addled starlets look at a mountain of white powder with less lust than she was feeling for her new benefits package. She wondered, *A sign of the times . . . or old age?*

But there were negatives. Her co-workers' lack of knowledge—and interest—in history alarmed her, she couldn't deny it. She tried not to think about Jude.

Erinn pulled into her driveway, shut off the engine, and dropped her head onto the steering wheel. She sometimes forgot how much she loathed humanity, but her first eight hours in the workplace had brought it all back. She was going to have to get used to the whole concept of communal creativity. As a writer, Erinn had always worked alone—and from her desk at home, wherever home may have been at any given time.

At APE, Erinn found trying to concentrate in a busy office, with its newsroom-style bull pens, a real challenge. Staff members would randomly shout out show ideas to one another, and each concept was discussed, embraced, or dismissed at full volume. Erinn recalled Gilroi pitching an idea about General Washington having a moment of reflection before taking his men into battle, and Carlos's reaction was to pretend to be throwing up in the trash can. Gilroi gave him a playful whack on the head. Erinn tried to think back to a time when she was ever that playful, but came up blank.

And why should I be playful? This is the Revolutionary War! This is the core of human drama! This is the History Network!

Erinn sat back in the driver's seat but still couldn't bring herself to open her eyes. She knew that reliving all the slings and arrows of the day was probably not in her own best interest, but as a writer, it was her duty to analyze everything that had happened. She had kept an eye on Jude, sitting at the next computer station. He seemed to spend as much time playing video games as he did researching. He caught her eye during one of his games, but didn't appear guilty in the least. Erinn pointed to her own computer screen.

"This is a great Web site on the Revolutionary War, if you're interested," she said.

"I'm not."

"I guess you already know everything there is to know about the war then?"

"No," he said, turning away from his game and looking at her. "But that's your department. Your job is to find out everything there is to know and write the script. My job is to come in and tell you how to shoot it. This director gig is a wonderful thing."

Jude smiled and went back to his game while Erinn stewed.

Finally, Jude shut down his computer, stretched, and asked Erinn how her research was progressing. She picked up her notebooks, graph sheets, and printed-out articles. She moved closer to him and pointed to a timeline she had created.

"I think it's important to give the audience a timeline of the war," she said. "I don't think all Americans have a real grasp of how long this conflict lasted."

"Erinn, we're covering one battle. You're over-reaching."

"But people need to understand the ideology behind the conflict."

"No, they don't."

They stared at each other.

"Erinn, people don't care."

"Then we make them care. If you give them something good, people will watch it."

"If you give them crap, they'll watch it, so why kill yourself?"

She let out a ragged breath. Jude suddenly shot out of his chair to follow a twenty-year-old intern into the office kitchen.

Erinn continued her research, which she found incredibly stimulating, and tried to envision how the shoot might go. She had so many ideas she felt light-headed. She tried not to let Jude's words—"My job is to come in and tell you how to shoot it"—nor his philosophy—"If you give them crap, they'll watch it, so why kill yourself?"—dampen her enthusiasm. She had to listen to him, she knew that; he was the director, after all. A shallow, soulless, superficial director, but the director, nonetheless. She would have to deal with him whether she liked it—or him—or not.

Her cell phone rang. She jolted upright, and realized she was still in her driveway. Erinn hurried to put the hated earbud in place, but all she managed to do was get it ensnared in her hair.

Realizing the car was stationary, and California's hands-free law no longer applied, she left the earbud dangling in her hair and just answered the damn phone. It was Mimi.

"How was your first day?" Mimi asked. "Why didn't you call me?"

Erinn knew instinctively that Mimi had already checked out the situation with Cary, and the fact that Mimi wasn't walking on eggshells was a good sign.

"I think it went well," she said.

"What did you think of the people?"

"Unspeakably unschooled . . . but salvageable. Most of them."

"What about your partner? Did you like him?"

Erinn couldn't resist asking, "How did you know my partner is a 'he'?"

Mimi sputtered on the other end, but Erinn took pity on her and continued, "I know that you know that my new partner is that well-muscled egomaniac who came over to look at the guesthouse. You can stop with the subterfuge."

"Subterfuge?"

"Yes, subterfuge. It's from the Latin, *sub-ter-fugierie*."

"Yes, Erinn. Thank you, I know what subterfuge means. And how do I know? Because you have told me a thousand times. But OK, you're right. Cary gave me the poop."

Erinn winced at her agent's choice of words. Clearly, the expression her agent was grasping for was "Cary filled me in," or the clichéd but perfectly serviceable "Cary gave me the lowdown," or even the industry-tinged "Cary gave me the breakdown."

"I'm not sure what to make of this Jude person," Erinn said as she heaved herself out of the car. "He seems to have a very unusual sense of humor."

"Translation: He makes fun of you and you don't like it."

"I *have* a sense of humor, Mimi."

"Yes, dear."

"I do," Erinn continued as she walked up the path to the front door. "But like everything else, comedy has rules—and he doesn't seem to follow any of them."

"You'll warm up, I'm sure of it."

"I wouldn't count on it. Do you want to hear what he did today?"

"More than you know."

Erinn stopped on the front step. "In a moment of misguided good will, I asked Jude if he wanted to show me the office. We started walking down hallway after identical hallway, with Jude bleating out, "Here's where they do home and gardening, here's where they do travel destinations, here's more History Network, here's where they're doing a documentary on Saint Paul."

"Oh God."

"Yes! Well, of course I thought, this is a perfect time for a stirring intellectual discussion."

"Oh God."

"I said to him, 'Oh? And what is the position of documentary writers on Saint Paul?' And do you know what he said to me? Of course you don't. He said . . . 'I don't think they have a position.' Then he asked me if I had a position!"

"Oh God."

"I said of course I have a position! And he asked me what that might be."

Mimi whimpered on the other end of the phone.

"I said I held Saint Paul personally responsible for all the small-minded, superstitious misogyny that permeates the world today. Well, half the world. And do you know what he said? Of course you don't. He said, 'I don't think anybody here thinks that.' I was ready to walk out the door."

"But you didn't—right?"

"Jude followed me to the elevator, and as I stepped inside, he said, 'I'd love to keep this going, Erinn, but the documentary is for the Travel Channel. It's about the *city* of Saint Paul.' And then the elevator door slammed."

Mimi snickered.

"It's not funny," Erinn said.

"I know, honey," Mimi said. "But it could be worse. Trust me."

"I'm not sure if the fact that I'm going to be traveling around with *just* Jude is going to make things better or worse."

"It is what you make of it."

"Thank you, Yoda."

"Was that a pop culture reference—after only one day in TV production?"

Erinn smiled. "I can sling thirty-year-old pop culture references with the best of them!"

They hung up as Erinn let herself into the house. She sniffed the air—the aroma transported her back to Italy, and for a moment she was lost in the delectable soup of memory. Caro brought her back to the present with a grating meow. He stared up at her and abruptly turned his back on her. Erinn followed the cat—and the dull clanging sounds of pots and pans—toward the kitchen.

She found Massimo, wearing a white dress shirt rolled at the cuffs, charcoal-gray trousers, and leather shoes, confidently whisking, stirring, and boiling. He didn't seem to be aware of her, and as she looked on, she wondered: *Did I take leave of my senses and offer my house to this man? He was supposed to move into the guesthouse . . . not the kitchen!*

The cat jumped up on the counter, and Massimo and Erinn both reached for him, each calling out, "Down, Caro!"

Massimo reached the cat first, scooped him up with one hand, and dropped him on the floor. The other hand continued to stir the divine-smelling sauce. He smiled over his shoulder at Erinn.

"Your timing, she is *perfetto*!" he said. "Dinner will be ready in a few minutes. I did not know if we eat in the kitchen or in dining room, so I did not set the table."

Erinn noticed a neat stack of her Tuscan dinnerware on the counter. The impertinence of this man, casually commandeering her kitchen. She paused, weighing her options. She knew she should set some rules right here and now . . . but on the other hand, the smell of that sauce. . . .

"The dining room," Erinn said. "I'll set the table."

She grabbed the place settings and moved into the dining room, avoiding the slightly accusatory look from her cat.

We'll have to straighten this out, she thought, *but there's no sense wasting a good dinner . . . especially after the day I've had.*

Massimo decanted a spicy Chianti and served up perfect portions of pasta Bolognese. He then expertly grated fresh Parmesan—no!—fresh Romano cheese—on top and sat down at the table with Erinn. Sneaking a quick peek into the kitchen, she noticed that it was already spotless—as was his shirt. Erinn was a good cook, but she could not spend any time in the kitchen without looking as if she'd taken a bath in food. Erinn took a bite of the pasta and smiled. The food was perfection. She could feel the cares of the day melting away, but then noticed the candles on the table were unlit. She went to the sideboard to retrieve a flame lighter and returned to the table, turning down the dimmer on the wall on her way.

"My mother always said, wine and women always look better by candlelight," Erinn said, lighting the wicks.

As she sat back, Massimo saluted her with his wineglass.

"Your mother is very wise," he said. "But this woman and this wine do not need to hide behind candles."

Caro sneezed derisively. Erinn was silently grateful she had turned the lights down, because she could feel herself flushing.

"I took this day away from work," Massimo continued. "I say to myself, Massimo, you are moving today and the lady of the house has a new job. *Basta!* Enough for one day."

"Are you settled in the back?"

Massimo furrowed his brow and looked sadly at Erinn.

"The kitchen, she is very, very small, Erinn," he said. "There is no room for my pots and pans. I remember how wonderful are your pots and pans, and I say to myself, Massimo, this fine lady will never mind if you keep things in her house. She knows quality."

Erinn gulped at her Chianti. "How did you get in?" she asked, as casually as possible.

"I . . . *comme si dice* . . . put a credit card in the lock," he answered just as casually. "It is very easy. This is a nice city, Erinn, but it is good to have a man around."

"To keep other men from breaking in?"

"*Sì.* A sign from God that I am here, no?" he asked.

Erinn took a sip of wine, which warmed her.

"Well, I'll be going to Philadelphia for work very soon. Since you know your way around the kitchen, you can feed Caro while I'm away."

Massimo saluted Erinn with his wineglass.

"When do you leave for Philadelphia?"

"In ten days," Erinn said. "I have a lot to do before then. These shoots are not as easy as they look."

"Ah! I wish you did not have to go! This television, she is unworthy of you. You are an artist!"

Erinn was again grateful for the low lighting. She could feel herself glowing.

After dinner, Massimo suggested they look at one of his short films. It was in Italian, but Erinn was eager to shake the cobwebs out of her brain and watch. It had been a long time since she needed to sustain an understanding of the language.

Massimo poured them each another glass of wine and took Erinn's hand as he led her to the sofa. He sat very close to her, but in such a casual way that it seemed the natural order of things. Massimo was such a sweet man—a little pushy, maybe, but sweet. Memories of another sweet Italian man threatened to invade the evening, but Erinn was very practiced at keeping them at bay. Erinn concentrated on the movie in front of her.

The plot was something about a curvaceous young Italian woman traveling through Italy. She seemed to spend most of her time changing in and out—mostly out—of clothes. Massimo played a street vendor and was on screen all of ten minutes. He was selling the woman a shawl, and she stripped down to a skimpy, transparent

T-shirt to try it on. Having spent so many years in the theater, Erinn was completely comfortable with nudity, but this seemed a bit excessive. She glanced at Massimo, who looked lovingly at his masterpiece flickering on the screen in front of them.

"She is beautiful, no?"

Erinn wasn't sure if he meant the film or the woman, who was once again divesting herself of her clothes on her way into the Adriatic Sea. Erinn took in the beautifully shot Italian landscape and the impossibly blue water. The sunset was perfect—a gift from the filmmaker's god.

"Yes, she is beautiful," said Erinn.

CHAPTER 7

Erinn was hoping Massimo would stay away from the front door, but as Suzanna pulled up, Massimo stuck his head out and waved. As Erinn started down the path, Massimo grabbed her and kissed her on both cheeks. Erinn got in the truck and slammed the door.

"Nothing is going on," Erinn said. "He's just trying to be helpful."

"Did I say anything?"

"You just make me feel defensive," Erinn said. "And silly."

"Are you nervous?" Suzanna asked.

"No! I can handle him!"

"Not Massimo, work!"

Suzanna was driving Erinn to the airport. Erinn had only packed a small bag of personal belongings, but Suzanna had to bring her husband's truck to fit all the camera equipment.

All the preparation for the Revolutionary War shoot was wrapped up and all the crew—Gilroi, Carlos, and Jude—were meeting at the airport. The plan was that they would all fly to Philadelphia together. After that, Erinn lost track of the plan. It appeared that once they hit town, they could either stay together for the big location shoots or fan across the area, shooting their pieces simultaneously. The lack of a concrete schedule made Erinn nervous, but the more seasoned crew seemed to be quite comfortable with the idea, so she decided to wait and see how things worked—before making changes. Erinn tried not to be judgmental, but the casual approach the men took to the assignment disturbed her.

"I'm ready for the shoot," Erinn said, grateful for the change in topic. "I'm just not sure if anybody else is."

"You don't have to worry about anybody else. Just do your job."

"Well," Erinn said, changing the subject, "at least I don't have to worry about Caro for the two weeks I'm away. Massimo will look after him."

A leaden silence filled the very small cab.

"I would have been happy to look after Caro," said Suzanna. "But I guess since Massimo practically lives in your house, this is fine."

Erinn bristled. She wasn't avoiding the topic of Massimo after all. "Massimo does not practically live in my house. He uses the kitchen from time to time."

"From time to time?"

"Well, OK, from meal to meal. But he's a wonderful cook, and he doesn't take advantage."

"Oh? He's taken up all your cabinets and half your refrigerator!"

"He has leftovers from the restaurant!" Erinn said. "You're just annoyed that I found him myself and you didn't get to save me."

"Well, I wouldn't have picked him myself, that's for sure. He doesn't even have a real job!"

"How can you say that? He's a cook!"

"You said he was a chef," Suzanna said.

Erinn twisted uncomfortably in her seat.

"He is an artist. I don't care what his label is."

"Bella Bella is a little dive on Pico Boulevard," Suzanna snorted. "I guess the difference between *cook* and *chef* is a fine line in translation."

"Cook, chef . . . the rent gets paid," Erinn said.

"Oh, well," Suzanna said. "Some people don't consider a tea shop a real restaurant, either."

Erinn was grateful for a truce.

"Have you been watching television like I told you to?" Suzanna asked. "Getting a sense of what people want these days?"

"Yes, and I don't think it did one bit of good. All it did was reaffirm my opinion that TV has gone to hell in a handbasket. These reality shows—my God! What a waste of time and money."

"Erinn, if you're going to make it in TV, you're just going to have to be more adaptable."

"I am adaptable," Erinn said. "Not a word that springs to mind when thinking of me, I grant you, but I am."

"Whatever you say, Erinn. Anyway, we're here," Suzanna said, as she pulled up to the curb.

She wanted to help Erinn load all the equipment onto a cart. Erinn maintained that it was too much for a pregnant woman and insisted that she had done enough and she should get back to her shop. Erinn endured a hug from her sister while scanning the check-in line for other crew members. Suzanna abruptly held Erinn at arm's length with tears in her eyes.

"Don't screw up, for God's sake, Erinn."

Suzanna drove off just as Erinn spotted Gilroi at the front of the check-in line. He was standing with a good-looking man in his forties. They leaned into each other intimately, and Erinn smiled. She remembered back in her heyday in New York, when gay couples could not show public affection. It was always so unnerving to live in the theater, where being gay was completely accepted, and then heartbreaking to watch her gay co-workers' transformation as soon as they headed into the world . . . or even out to the street. She remembered a time when two of the most affectionate men she knew—they were always all over each other during rehearsal—left the hall and parted on the street. They stood there gazing at each other and then theatrically shook hands. It was their "heterosexual good-bye," they said, making a joke of it. But nobody—least of all the two of them—really thought it was funny.

Erinn watched as Gilroi's partner kissed him good-bye and grabbed a cab. Erinn wondered if Gilroi was too young to have felt that kind of prejudice. From his body language and theatrical facial expressions, it was clear Gilroi was arguing with the beleaguered check-in attendant. Gilroi caught Erinn's eye and signaled her to join them. She pushed her cart to the front of the line, oblivious to the glares from the other passengers lining the curb.

Gilroi turned to Erinn.

"He says I can't bring the camera case on the plane. It won't fit in the overhead. I have to get it on board! I can't check the *camera*!"

Erinn knew that Gilroi was right. Even in a protective case, the camera was much too delicate—and expensive—a piece of equipment to leave to the underbelly of the plane. A cab pulled up to the curb while Erinn was mulling over the situation. Carlos unloaded his equipment next to Gilroi's. A passenger a few heads back shouted that it wasn't fair for these "movie people" to cut into line.

Erinn stared the man down.

"For your information, we're TV people, not movie people. Furthermore, we have a problem to solve and it will save everyone—including you—time if we solve it once, instead of three times. So I'll thank you for your patience."

Turning back to the problem at hand, Erinn detected a look of respect shoot from one production crew member to the next. Erinn, feeling empowered, turned to her cohorts.

"The problem seems to be that the camera cases are too big for the plane . . . not the cameras themselves. We all have carry-on bags. Let's re-pack. We'll put the cameras in our carry-ons and pack our carry-on things in the camera cases." She turned to the check-in attendant. "Does that work for you?"

"Yes, ma'am," he said as the crew got busy stuffing and shuffling belongings.

Gilroi gave Erinn a quick, approving squeeze.

"Good work, Sawyer! You started out a youngster, but you came back a star."

"Thanks, Gilroi. But that quote is wrong."

"It can't be. I know my movie quotes. It's from *42nd Street*."

"Yes, it is from *42nd Street*," Erinn said. "Nineteen thirty-three. But the quote is 'You're going out a youngster, but you've got to come back a star!' "

Gilroi smiled, impressed.

"Louie, I think this is the beginning of a beautiful friendship."

Erinn smiled back. Slowly, she was making inroads. Although impressing Gilroi was easy . . . ten years in the theater meant she could match movie and Broadway play quotes with the best of them.

When the equipment had been checked in to everyone's satisfaction, the group managed to get through security without incident and headed toward the gate. Erinn looked at her co-workers and was pleased that they had turned to her in a time of crisis. Clearly, her unruffled demeanor and authoritative persona were a calming influence. Carlos fell in step with Erinn and put his arm around her shoulder.

"Thanks, Momma," he said. "It's always cool to have the old guard around when things turn to shit."

Erinn blinked in surprise. *Momma?* She looked up at Carlos, who loped along easily beside her.

Maybe it's a Latino thing.

She stole another look at Carlos as he checked out every pretty young woman who walked past them.

No, it's an old thing.

It wasn't until everyone was clustering around the boarding area that Erinn realized they were one director short.

"Has anyone seen Jude?" Erinn asked.

"He'll be here. He always does this," said Gilroi.

Erinn boarded the plane with the others. She tried to settle in to her aisle seat. She looked over at Carlos, who was sitting by the window, flipping through United's in-flight magazine. The empty middle seat, where Jude was supposed to be sitting, yawned between them. The rest of the Apple Pie crew was ready to fly to Philadelphia where they would spread out and conquer the entire Revolutionary War in a span of ten days. Could they shoot without a director? Erinn looked around the plane and saw Gilroi calmly reading a newspaper and listening to his iPod a few rows ahead. No one seemed alarmed that Jude was not on the plane. Erinn tried to shake thoughts of a coup from her brain.

"Passenger Raphael, please report to gate forty-six. Passenger Jude Raphael."

Erinn listened tensely to the flight attendant making her loudspeaker announcement. She thought the flight attendant sounded magnificently bored asking Passenger Jude Raphael to get himself to the plane. Erinn was wondering if the attendant just added a plaintive plea to her voice, maybe that would inspire him to get a move on, wherever he was.

Stop thinking about this scenario, Erinn admonished herself. *Jude's the director, not you.*

Well, I am if he doesn't get his ass on this plane.

As the seconds ticked by, Erinn's mood lifted. If he didn't get on the plane, she was sure she could convince Cary that it only made economic sense to give Erinn a shot at directing.

Squash those thoughts!

"Passenger Raphael, last call. Passenger Raphael. Flight 260 to Philadelphia will be leaving in one minute."

"Should I call the office?" Erinn asked Carlos, trying to sound professionally concerned.

Carlos looked up and pulled one earbud out of his ear. Erinn smoldered.

"This requires two ears."

Carlos grinned and good-naturedly yanked out the other earbud.

"OK. What's up?"

"Should I call the office?"

"What about?"

"Jude."

"Oh, Erinn. Just chill."

Carlos nestled the earbuds back in place.

Erinn stared at him and thought about the new words she'd picked up during the two weeks she'd been at Apple Pie. Because she was self-taught, she didn't really know much production-speak, but every time she heard a word she didn't know, she wrote it down.

Now, when someone asked for a "stinger," she knew to grab an extension cord, and if "barn doors" were called for, she knew that it was a lighting fixture with metal flaps that opened and closed. "Beefy Baby" had nearly stumped her, but it turned out to be an aluminum stand with some heft to it.

Erinn looked around the plane. She caught Gilroi's eye. He seemed to read her mind.

"Don't worry. He always shows up by the time we have to shoot."

Erinn sat back in her seat and closed her eyes. She admonished herself for her fantasy of how great it would be if he *didn't* show up. A tap on her shoulder brought her back to reality. It was Jude, holding a Burger King bag. He indicated the seat next to her.

"I think that's my seat," he said.

Erinn got up and let him in. She was determined not to say a word, but silence was not one of her virtues.

"You almost missed the flight."

"No, I didn't," he said, biting into his greasy burger. "I can't stand getting on the plane and just sitting, so I always wait until they're ready to close the doors before I get on. I still had a good seven minutes."

"The flight attendant said 'last call.' "

Jude shrugged. "They call your name four times before they lock you out. I was cool."

She glanced over at Carlos, who was pretending to read but who was smirking. Erinn loathed being smirked at and she stewed.

The flight attendant, a young woman in a snug uniform and a name tag that read *Marla*, leaned over Erinn to speak to Jude. Erinn, annoyed, flattened herself against her backrest to make room for Marla's industrial-strength breasts. Marla and Jude flirted effortlessly over Erinn, which annoyed her even further.

"Glad to see you could join us," Marla said.

"Wouldn't have missed it."

"We almost lost out on your company for Burger King?" Marla shook her curls.

"Hey! Breakfast is the most important meal of the day."

Marla giggled and removed her breasts from Erinn's personal space.

Erinn pulled out her book and determinedly began reading. Jude chomped his fries noisily beside her and suddenly nudged her as Marla started her pitch to her bored, captive audience.

"You're supposed to give her your undivided attention," Jude said. "Since you seemed so hell-bent on following all the airline's rules."

Erinn looked fleetingly at Marla, who was pretending to put the oxygen mask over her head without messing up her hair. Marla smiled hugely at Jude, who smiled back. The grease on his lower lip shone in the cabin light.

"I think you can give her enough undivided attention for both of us," Erinn said, as she returned stubbornly to her book.

Erinn snuck a peek out the window as the plane soared over the Pacific Ocean. She loved taking off from Los Angeles International Airport. North, south, east, or west—wherever you were going, the jet flew straight out over the water before heading in any specific direction.

Starting out over the water . . . it's like some sort of baptism.

Her thoughts were interrupted by Jude's voice.

"I love flying over the water," he said. "It's like . . . you're given a clean slate . . . ya know?"

CHAPTER 8

Erinn held her carry-on tightly to her chest and concentrated on her breathing as the Apple Pie production crew clustered around the luggage carousel. She had made sure that her camera came through the flight all right and then turned her attention to her teammates. They grabbed and sorted the gear as if the bags were stuffed with marshmallows instead of thousands of dollars' worth of production equipment . . . and that was the price tag *without* the cameras!

"Don't worry," Carlos said. "The gear is fine. We pack the shit out of this crap before we leave town."

Erinn blinked. Somewhere in that sentence was reassurance, she sensed.

As the motley crew made their way to the rental car pickup station, Erinn wondered how people who spoke of "packing the shit out of crap" could possibly be expected to turn out a cohesive narrative. And yet, here they were. Once inside the rental-car van, they rumbled along toward Hertz, the team members seamlessly split off into pairs. She was apparently with Jude. When the driver called "Hertz Gold," Gilroi and Carlos stood up.

"That's us."

They looked at Jude.

"You riding with us?" Carlos asked.

"Did you sign up for Hertz Gold?" Jude asked Erinn.

"I didn't know there was such a thing as Hertz Gold," Erinn said, trying to sound as casual as possible.

Her teammates stared at her in disbelief.

Averting her eyes, she caught the eyes of the driver, who look equally mystified. How could one live in the twenty-first century—their looks seemed to say—and never have heard of Hertz Gold?

She grasped for something to say that might redeem her, but nothing came to mind. Jude turned to the other men.

"That's cool," he said. "We'll see you at the hotel."

The men unloaded their gear, and the van doors shut."Why didn't you sign up for Hertz Gold, dude?" he asked. "Gilroi and Carlos kick your ass as a producer, you know that?"

"Why didn't *you* sign up for it if you care that much?"

"You're the producer . . . it's your job."

"Anything that you don't want to do is the producer's job."

"That's right," Jude said. "That's the natural order of things."

The van lurched to a stop, the doors swung open, and Jude and Erinn got out. She knew that it was the producer's job to keep track of all the gear, and she had heard that it was also the producer's job to carry all the gear. Erinn hoisted all the camera gear onto her shoulders and was about to reach for her own bag when Jude intercepted it.

"Let me help you with that," he said.

Erinn held tightly on to her load.

"It's my job. I've got it," she said.

"Humor me," he said, as he effortlessly took the two heaviest bags off her shoulder and started toward the Hertz kiosk. While they were in line, Jude got a phone call on his cell.

"Aw, shit. OK, thanks," he said into the phone. "Well, we'll see what we can do from this end. . . . Don't be so sure . . . I think she's up to it."

He winked at Erinn.

"What?" she asked.

"That was Carlos. They weren't able to get a free upgrade," he said. "Now we have to see if we can get one . . . we meaning you, Ms. Producer. It's a little contest we have. No pressure, though."

Erinn felt herself getting hot. No pressure indeed. She hadn't rented a car in years, let alone negotiated an upgrade. But she knew that this was a test—a test she had to pass. Erinn stepped forward, steeling herself. She was *BATTLEready!*

She and Jude handed over their licenses, and Erinn checked off the necessary, mystifying boxes regarding insurance. She noted that the car assigned to them was a Ford Focus.

"A Focus, you say?" Erinn began, having no idea what a Ford Focus was, but since it was considered a compact, she figured she was fairly safe in assuming the car was small. "That sounds a bit small for all this gear, wouldn't you say?"

As she gestured toward the luggage, Erinn caught a quick view of Gilroi and Carlos heading into the kiosk. They were here to see if she could get an upgrade, no doubt. Her knees started to shake. She could already feel the humiliation if she fell short. Erinn's three fellow crew members looked at her impassively. *You must not fail,* she told herself. Her fortitude wavered as she returned her gaze to the extremely bored clerk, who merely shrugged. Erinn redoubled her efforts. She was getting annoyed.

"May I speak to the manager, please?"

The clerk shrugged dismissively and called for "Dennis" over the intercom. The fact that Dennis was standing right next to him didn't seem to matter. Neither the clerk nor Dennis seemed to find anything the least bit weird that the clerk could have just as easily tapped Dennis on the shoulder. Erinn turned back and exchanged some superior eye contact with her co-workers. At least *they* seemed to get the joke. Erinn felt an odd need to close this deal. She knew she could really win some points with these guys if she came through . . . especially since the old pros had failed.

"May I help you?" asked Dennis.

"Well, I don't know, Dennis," Erinn said, trying to come up with an instant strategy. "I don't know if you can help me or not."

The Apple Pie team feigned assorted casual postures, but Erinn knew they were all ears. Carlos had even removed his earbuds.

"What seems to be the problem?" Dennis asked.

"Well, Dennis," Erinn said, "I'll tell you what the problem is. My company will only pay for us to get a compact car. All our gear is not going to fit into a compact car. Which means, we're going to have to leave our equipment in the backseat, exposed for anyone to see. Now, I know Philadelphia is not New York. I know Philadelphia is a wonderful, safe, secure city. But it is a city, Dennis. And bad things happen in cities. Things can get stolen in cities. And I am just wondering if you think it's in the best interests of Hertz, Dennis, for you to risk very expensive camera equipment being stolen from one of your cars, when you could easily avoid the risk by giving us an upgrade."

"You have insurance. We'll take the risk."

"Really, Dennis? Are you sure that's wise? We're from a television show . . . and my team over there . . . they see a story in everything."

Dennis scowled at the men in their ratty clothes. He turned to the clerk.

"Give her an SUV—with dark windows," he said, looking back at Gilroi and Carlos.

"I suppose they need an upgrade, too?"

"Oh, no," Erinn said. "They are Hertz Gold members. They'll be fine. . . . They'll be just fine."

"Oh! Snap!" Carlos said. "We've been p'wned!"

While she had no idea what Carlos was saying, Erinn understood by Jude's laughter that she had been wildly successful—on many levels—in her first task as a producer.

Jude loaded up the cargo and luggage into a new bright-red Ford Explorer while Erinn punched the hotel's address into the GPS. A horn sounded and she looked up to see Gilroi and Carlos drive by in their Ford Focus. Carlos was at the wheel and he yelled good-natured obscenities. Gilroi's head was attached to his BlackBerry, but he did look up long enough to give a distracted wave. Erinn wondered if there was a protocol for who drives . . . producer or director? Since the producer seemed to do everything, did that mean the producer always drove? Or that the director got his choice?

Jude suddenly plopped down in the passenger seat, pulling gloves on over his extremely frozen-looking fingers. Erinn remembered frozen fingers from her New York days and smiled fondly at the memory of thinking your digits were going to fall off on the sidewalk at any minute.

You never think your fingers are going to fall off in Los Angeles.

"How do people live here?" Jude asked, teeth chattering.

Erinn took a deep intake of breath, but before she could say anything, Jude held up a gloved hand.

"Let's just go," he said. "I forgot who I was talking to."

"To whom you were talking," Erinn said.

Jude looked at her.

"To whom you were talking," Erinn repeated. "You ended that sentence with a preposition . . . you know, *to, with, at* . . ."

"Kill me," Jude said almost to himself, resting his head on the frosted window.

"Oh, don't be so hard on yourself," Erinn said, secretly delighted that this young man would care so deeply about a grammatical error. "Here's a little anecdote that will help you remember. . . ."

Jude wrapped his scarf tighter around his neck. Erinn waited for him to stop fidgeting—all her people skills were coming back to her!—and she began her story.

"A freshman was crossing Harvard Yard with a map of the school in his hand. Lost, he stopped a professor and asked, 'Excuse me, Professor, but do you know where the administration building is at?' The professor looked at the student and said, 'Well, yes, young man, I do know, but I must remind you that here at Harvard, we never end our sentences with prepositions.' The student looked embarrassed and said, 'I'll remember that, Professor. So, tell me, do you know where the administration building is at, *asshole*?' "

Jude didn't move and Erinn thought he had fallen asleep. Slowly, he lifted his head off the window and stared at Erinn as if he'd never seen her before.

"That's hilarious, Erinn," Jude said. "That's fucking hilarious."

Erinn was waiting for him to tell her the story sucked, but he genuinely seemed pleased. It was a little unsettling that he didn't actually laugh at the joke, while pronouncing it hilarious, but perhaps that was professional courtesy.

"Let's get going," Jude finally said. "Did you put in the address of the hotel?"

"Yes," Erinn said as she started the engine. It appeared that she was going to do the driving.

"Great," Jude said, peering at the GPS on the dashboard. "Where's the hotel at?"

Erinn froze. "Where's the hotel *at*?" Had he not even listened to her? There was a horrible silence as the two of them stared straight ahead. Erinn risked a quick look at Jude, who was looking back at her.

"Where's the hotel at—asshole!" they both said.

This wasn't quite the bonding Erinn was hoping for, but, she thought, baby steps. Baby steps and profanity.

The British-accented GPS relentlessly led the charge toward the Nortown House Hotel on 8th Street. The expressway was unusually clear, but once the SUV hit Center City, it was stop and go all the way through town.

"The hotel is between Walnut and Locust," Erinn said, trying to make conversation when she suddenly realized she and Jude hadn't spoken for almost the entire ride into town. "All the east-west streets in Philadelphia are named after trees."

"Is that so?"

"Yes. William Penn was the founding father of the city and he was a Quaker."

"And . . . that has to do with naming all the streets after trees how?"

Erinn's brain quickly unscrambled Jude's sentence and decided that he must be interested, so she continued.

"He thought that naming the streets after people was immodest. He had the east-west streets named after trees and then numbered the north-south streets."

"Huh," Jude said, looking out the window.

"Of course, that was two hundred-odd years ago, so some of the street names have changed. Mulberry Street became Arch somewhere along the line."

"I know Arch Street," Jude said, turning to look at her. "Betsy Ross lived there."

Erinn tried to hide her amazement that Jude knew this fact.

"We used to sing this song in grade school," Jude continued, then burst into song. "Betsy Ross lived on Arch Street near Second . . ."

Erinn shook the cobwebs out of her brain. She knew this song as well.

"Her sewing was very, very fine. . . ." she sang.

"Arrgh . . . what's the next line?" asked Jude.

"General Washington went up to see her!" Erinn added mellifluously.

"To order a brand-new flag," Jude sang in a surprisingly strong voice.

"Six white stripes and seven pretty red ones."

"Thirteen white stars in a field of blue."

"It was the first flag our country ever floated."

"Three cheers for the red, white, and blue!" they sang together.

"I gotta tell you, Erinn, you are nothing like anyone I've ever gone out on the road with. Betsy Fucking Ross. Wow."

"You know, some people dispute the claim that Betsy Ross actually sewed the first flag," Erinn said.

When Jude didn't say anything, she felt perhaps she'd gone too far. She knew she had a habit of coming on like a know-it-all. She'd had the problem since she was a child, but in all these years of self-imposed isolation, she hadn't really thought about it. Now, all her insecurities were rearing their thorny little heads.

"I'll give you this, Err, you really know your shit."

Erinn cringed at the "Err" nickname, but decided, under the circumstances, to let it go. She and Jude had just had an entirely civil conversation—and she'd actually taught him something without annoying him.

Erinn maneuvered the SUV onto 8th Street and pulled seamlessly up to the curb in front of the Nortown House Hotel. Valets attacked the car with gusto, pulling out bags and gear. Erinn had forgotten the speed at which Eastern people moved. Erinn noticed that Jude, hopping up and down from the cold, waited on the curb for her while she signed over the car. A well-trained professional, Jude never took his eyes off the camera equipment.

"It's freezing out here. You go on in," Erinn said. "I'll watch the bags."

"Nah. I'll wait with you," he said. "We're a team, remember?"

Erinn bit her lip. She was overcome by this offhand remark. It had been a long time since she'd moved through life as part of a "team" . . . if you didn't count her sister—which she didn't. Or her cat—which she did, but under penalty of death would not admit.

The valet, with a cart piled high with gear and luggage, followed Erinn and Jude into the lobby. The producers of *BATTLEready!* were in charge of finding and confirming lodgings in each city. Erinn, as the newest producer, had been appointed producer-in-charge of Philadelphia. Given their budget, finding a great hotel had taken some work. Carlos had once booked the rooms for a shoot in Philadelphia, and he suggested the Holiday Inn by the convention center. The rooms were cookie-cutter, but the building was newly renovated, there was a gym on the premises, and the Inn was attached to a shopping center. If you bargained hard, said Carlos, the management would throw in a microwave and mini refrigerator. Erinn listened politely, but she knew old cities like Philadelphia had too many fantastic historic hotels to get stuck in a "chain."

After painstaking research, Erinn had chosen Nortown House, a historic landmark that looked well appointed but also had all the modern conveniences a production crew might need—high-speed Internet access, FedEx delivery and pickup, and continental breakfast. The hotel also served afternoon tea, but Erinn knew that wouldn't be a selling point for the people with whom she was traveling. Still, it appealed to her, and maybe she could gently issue in a calm afternoon or two. As she looked around, she was relieved to see that the hotel lobby was even more impressive than she had hoped. She knew that Gilroi and Carlos were probably already checked in, and she imagined their satisfaction at Erinn's selection.

Jude let out a groan as the warm air hit them.

"Gak! It's boiling in here," he said, shedding coat, gloves, and scarf.

"Don't complain. You're going to be spending days on end in a log cabin at Valley Forge, don't forget."

Jude followed her to the check-in desk. Erinn got out her freshly minted company credit card and handed it to the woman behind the desk, who wore a discreet name tag. It said merely *Susan*. Erinn was relieved to see that. She was not a big fan of informational name tags, such as *SUSAN* in large letters and *Mexico City* in smaller letters underneath. Apparently, some advertising agency or customer service survey deemed it important to add the clerk's city of origin as a way of—what? Bonding? But if you weren't from Mexico City, which most people weren't, what difference could this possibly make to anyone?

If informational name tags annoyed her, she positively detested the sprightly *Hi, my name is Susan. Use your words,* Erinn would think every time she glanced at one of those cheerful placards.

"Hello, Ms. Wolf. Welcome to the Nortown House Hotel," Susan said. "I have you on the second floor, as you requested."

Erinn had not specifically asked for the second floor, merely a lower floor—she hated elevators—but she let that go.

"Facing east?" asked Erinn.

The management-course smile on the young clerk froze into place.

"East?"

"Yes, east," said Erinn. "When I called, I specifically asked for a room with a sunrise view."

"Excuse me," Jude said.

Jude bumped Erinn to the side. She was ready to take umbrage with his knight-in-shining-armor routine. It was one thing to wait with her and the luggage, but this was quite another. She was the producer! She could handle this herself!

"I can see this is going to take some time to get straightened out," Jude said to the clerk. "So if you can just tell me where my room is . . . my name is Jude Raphael . . . you can get back to the eastern-facing room in a minute."

Erinn kept her face composed. She'd made bigger miscalculations in her life. She thought about Massimo, and how he would never barge in front of woman for any reason. Jude suddenly turned from his transaction and looked at her incredulously.

"There's no gym here," he said.

"That's correct," Erinn replied.

"You booked us into a hotel with no *gym*?"

"This hotel is a historic landmark, Jude," Erinn said. "You have to give up some of the less important things for atmosphere."

"Is that so? Well, Ms. Producer, you haven't been on any of these twelve-hour-a-day shoots before, so I'll ignore your snarcastic attitude. But a gym is a necessity, not a luxury. You'll see."

Erinn watched Jude as he went up the staircase two steps at a time. Clearly, the man could skip a few days at the gym to no ill effect. He was obviously a fanatic.

And what did he mean, she had a "snarcastic" attitude? This was some urban hybrid of "snarky" and "sarcastic" that was supposed to send her reeling. If she hadn't been so annoyed, she might have even admired the compound.

Erinn stepped up to the desk, ready to resume her battle for the eastern-facing room. Susan smiled at her brightly. Erinn was always suspicious of bright smiles under these sorts of circumstances. They usually meant "Hi, I'm not going to be in the least bit helpful." Erinn decided to be firm.

"I know it's an unusual request, but I get up early and I like to rise with the sun," she said. "I do my best work then. It's important."

"I understand!" Susan said, furrowing her brow and looking at her computer screen. "Well, it looks like your co-workers chose most of the lower floors, but I can give you an eastern-facing room on the sixth floor, or I have one western facing room on the second floor. Which would you like?"

Erinn let out a sigh. Why did it always go like this? She had asked for an eastern-facing room on a lower floor, and now the hotel was trying to convince her they would be doing her a favor by honoring *one* of the requests.

"All right, I'll take the sixth floor," Erinn said.

In her peripheral vision, she saw the bellhop grabbing the camera equipment. She wheeled on him.

"That's all right," she said, taking the heaviest bag from him. "This is very delicate equipment. . . . I'll carry it myself."

"It's six floors and you have four very heavy bags, ma'am."

"I realize that," Erinn said, knowing full well where this conversation was headed. "I'll just take the cart into the elevator and I promise I will return it to the lobby immediately—with a tip."

"That's just it, ma'am. There is no elevator."

Erinn felt as if she had suddenly grown roots and was anchored to the spot. She had booked a hotel with no elevator for two production teams, each one hauling almost seventy pounds of equipment. She caught Susan's eye. No wonder all her co-workers chose the lower levels! Erinn shook herself from her spot and handed the heavy bag back to the bellhop. The two of them divvied up the bags and started the long, hard climb to the sixth floor. After the third floor, Erinn stopped to catch her breath. She flattened herself against the wall when she saw Carlos in the hallway. He didn't notice her, but he had stopped and was attempting some back and shoulder exercises.

If her teammates didn't need a gym when they got here . . . they'd certainly need one by the time they left.

Finally, Erinn and the bellhop stumbled into her room. She fished a twenty-dollar bill out of her bag. Her per diem really didn't allow for such extravagances, but Erinn felt it was her duty to make it up to all the staff, who were now going to be hauling equipment around for the next several weeks. Erinn remembered from her traveling days that word of a huge tip would get around. Well, at least in India. Philadelphia was still a wild card. The sweating bellhop took the tip, gasped out a "Thank you," and staggered from the room.

CHAPTER 9

Erinn looked around. Well, even with no gym or elevator, the hotel made good on décor. Through sheer force of will, she had negotiated mini-suites for every member of the crew (something she hoped they'd remember when condemning her for the hotel's shortcomings). Erinn was surprised to see that the colonial feel of the exterior and lobby didn't extend to room décor. The suite was tastefully appointed in sleek, modern furniture and bright colors. Erinn felt sure that she would be completely comfortable in the place for the next three weeks . . . that is, if she could continue to get the equipment up and down the stairs. She spotted her precious east-facing window. The shades were drawn, and it would be dark outside anyway, but she went to the window and drew back the curtain. It took a while for Erinn's eyes to adjust to the darkness outside. And then she realized she was looking at a brick wall. If she stretched all the way out, she could almost touch it. She was in a sixth-floor walk-up with a ton of equipment . . . and there would be no sunrises.

Unpacking took close to an hour. She got her clothes out of the suitcase and into the chest of drawers and closet in ten minutes, and spent the rest of the time setting up her command post. In her mind's eye, her desk faced the eastern morning light, where she would drink coffee and set up the day's schedule . . . but clearly, she was not going to glean any inspiration from the brick wall out her window. On the bright side, the suite was amazingly light and airy, so Erinn set up the dining room with a computer, printer, history and tour books. She staged the camera equipment, batteries, chargers, and lights on the desk.

Surveying the rooms, she felt she was *BATTLEready!* She went into the bathroom and started the tub. Erinn had been dreaming of a long, hot soak in the tub since she'd gotten off the plane. The water rushing into the bathtub was loud, but not loud enough to drown out the sound of the room phone ringing. She came out of the bathroom, but couldn't locate the phone. It had been on the desk, but she had deemed it superfluous and stashed it out of the way. Now she couldn't find the damn thing. She jumped facedown on the mattress and hung over the edge of the bed, looking underneath. Many dust bunnies, no phone. With the blood rushing to her head, the pressure pulsing behind her eyes, she groped wildly under the bed. The phone stopped ringing. Erinn lay back on the mattress, trying to let the blood settle back in her body.

Her cell phone rang. Thankfully, it was in her pocket. Without opening her eyes, she answered it.

"Hello?"

"Hey," Gilroi said. "I rang your room. But I didn't get an answer. It just went dead."

"What went dead?"

"The phone."

"A phone can't go dead," Erinn said. "It's not a living, breathing thing. It merely stopped ringing."

"Erinn, you know that expression, 'Never apologize, never explain'?"

"Of course I do . . . Edwin Milton Royle."

"What?"

"Edwin Milton Royle wrote that in nineteen sixteen in his novel *Peace and Quiet*."

"Uh . . . really? 'Cause I think you might be wrong."

Erinn tried to stifle a giggle. She might be *wrong*?

"Oh really?" she asked.

"Yeah . . . because John Wayne said it in the nineteen forty-nine film *She Wore a Yellow Ribbon*."

Erinn had forgotten that Gilroi's point of reference was either the movie theater or Broadway theater.

"Well, whoever said it, what about it?" Erinn asked.

"Maybe you should practice the 'never explain' part."

Erinn sat up.

"What can I do for you, Gilroi?"

"Oh, well, I was wondering if you ordered oxygen tanks for those of us you so thoughtfully stored on the upper floors of this *relic*."

"You're only on the third floor!"

"There's no elevator! What were you thinking?"

Erinn was silent. Never explain? Fine.

After a moment, Gilroi said, "Hello? Hey, Erinn . . . are you there?"

"Yes . . . I was just following your advice. Royle's full quote, in case John Wayne didn't use it in its entirety, is 'Never apologize, never explain. Get it over with and let them howl.' I'm letting you howl."

Gilroi laughed."Darling, you are so adorable," Gilroi said. "Listen, I didn't actually call to bust your chops. The producers are all getting together in about an hour to go over our strategy for this shoot. There's a cool Irish pub around the corner called the Black Sheep. We're meeting in the lobby in a half hour. *Ciao*."

"Sì. Lo vedrò fra mezz'ora," Erinn said instinctively.

Gilroi laughed and hung up. Erinn raced back to the bathroom and shut off the tap—catching it just before the tub overflowed. She stared at her reflection in the water. Unfortunately, she looked as tired and as irritated as she felt.

After her bath, Erinn felt a little better and traipsed down the six flights of steps to find Carlos prowling the lobby. She guessed that the charms of a historic landmark hotel probably didn't thrill the young producer.

"Hey, Erinn," he said with a brilliant smile.

On second thought, perhaps she was wrong.

"Hello, Carlos."

"This hotel blows."

OK, so she was right the first time.

Well, at least I can still read people.

"No gym, no—" Carlos said.

"—elevators, no bar, no swimming pool."

"Exactly. This place is a pain."

"Well," she said. "It's been said, 'Pain is inevitable; suffering is optional.' "

"Whatever."

Gilroi glided down the stairs to join them. He was ready to hit the cold streets in a camel's hair coat and brown cashmere scarf.

"I love this hotel, Erinn," Gilroi said, pulling on his gloves. "I felt like Scarlett O'Hara coming down those stairs. And here you are, Carlos, my Rhett Butler, waiting for me."

"Bite me," Carlos said. He turned to Erinn. "He does this everywhere we go. I've been Ricky to his Lucy, Romeo to his Juliet, Stanley to his Stella. He never stops."

"Well, I can dream, can't I?" asked Gilroi.

The two men laughed comfortably. Erinn was reminded again of how times had changed. She realized that keeping herself cloistered all these years had been to her detriment in many ways. Good things were happening all around her and she hadn't been aware. It was wonderful for her to witness a gay man and a straight man completely comfortable with each other. Of course, thinking back to her first meeting with Jude at the guesthouse, this loosening of prejudice also made way for labels like *gay* and *retard* to effortlessly join the lexicon, which Erinn found disgraceful. Well, this was a producers-only meeting. Jude wasn't here, and she wouldn't think about it. *I'll think about it tomorrow,* Erinn quoted Scarlett O'Hara to herself. She was sure she'd be matching Gilroi quote for quote in the days ahead, and she smiled. She loved a challenge.

Gilroi held the door for Erinn and ushered them all out into the snapping wind. Erinn breathed in the cold East Coast night air. Memories of New York, and of being young and happy, tried to flood her, but she was an old hand at shoring up those emotional levees. She forced herself to concentrate on the two producers walking slightly ahead of her. Carlos did a double take every time a pretty woman walked by. Gilroi turned back to Erinn, smiling.

"He always acts like he just got out of prison."

Erinn knew it would be to her advantage if she could loosen up and join the fun. *OK*, she thought, *here goes!*

"As if . . ." she said.

The two men stopped and looked at her. Gilroi arched his eyebrow.

"As if . . . ?"

Erinn hoped the smile she had plastered on her face was coming off as jovial, but her teeth felt frozen in their collision with the evening air.

"He always acts *as if* he just got out of prison."

Gilroi's eyebrow collapsed and he and Carlos looked at each other. Erinn realized that this probably wasn't the right approach, but unlike writing, you couldn't just delete a comment and start over.

Carlos suddenly yanked open a door and disappeared inside. They had arrived at the Black Sheep. Gilroi shook his head in disgust.

"Don't mind Carlos's lack of manners," he said. "He ain't no Jeeves."

As Gilroi opened the door for Erinn, Carlos popped his head out.

"What's with you guys? Come in! It's freezing!"

"We're coming, Prince Charming, we're coming," Gilroi said.

Erinn was happy to find herself back in a uniquely East Coast bar. Lots of old brick and gleaming wood. The bar was packed, and Erinn wondered how on earth they where going to be able to conduct a business meeting above the dim.

"I'll get the first round!" Carlos shouted. "Please-Don't-Call-Me-Tin-Lizzy, what'll you have?"

Erinn bristled at the nickname, but there was obviously no getting around it with these kids. One thing she took to heart while researching *BATTLEready!* was "Choose your battles," so she just smiled and ordered.

"I'll have a Blackthorn," she said.

Carlos bent down, putting his lips to her ear as if she were a child.

"Can't hear you," he said.

"A Blackthorn!"

"What is that?"

"It's a hard cider. This is a pub. They'll have it."

"OK, Miss Continental Divide. Gilroi, what'll you have?"

Gilroi ordered a glass of Sterling cabernet, and Carlos set off for the bar, muscling his way through the crowd.

" 'Miss Continental Divide'? What does that mean?" Erinn asked.

Gilroi shrugged.

"I think he meant . . . you're so continental ordering a cider. His grasp of sarcasm is kind of iffy."

Erinn took a deep breath. Gilroi had made a droll comment about sarcasm! She beamed at her companion. Here was someone with whom she could carry on an intelligent conversation, someone who would understand her. She felt as if she were stranded in the middle of the ocean and had been thrown a life raft. They watched Carlos making his way back to them with their drinks. Even in the loud bar, Erinn could hear Gilroi suck in his breath.

"Carlos doesn't wear underwear," Gilroi said. "You have to love that in a traveling companion."

Erinn nodded mutely. OK, intelligent conversation might be spotty. But it was a start.

Carlos put their drinks down and they all settled in to go over the next few weeks' schedule. Carlos and Gilroi pulled out BlackBerrys—the calendars glowed in the dark. Erinn pulled out a lime-green Filofax, a gift from Massimo. The two men stared at it for an instant, and then got back to business.

"OK," Carlos said, "tomorrow we all shoot together, right?"

Erinn and Gilroi nodded in agreement. Erinn hated to admit it, but she was relieved when she found out they would all start shooting together. She was incredibly nervous about the prospect of handling the camera, Jude, and keeping track of the schedule all on her own. Cary had driven home the point that overtime was not to be tolerated.

"The directors don't care about overtime," she said. "It's the producer's job to keep the production moving."

Since the director was in charge of how much they shot, Erinn wasn't exactly sure how she was supposed to keep any director—but especially Jude, who seemed to march to his own drummer—on track. But now she could watch these two old pros at work and by the time she was out in Valley Forge with Jude, she'd have a better idea.

They had a full day planned. They would meet Lamont Langley, the actor who was to play George Washington, in front of Independence Hall practically at dawn to give him his costume and lay out the day's shooting. Because the crew was shooting a documentary, and the action would be covered by a voice-over, there was no dialogue, so once the actor was in costume, they could commence shooting right away.

"Good thing Lamont doesn't have to learn any lines," said Gilroi, looking at Erinn. "He drinks big-time." Erinn didn't mention that she knew Lamont from her Broadway days. Lamont drank then, too, but somehow, when they were young, it just seemed theatrical, whereas now it sounded sad. While he never acted in her play *The Family of Mann*, they certainly ran in the same circles and were both considered (if Erinn did say so herself) highly desired company. Now no one knew her, and Lamont was reduced to non-speaking roles in a castoff HBO powdered wig. She couldn't wait to see Lamont. It would be good to see a familiar face. They could compare notes—Erinn was sure he was as surprised as she was to find himself in this brave new world.

Carlos was laying out their shooting schedule. He kept stressing they needed to stay flexible. Erinn couldn't understand the concept . . . how could you keep a production moving if you didn't adhere to a timetable? Cary's admonishment that the producer was in charge of keeping the company out of overtime played in her head. Maybe while they were shooting on the Delaware River and Carlos was in charge, *maybe* the crew would be flexible. Maybe when they were in bucolic Chadds Ford, when Gilroi was running the show, *maybe* the crew would be flexible. But in Valley Forge? No way. If ever there was a time for inflexibility, it seemed to Erinn that fieldwork on a production was it.

She was committed to inflexibility and said so.

"You can't predict the weather," Gilroi said.

"What has the weather got to do with it?" Erinn asked.

"Everything," Gilroi said. "We're shooting in town, because there's no snow on the ground. But when it snows, we've got to go to our battlefields. How were you planning to shoot the scenes in Valley Forge if there's no snow on the ground?"

Erinn was alarmed that she hadn't thought about that. In her mind's eye, there was always snow on the ground when she visualized her shoot at Valley Forge. Insecurity washed over her. How stupid could she be? How could she not have anticipated this? When she'd left New York, at least she had had some success to cling to. What if she failed at this new job right off the bat? She forced herself to listen to Carlos and Gilroi block out the events of the next few days. She would have to be alert.

If the weather held—Carlos tapped on his BlackBerry—they would execute Plan A, which meant that they would shoot in the city. If it started to snow, they would shift to Plan B. Plan B involved each producer heading out solo to his or her respective battlefield and shooting scenes called "B-roll" . . . a staple of History Network reenactments . . . lots of beautiful camera angles and artistically framed scenery to be used under dramatic voice-overs.

She sipped at her cider. Gilroi suddenly lit up.

"Oh my God! Oh my God, I love this song!"

Erinn listened to the background music. They were playing "Jump, Jive an' Wail." Erinn smiled. She had to shout above the crowd.

"I love this song, too."

Gilroi stood up and held out his hand.

"Come on, Erinn, let's dance."

Erinn looked around the pub. She pointed out that no one was dancing. Gilroi didn't care. He loved to dance, and there was a great tune playing.

"OK, Ms. Nineteen Eighties Playwright . . . don't tell me you can't swing dance!" yelled Gilroi over the music.

Erinn pretended she didn't hear him. But it was obvious that Gilroi knew that everyone who had been in New York in the eighties had learned to swing dance.

"I'll take that as a *yes*. . . ." Gilroi said.

In an instant, Gilroi had her on her feet, and muscle memory kicked in. Erinn was transported back to New York, when she was young and successful and spent half her nights happily dancing. Her insecurities fled as she swirled around. The room was a blur, but once in a while the startled face of a young pub patron smiled at her. She jumped, jived, and wailed as if her life depended on it.

When the song ended, Gilroi escorted Erinn back to the table, where Carlos was waiting.

"That was cool, Erinn," Carlos said. "I wouldn't have thought you were a dancer."

"Oh, don't be fooled by Ms. Tight Sphincter here," said Gilroi, kissing Erinn on the head. "I heard the eighties in New York were just madness! I'll bet she has stories that would blow us away."

Erinn sipped her hard cider. "More Than You Know" played over the sound system.

CHAPTER 10

If the Revolutionary War were run anything like BATTLEready!, *we'd probably still be British*, thought Erinn. For all the advance planning she'd done, it turned out that Carlos was right—flexibility was key! Well, she would make good on her promise to Mimi that she was indeed flexible. She looked out the window at the snowstorm that was blanketing the city. Plan A, their concept to start shooting in front of Independence Hall, was scrapped. It was on to Plan B. All the producers would go their separate ways and get some desolate footage of snow-swept hillsides and battle stations. In a day or two, if the snow didn't melt, they'd start shooting their scenes with costumed actors.

Erinn called the front desk and asked that the SUV be pulled up in front of the hotel. She grabbed her camera bag, struggled into her L.L. Bean gray down parka, gloves, and hat, and waddled out the door and down the steps to the lobby. Carlos, Gilroi, and Jude were all in the lobby leisurely drinking coffee. They watched her come down the stairs, lugging her camera bag.

"That's a look, Tin Lizzy," Gilroi said, giving her down-clad figure the once-over.

"Well, it's going to be cold out there!" Erinn said, digging in her pocket for the valet stub.

"You're going out?" Carlos asked.

"Of course I'm going out. I have to shoot B-roll of the battlefield," she said.

"Erinn, have some coffee," Jude said. "It's freezing out there. We're not going anywhere today."

"Excuse me," she said. "You weren't at the meeting last night."

"Well, *I* was at the meeting last night, and I'm with Jude," said Carlos. "It's too cold out there."

"Too cold?" Erinn said. "That's what this shoot is all about. We need to capture the misery of those poor benighted soldiers. We owe it to them to get out there and do our best work."

"I'll do my best work from here," Jude said.

"Fine," said Erinn. "You Southern Californians can sit here. I'm going to work."

"Southern Californians? Shows you what you know," Gilroi said. "I was born in New Jersey. Was brought up there."

"Oh please. That line is from *Butch Cassidy and the Sundance Kid*, nineteen sixty-nine," Erinn said. "Really, Gilroi, you're going to have to get some more obscure material."

Gilroi laughed and returned to his coffee. Erinn looked out the window and saw the Ford Explorer. Great wafts of icy snow pushed aggressively over the hood. *Even the car looks scared*, thought Erinn. She started to have second thoughts.

"Well, I guess if you have an SUV, you might be able to get through," Carlos said. "Too bad we're stuck with a Focus. It won't take us anywhere in this weather."

Erinn doubled her resolve.

"Seriously, Erinn, it's dangerous out there," Jude said. "Just chill."

"I'll chill in Valley Forge," Erinn said and turned on her heel.

Erinn got in the driver's side and started the car. She was punching in the address of the battlefield when the passenger door opened. A man in a dark jacket climbed in. Under the jacket, he wore a sweatshirt with the hood pulled up.

"Just drive," he said.

Erinn sat frozen at the wheel. The man spoke again.

"Come on, Erinn. If we're going to do this, let's do it," Jude said from under the sweatshirt hood. "I don't want to get stuck in Valley Fucking Forge because you were too lame to stay inside."

"Look, Jude, it's very nice of you—"

Jude put his hand up, blocking her words.

"Just. Drive."

Erinn put the car in drive and headed north. She thought of mentioning that there was no traffic on Route 76, but Jude was clearly not in the mood for small talk. She looked at the scenery, but the snow had kicked up so much that she could only see three feet in front of her. Her vision was so obscured that she almost missed the sign for Valley Forge, but luckily, the GPS squawked, and she just managed to get off the highway with a sharp right turn. She glanced over at Jude to see if he'd noticed, but he was sitting with his head back against the seat, eyes closed and arms folded.

Thankfully, the GPS, with "her" calm English accent, guided Erinn through the park. If she had been on her own, Erinn realized, she wouldn't have been able to find anything—the entire park was white. She was trying to find some picturesque log cabins, but all she could see were large snowy lumps dotting the landscape. Her cell phone blared inside her pocket, and she was so startled, she almost drove off the road.

Pulling over, she fished her cell phone out of her coat. Erinn flipped it open and read the caller I.D. It was Massimo. Feeling a little shy, a quick look at Jude let her know he was still not participating in their adventure. He hadn't moved a muscle.

"Buon giorno, Massimo. Come andate?" Erinn said.

"Buon giorno, dolce amica," came the deep baritone on the other end of the phone. "I have called to speak of Caro."

Erinn's stomach lurched.

"Is there something wrong?"

"No, no," he said. "I just want to know if he eat . . . the people's food."

"People's food?" asked Erinn. "Oh! People food! You mean, not cat food?"

"*Sì* . . . I make such beautiful dinners and I have no one to share. I wish to share with Caro."

"That's fine," Erinn said. "Everything else OK?"

"Life, she goes on."

Massimo started to cut in and out on the phone. Erinn shook it.

"Hello? Can you hear me?"

Nothing. Erinn shook the phone again, but this time noticed the bars on the phone face were blinking.

She yelled into the phone, "Massimo, I have to go. The phone is running out of battery."

She hung up and looked at Jude. He was clenching his teeth."OK, let's calm down," said Erinn. "I'll just grab some quick shots and we'll head back."

"Shots of what?" Jude asked, looking out the window. "There's nothing to see!"

"Excuse me, are you now telling me what I should be shooting?"

"No . . . but I could if I wanted to . . . that is my job."

"No, it isn't. You direct the scenes with the actors. I'm the producer with the camera. I direct my own B-roll. Feel free to stay in the car."

Erinn got out of the SUV and slammed the door. The wind was howling so violently that she had to hang on to the door handles as she made her way to the tailgate. She felt the latch under her gloved fingers and gave it a pull. Nothing. She tried again. The latch wouldn't budge. She gripped her glove in her teeth and pulled it off, hoping that she'd get better traction with bare fingers. She tried the latch again and still it wouldn't open. She could hear Jude coming around the passenger side of the Explorer.

"I think the latch is frozen," Erinn yelled to Jude over the yowling wind.

"Try the key!" Jude yelled back. "Maybe it's just locked."

Erinn felt a twinge of annoyance. The back couldn't be locked, could it? The key was still in the ignition, so she trudged back to the driver's door, reached in, and tweaked the key fob. She looked in the rearview mirror as Jude effortlessly opened the tailgate and grabbed the camera bag. Erinn sprang back to the rear of the car and snatched the camera.

"I've got it from here," she said. "Thanks."

"Erinn, don't be insane," Jude said, trying to take the camera case out of her hands. "You've made your point. Now let's go."

"Oh? And exactly what is my point?"

"That you're the teacher's pet. The good little camera girl who won't let a blizzard stop her. Now let's go!"

Jude forced the camera bag out of Erinn's hand. His eyes suddenly took on a horrified light. Erinn instinctively panicked, but she wasn't sure why.

"What's the matter?" she asked.

"This car automatically locks itself," he said. "Are the keys still up front?"

Erinn slipped and skidded her way back to the driver's door and flung it open with relief. She grabbed the keys and held them aloft. Even through the raging snow, she saw the relief in Jude's eyes. "That would have so sucked!" he said.

The wind picked up suddenly and Erinn almost lost her balance. She realized that the ground was starting to freeze underneath them. She admitted to herself that there was no point in being out—she'd never get a shot worth having, even if they didn't freeze to death.

"When defeat is inevitable, it is wisest to yield," Erinn yelled to Jude.

"Whatever, dude. Let's bounce."

Jude threw the camera gear into the back and felt his way to the passenger side. They both got in and Erinn started the car. She hoped Jude would stay quiet. She was feeling so shaky—not from the cold, but from the realization that she was not being a good producer. *This was complete madness coming out here,* she said to herself. What exactly was she trying to do, get them both killed? To put it in Jude's vernacular, she sucked!

Jude put on the heater and settled back in his seat with his eyes closed. He didn't say a word. Erinn tried to pull out onto the road, but the wheels just spun on the ice. Erinn and Jude looked at each other.

"Are we stuck?" Jude asked.

"We can't be," Erinn said. "This is an SUV. It must have four-wheel drive."

"Not necessarily," Jude said. "Do you see any kind of lever or button or anything that would let you switch to four-wheel drive?"

Erinn frantically looked around, but she didn't see anything.

"No. There isn't anything. Are we doomed?"

"*Doomed?* Jesus, Erinn. You are a glass-empty kind of girl, aren't ya?"

"Actually, I'm a 'The glass is the wrong size' kind of girl . . . woman . . . but I think that's beside the point right now. What should I do?"

"Start rocking the car. Put it in first, then reverse, then first, then reverse. Then give it a little gas and see if we can get out of this."

Erinn started shifting gears and made a mental note. Next time, she wouldn't settle for anything less than an SUV with four-wheel drive.

Miraculously, the car suddenly shot forward. She gasped and Jude slapped her on the shoulder approvingly. Erinn turned slightly toward what she hoped was the road—it was so covered in snow that she couldn't actually see a road, but it must be there. Making sure no one was coming—*Fat chance*, she thought—she started inching the Explorer through the ice and snow. She was creeping forward, when the car became completely unresponsive and started sliding toward the right. Pushing the gas did nothing. Turning the steering wheel did nothing.

"Oh, no," Erinn said.

"What?"

"The car has lost traction. We're skating on the ice."

"Holy shit!"

Erinn frantically turned the wheel to the right and then to the left. The car continued to slide.

"Oh my God!"

"Stay cool, Erinn. We're on flat ground. Nothing can happen. Just chill."

Erinn tried to relax, but the car kept sliding sideways, the weight of the vehicle causing it to pick up speed. Clearly, they weren't on completely flat ground or the SUV wouldn't be hurling itself sideways, but Erinn decided now was not the time to argue this point.

Erinn felt the vehicle tipping. She was jolted violently sideways and caught, suspended, by the seat belt. She craned her neck to look at Jude, who was looking up at her from the passenger seat. The SUV was completely on its side, like a gigantic dead beast.

"Now we're doomed," he said.

Erinn tried without success to free herself from the seat belt. With every gyration, the belt tightened around her neck. She tried to hold still. She craned her neck and watched Jude brace himself against the passenger door with his right arm. This gave his seat belt some slack and he was able to release the lever. He thudded against the passenger door, but at least he was free. Erinn felt her breastbone pressing into the seat belt as she hung sideways. She watched as Jude twisted himself around, crablike, and faced her. She looked into his eyes.

"The camera case," she said.

Jude sat back on his heels.

"Dude," he said. "Seriously? Forget the gear right now. We're in deep shit."

"The camera . . . ," Erinn breathed heavily. "Check the camera. . . ."

"What are you, one of those freaks who needs to record their own death?"

"His or her own death," Erinn corrected, gasping. " 'One freak' is singular."

"You are so pushing your luck, lady," Jude said.

Erinn was running out of breath, and she hung limply forward.

"Come on, Tin Lizzy," Jude said, wedging his back against her.

He must look like Atlas with me on his back instead of the world.

She had her eyes closed, but she vaguely sensed that he must be standing on the passenger window . . . or the passenger armrest. What if he broke one of them? Would the rental company charge them? Had she bought the right insurance? Weren't they in enough trouble having skidded into a ditch?

Erinn heard Jude's voice through the fog. His back was to her.

"When I lift you up, you need to unhook your seat belt. Come on, Erinn, you can do this."

Jude gave the faintest of pushes, but not enough to lift her.

"Crap," Jude said. "I can't get enough traction with the console in the way."

Jude turned around so that he was facing her. Their eyes met.

"The camera case," she said.

Jude ignored her and tried to lift her off the seat belt, but there was no way around the console.

"Shit! Crap!" Jude said.

"Jude . . . there's a knife . . . ," Erinn croaked.

". . . in the camera case!" he said.

Erinn could hear him scramble to the back of the SUV and unlock the camera case. She was reminded of sounds one hears when one is drifting off to sleep. Every noise sounds strangely amplified—and yet the sound is of no interest. She had the vague sensation of falling and, when her head cleared, she was lying on Jude, up against the passenger window. Jude was panting for breath, knife held aloft. She could hear the slit seat belt clanking behind her.

She reached around Jude's neck. His expression changed, softening. She touched the passenger window behind his head.

"Thank God it's not broken."

"Lady, I have a knife."

Erinn was suddenly very aware that she was pressed up against Jude. She tried to lift herself off him, but each time she thudded back against him.

"Hold on, Rocket, before somebody gets hurt," Jude said, releasing the knife.

He tried to help her get some sort of footing, but no luck. Try as she might, she could not help but be aware of the rock-solid abs underneath her as she braced her hands against them, pushing off again and again. Every time she was even remotely aloft, she would crash back down against Jude, who would let out a painful-sounding "oooph."

Finally, she managed to grab hold of the headrest and pull herself off Jude. She hugged the headrest and tried to feel her way around him, trying not to kick him in the . . . Erinn shook the image out of her head, editing herself. She tried not to kick him as she squirmed upright. By the time she was safely off him, she had somehow pulled herself into the backseat. Well, she thought, more accurately, she had pulled herself onto the back window. As her body brushed by Jude on her journey into the back, she tried to keep her butt, breasts, and gut out of his face. She thought fleetingly of meeting him for the first time and his comment about her "spare tire." It didn't really bother her, she told herself, but she did find it interesting that she should remember that at this particular time.

Jude looked into the backseat. He leaned his elbows on the console and was breathing heavily from the exertion of freeing her.

"Thank you," Erinn said.

Jude just held up his hand in a gesture that could have meant anything from "That's fine" to "Never speak to me again."

Erinn scanned the back of the SUV and saw that Jude had carelessly flung her expensive camera aside while looking for the knife. The camera hung upside down, dangling from its strap. *It must have gotten caught on a clothes hook,* she thought, freeing it and cradling it gently. She was annoyed with Jude for manhandling the camera but decided to keep her own counsel on this. He had, after all, just saved her life. She picked up the camera and turned it on. She held her breath, waiting for the red light to glow. It did. *Thank God it still works,* she thought.

"Erinn, you need to call AAA or the police and have somebody come get us. It's not going to get any warmer, and it'll be getting dark in a few hours," Jude said.

Erinn turned off the camera and started fishing around in her pockets for her cell phone. She tried hard not to panic as she patted a tissue, a mint, and a few bobby pins—nothing remotely resembling a phone. It must have fallen out when the vehicle rolled.

Erinn climbed back to the front seat and started searching. Jude, without asking, divined what the situation was, and started feeling around by his feet.

"Here it is," he said, picking up the phone, which was sitting between his feet on the passenger window. Erinn held out her hand for the phone, but Jude was looking at it with a furrowed brow. He started jabbing at it.

"Jesus Christ, Erinn. Your phone is dead."

Why did these kids insist that phones were "dead," as if they were beloved pets? A little charge and the phone would be as good as new. So it wasn't "dead" on any level—no matter what your philosophy of life or death. Not even reincarnation. She was about to bring this up, but thought better of it, considering Jude's foul mood.

"I'm not used to cell phones. I forgot to charge it last night. Which is actually pretty amusing, since I charged all the batteries for the camera!"

"Well, plug in your car charger. We can't be out here with no phone."

"I don't have a car charger."

"Oh, this is great."

"Well, we can use your cell phone."

"I don't have it with me."

"Why not?"

"It's in my room. My plan for the morning was to hang out with the guys in the lobby until we could head out to a gym."

Erinn took a deep breath.

"Well, there's only one thing to do," she said.

"Which is?" Jude asked.

"Grab some shots while we're here."

"Are you nuts?"

"What are we going to do, Jude? Sit here and hate each other?"

"Hate *each other*?" he said. "You have no reason to hate me. I just saved your sorry ass."

"If you look throughout history, you will find that *hate* and *no reason* make very companionable bedfellows," Erinn said. "Now help me get this door open so I can get to work."

Erinn and Jude both pushed at the driver's side door over their heads. It creaked open like a hatch and Erinn climbed out with a little shove from Jude. She gave Jude the camera. It took all her strength to hold the door open far enough to squeeze out. Jude handed her the camera and hopped out after her.

Erinn looked around at Valley Forge as the snow continued to fall around them. The wind was still blowing, but lightly, and the snow drifted silently over the fields. There were probably telephone poles, or street signs, or cars, or other signs of modern life in front of them, but under the gossamer white blanket, it just looked peaceful and unchanged by time.

"This must have been what it looked like during the Revolution," Jude said.

Erinn shrugged, and turned on her camera.

"Not really," she said. "All those footprints, and horses, and garbage . . . it would have been hideous. The snow would have been gray or brown almost as soon as it hit the ground. But for television, this couldn't be better."

Jude suddenly reached in front of her and pushed a button on the camera. She looked up.

"Just making sure the camera microphone is on. I want witnesses for how annoying you are," Jude said.

He trudged off a few feet while Erinn continued to pan the horizon slowly. She turned back and caught Jude in her viewfinder. The snow and fog made him look shadowy and a bit ethereal. Erinn's pulse quickened when she realized you couldn't tell if this was a modern man walking though Valley Forge or a soldier or a ghost. She continued to shoot happily. *I'm probably going to win a Tony for this footage,* she thought. *Or whatever might be the TV equivalent.*

CHAPTER 11

Although it appeared to be totally silent as Erinn created snowy vignettes with her lens, there *was* sound. The wind whispered. The snow actually sounded as if it were breathing as it drifted, hissing softly, across the fields. Erinn stopped shooting long enough to dip her nose into her scarf—it was getting really cold. When she returned her eye to the viewfinder, she heard a click—the camera had shut itself off. Panicking, Erinn unbuttoned her coat and thrust the bulky camera inside, trying to warm it up. She couldn't see Jude in the whiteness, but knew he was out there somewhere.

"The camera is frozen," she said.

"Join the frickin' club!" came a disembodied voice, unmistakably Jude's.

"I have some weather protection for the camera. It's in the car. You'll have to help me get it out."

Erinn, trying to keep her balance, headed toward the snow-covered mound that was their SUV. She was ungainly walking through the ice and snow while trying to protect the camera, but she held onto it for dear life. The last thing they needed was for her to drop the camera. As if reading her mind, Jude was suddenly beside her, steadying her.

They reached the Explorer. They blinked morosely at the undercarriage, which, even in the snow, stared back at them at eye level. Erinn stared at it, trying to decide how best to get back inside. Should she scramble up the tires? And even if she managed to hoist herself onto the side of the car that was pointing toward the sky, how could she pry open the door? Should she stand behind the door and pull—or in front of the door and try to push it?

"You'll have to jump up there and open the door," Erinn said. "The weather gear is in the camera case."

To Erinn's relief, Jude effortlessly pulled himself up on the SUV's side. He squatted in front of the door and reached down. It seemed he had opted for the "pulling the door" move. Erinn shivered. The snow and wind were picking up again. She cradled the camera inside her jacket.

"The door is locked!" Jude yelled down to her. "Throw me the keys."

Erinn patted her pocket. No keys. She patted another pocket. No keys. She started to feel dizzy.

"Look in the car," she yelled up to Jude. "Maybe I left them inside."

"You did," said Jude. "I can see them."

Erinn leaned her head against the left front tire. She was startled when Jude suddenly jumped down beside her.

"The car locked itself, dude," he said. "I mean, we talked about this! How could you let this happen?"

"Me?"

"Yes, you! You were driving."

"Well, thanks for the support, *partner*."

"I can't believe this. God knows what would have happened to you if I hadn't come out here with you. You'd still be hanging by your seat belt, *partner*."

Erinn stared at Jude.

"I . . . I . . . I guess I am responsible for this," she said. "I haven't done one thing right. And we haven't even started shooting yet. When we get back, you should call Cary and have me fired."

"*If* we get back."

"What do you mean by that?"

"Look around you! We're in the middle of nowhere, without a phone, and we're locked out of a car that's lying on its side. We're fucked, Erinn—seriously fucked."

Erinn could feel tears stinging the backs of her eyes, and she looked at the sky, trying to blink them away.

"Christ. You're not going to cry, are you?" asked Jude.

Erinn took umbrage. She was not the crying type. Jude surely realized this.

"No," she said. "I don't cry."

"Good. Because I hate it when girls cry."

"I'm a woman . . . not a girl," Erinn said. And burst into tears.

"OK, OK. *Woman*. I got it. Please don't cry. Your tears might freeze and then you'd really be screwed."

Erinn tried to shore herself up. She took a few deep breaths, which was difficult. The wind was so cold it froze her lungs.

"I'm OK. I'm sorry."

"No need to be sorry, Tin Lizzy. We're cool. We'll think of something," Jude said, then put out his hand. "Give me the camera."

Erinn tightened her grip on her prized possession.

"What for?" she asked.

"I'm going to have to throw it through the window, so we can get back inside."

Erinn looked at Jude as if he'd lost his mind.

"Throw something else through the window," she said.

Jude looked around, spreading his arms to take in the vast whiteness all around them.

"Like what?"

"Like yourself. Just stomp on the window. Surely it will break eventually."

"Try again."

Erinn frantically looked around. There was nothing.

"Erinn, give me the camera. We've got to get into that car or we're going to die out here."

"If we smash the window, it really won't be much shelter," she said.

"Better than nothing. Seriously, Erinn," Jude said. "Don't make me wrestle that camera from you."

Erinn held tight to the camera. There had to be another option. She looked at Jude. Instinct kicked in and she sprinted away from him as fast as she could. Jude set out after her. Erinn was surprised at her pace. She wasn't sure if it was fear of losing her camera that kept her several paces ahead of Jude or the fact that lugging gear all this time had really toned her. Whatever the reason, she managed to stay ahead of him. She shot a quick glance behind her and stopped in her tracks.

Jude was gone! She looked to the right and left. Where was he?

Still hugging the camera, she squinted. The snow had fallen so thickly, she couldn't even see the outline of the beached Explorer. She cursed under her breath. Now she appeared to be stranded—and lost!

She listened. All she could hear was her pulse pounding in her ears. She took another step forward, but found herself suddenly face-down in the snow. Something enormous seemed to have fallen on her. A tree branch broken from the crushing weight of the snow? No, she thought, it couldn't be a branch, because it was fighting her. She realized that Jude had somehow jumped her. She was facing him and he was straddling her, trying to pull the camera from her grasp.

Holding tightly to the camera with one hand, she batted at him with the other.

"Stop it! Stop it! You can't throw this through the window. You can't!"

"Damn it, Erinn, give it up."

"You'll have to kill me first!"

Jude, straddling her, stopped fighting. Breathing heavily, he got up.

"I can't believe you," he said, panting. "You care more about that damn camera than you do about your life. Or mine."

Erinn sat up in the snow.

"Jude, I'm sorry. When you put it that way . . ."

She stood up and put a hand on Jude's shoulder. He turned and looked at her. Erinn thought that he looked very handsome with the snow clinging to the stubble of his chin. Shaking the thought from her mind, Erinn smiled weakly at him, trying to convey how very sorry she was for getting them into this terrible, terrible mess. Erinn opened her coat, and pulled out the camera. She held it out to him, trying to hide the resignation in her eyes.

Two hundred and thirty-two years later . . . this *will be the defeat at Valley Forge.*

Jude reached out his hand and Erinn put the camera in it, eyes closed, throat constricting. She felt the weight of the camera transfer from her hand to his.

"Psych!" Jude laughed, holding the camera aloft and running away from her.

He taunted her, running backward. Erinn opened her eyes and raced after him.

"Give me that camera!"

"You are such a loser! I can't believe I psyched out the great Erinn Elizabeth Wolf."

Jude continued to run lightly backward, teasing her. She ran on determinedly. She noticed that Jude had put the camera under his jacket, so at least it was safe and warm for the time being. She called out to him—

"Jude, look behind you!"

"Is there something big and scary behind me? Come on! You can do better than that!"

Erinn closed her eyes, and Jude, trotting backward, ran into something large and scary. He collapsed under an avalanche of snow. Erinn struggled toward him and started digging. Jude popped up, gasping for air.

Erinn launched herself on top of him without a word. She was getting that camera back if it was the last thing she did. And considering that the sun was going down and it was still snowing . . . it just might be. Jude fought his way out of the snow and easily blocked Erinn's flailing. He pulled the camera from his jacket and examined it.

"Just chill a second," he said to Erinn, sitting cross-legged in the snow. "Let me see if there's any damage to this thing."

Erinn stopped her feeble attack. She watched as Jude expertly manipulated the camera. He looked at her.

"I can't tell. It's still frozen."

He handed it back to Erinn, who cradled it under her coat. She stood up and looked around. The snow kept coming. She walked a few feet from Jude, scanning the horizon. There was no sign of the car. It lay buried deep in the snow somewhere. With all the running around she and Jude had done, she wasn't even sure which direction the car was in.

"Won't it suck if we like . . . you know . . . die . . . at Valley Forge?"

"Well, yes. But as they say, 'A good death does honor to a whole life.' "

"I don't think freezing to death after wrestling in the snow qualifies as a good death. I think it qualifies as a really stupid death. Got any quotes about really stupid deaths?"

Erinn turned around to face him. Why was he so hostile? Weren't they in this together?

"The trouble with quotes about death is that ninety-nine point nine hundred and ninety-nine percent of them are made by people who are still alive."

Jude looked at her in surprise. He smiled.

"That's hilarious, Erinn. That should be in *Bartlett's Quotations*."

"It is. Joshua Bruns said it," Erinn told him. "But if he didn't, I would have."

Jude stood up. He stepped purposely through the snow that had fallen on him. Erinn narrowed her eyes as she tried to focus and strained to see through the blizzard. She couldn't tell what it was at first, because it had been covered in snow. She wasn't sure, but she thought she knew what had caused the avalanche.

Her stomach flipped. She walked casually toward Jude, careful not to arouse his suspicions. She didn't want to hear about this if she was wrong. She walked very carefully, passing Jude as she went. He turned, confused, as he watched her make her way past him. Erinn reached her destination and clawed at the snow. She stopped and held her breath. She turned to Jude."It's a cabin!" she said.

Somehow, they had stumbled upon one of the historic log cabins that dotted the Valley Forge Park.

CHAPTER 12

"Awesome," Jude said as he dug his way toward her. "Now we just need to find a way to get inside."

Erinn had a death grip on her camera, should Jude decide he should dismantle it in order to find some inner working with which to pick the lock. Erinn continued to scrape away the snow until she had uncovered most of the door. She found a piece of rope tying the door shut.

"Wouldn't you think they'd have more security on this?" Erinn asked.

"We've just been sent a frickin' miracle, dude. Stop complaining."

"*Deus ex machina*," Erinn said.

"Oh, yeah, I forgot. You speak Italian. Very impressive. Especially under the circumstances."

Jude pushed his shoulder into the door and gave a shove. The door did not budge. It must be frozen! He stood a few feet back from the door. He ran toward it, but slipped in the snow, catapulting onto his back. He groaned. Erinn held out a hand and helped him back up.

"*Deus ex machina*. It's not Italian. It's Latin. It means 'God from the machine.' It's a plot device in which a surprising or unexpected event occurs. Just like this!"

Jude tenderly touched his spine and shook himself off.

"Fascinating."

"And I'm not complaining," Erinn said. "I'm speculating."

"Speculate when we're inside."

Jude walked up to the door and stared at it. Erinn watched him watch the door. Suddenly, Jude gave a frightening roar and kicked it with incredible force.

The door creaked open.

Jude pushed the door with both hands until there was enough room to slide through. He disappeared inside. Erinn stood silently in the snow wondering what she should do. Before she came to any conclusion, Jude's hand suddenly appeared in the doorway. She blinked at it for a few seconds, and then took hold of his fingers. She could feel the warmth even through her glove. He guided her into the darkened cabin. It was cold in the cabin, but just being out of the snow was a blessing. In a few minutes, her eyes adjusted to the darkness. She took in the interior—rough-hewn log walls, bales of hay lining one wall, large logs lining another. There was a boarded-up window. A stone fireplace rounded out the décor.

"We've got to stop meeting like this," Jude breathed behind her.

Erinn jumped. She whirled on him. Although she could only make out his outline, she could practically feel him rolling his eyes.

"Don't worry, lady," he said. "You're totally safe with me."

"You just surprised me," Erinn said, stung. "I know you don't have any carnal interest in me."

"Jesus, Erinn. 'Carnal interest'? Really? Who says that?"

"I do," Erinn said quietly.

She sat on a large bale of hay. She leaned back against the wall and watched Jude gathering some of the wood and hay. He tossed everything in the fireplace. He wasn't planning on starting a fire, was he? In a log cabin? Jude reached inside his jacket, pulled out a lighter, and lit the hay.

"Why do you have a lighter?" Erinn asked. "Do you smoke?"

"Once in a while. It's no big deal."

"No big deal? Don't you worry about getting cancer?"

"I'm just about freezing to death in a log cabin with a total nag. No, I'm not worried about getting cancer."

Erinn was silent. She stared into the fire. In an instant, the room lit up. Jude tended the fire until the wood caught. Erinn held her breath until it was obvious that the room wasn't going to go up in flames. Jude sat on a large log, looking pleased with himself.

"Wow, Jude. That was amazing," he said. "Your turn."

Erinn relented.

"That was pretty impressive," she said. "Thank you."

"Yeah. I actually have some skills, believe it or not."

"Have I given you the impression I don't think you have any skills?"

"You give the whole world the impression you don't think I have any skills. But I don't take it personally. You don't seem to have much faith in anybody but yourself."

"I will admit to being extremely self-sufficient. I don't think of that as a flaw."

"Yeah, well, you don't seem to think of any of your annoying qualities as flaws."

"My annoying qualities?"

"Yeah. Like . . . like, you're always correcting people. Especially grammar. You correct me, you correct Carlos and Gilroi—you even correct Cary, who is your boss. I mean, what does that tell you?"

"That people who misuse the English language outnumber those who don't four to one?"

"*No* . . . it means that it isn't enough that a person is smarter than everybody else—everybody else has to admit it."

"I do entertain ambitions larger than to be a regular Joe."

"Dude. Queen Victoria was more of a regular Joe than you'll ever be."

Erinn and Jude stopped speaking. He stared into the fire, and she thought he looked very young and angelic. Even if he did speak to her like a barbarian. "It's still pretty cold. We've got to do the body-warmth thing," Jude said.

He stood up and came and sat next to her on the bale of hay. His leg touched hers, and Erinn forced herself not to move away from him.

"Just relax," Jude said, sensing her discomfort.

"I have no interest in relaxing," Erinn said.

"You don't relax, you don't have any fun. This is some life you've got going on."

"You think you were put on earth to have *fun*?"

"You think you were put on earth to write one lousy play?"

Erinn felt breathless, as if the wind had been knocked out of her.

"It . . . it wasn't lousy."

"That's not what I meant."

"Don't you think I would write another *The Family of Mann* . . . if I could?"

"But you *shouldn't* write another one! You should write something new! And different. You need to get out there and mix it up a little . . . you know, experience life."

"I've experienced enough life, thank you. I'll have you know that when I lived in New York, I was considered somewhat of a wild thing."

They both stared into the flames and Jude slumped easily against the wall. The fire crackled lazily, and Erinn let some of the tension in her body relax.

"I can't really see you as a wild thing. And I'm a pretty imaginative guy," Jude said.

"I kid you not," said Erinn. "I went to Studio 54 when I was underage!"

"Wow! You snuck into Studio 54?"

Erinn smiled smugly in the darkness. She had him now.

"What's Studio 54?" Jude continued.

"Just the definitive nightclub for an entire generation!"

"I'm kidding," said Jude. "I've heard of Studio 54."

"Oh, right . . . from the history books."

Jude shrugged sheepishly. Erinn tried to ignore him. The banter seemed to be warming Jude, and he continued: "The grumpy and weird Erinn Elizabeth Wolf defining herself with a nightclub?" Jude said, looking up at the ceiling of the cabin. "Nope, I'm not picturing it."

The room was warming up all right, but Erinn didn't move away from Jude.

"It's true. I remember one night," she said. "It was winter, and the whole lot of us were drunk as a collective skunk. We climbed up to the top of the Empire State Building and spit over the side, to see if it would freeze on the way down."

"Erinn Elizabeth Wolf spitting on people beneath her—now *that* one I can picture."

"Very amusing," Erinn said, nudging him good-humoredly.

"Although I'm still working on you being part of a collective skunk."

Erinn turned to look at him.

"What do you think, I sprang fully formed—grumpy and weird—from the earth?" she asked. "New York City in the eighties—you should have been there."

"I was."

"That's impossible!"

"I was born in New York in 1981."

Erinn let out a great whoop of laughter. Jude smiled hesitantly and turned his face to her.

"What's the joke?" he asked.

"That I'm having a serious conversation with someone who was born in 1981."

"Well, you'll have to excuse me for not making the literary scene while you were there, but I was in kindergarten."

Erinn composed herself.

"Where did you live?"

"Hell's Kitchen."

"That . . . that used to be a very rough neighborhood."

"Yep, it was. My dad said living in a place like that builds character."

"You're lucky you never got shot!"

"Who says I never got shot? I'm kidding. My neighbors were partial to knives."

"How long did you live there?"

"Oh, through high school."

"Are your parents still there?"

"Who knows? My family isn't really what you'd call close. My parents are . . . free spirits. Last time I saw them, they were in search of the perfect consciousness, or the perfect wave, or the perfect cappuccino. I lost track."

"When was that?"

"Sometime when I was in junior high, I guess."

"You haven't seen your parents since junior high school?"

"Well, at first they were into having me around, then they weren't. I stayed with a bunch of relatives after that until I was old enough to leave."

"It must have been awful," she said.

"It wasn't awful . . . it was just, you know, my life. What can I say? It's why I love TV. I kept thinking that if I could just get on board *The Love Boat,* all my problems would be solved."

Erinn reached out her hand and put it on Jude's thigh. She patted it, in what she hoped came across as a maternal gesture.

"Jude! I had no idea. I'm sorry I misjudged you. I just thought you were a product of the West Coast."

"Ah, don't worry about it. I mean, my parents tracked me down on Facebook about a year ago. They don't want anything from me, and I don't want anything from them. It's cool."

"It sounds terrible."

"Really, it's OK," he said. He put his hand over hers. "What about you? You have any skeletons in your closet?"

"Oh, just the usual," Erinn said. "Nothing very interesting."

She hoped Jude wouldn't press her on this. He nodded. She wasn't sure if he accepted this or just decided not to push her, but he mercifully changed direction.

"So . . . if we don't . . . like . . . die here . . . what do you want to do next?"

"Professionally?"

"Yeah."

"Well, I don't know. I suppose if I'm going to stay in television, I'd like to create my own show."

"That's cool."

"As a matter of fact, I have an idea for a reality challenge show."

Jude's eyebrows shot up so fast Erinn was surprised they didn't fly out the window.

"I was reading an article in *Living History* magazine about volunteer lighthouse keepers. You can live at some of these lighthouses exactly as if you were living at the end of the nineteenth century. No electricity, Internet, or television, water pumped from a well by hand. Riveting!"

"So what's the hook?"

"So . . . you could get a group of these hideous, hedonistic cretins we call the younger generation, well, whom I call the younger generation and you call your peers, and see what they make of it. You could have teams."

"Like *Survivor*?"

"What is *Survivor*?"

Jude seemed to laugh, but he kept it to himself. Erinn didn't see what was so funny, but she didn't feel that he was laughing at her, exactly.

"This is still very much under wraps," she said. "You can't tell anyone."

"Who would I tell?"

"I don't know . . . but I am very wary of discussing ideas. You need to take this to the grave."

"What are you going to call this . . . lighthouse idea?"

Erinn hesitated. She was afraid Jude would make fun of her, and she was already venturing into unknown territory with this entire conversation.

"I was thinking of calling it *Let It Shine*."

Jude didn't say anything, but nodded. In the darkened room, she couldn't tell if he approved or not.

"You know," Jude continued, "maybe we could hang out sometime."

"Are you changing the subject?"

"Ummm . . . yeah. I'm not really in the mood to talk about my grave, under the circumstances."

Erinn flinched.

"Seriously, Erinn. What do you say? Can we hang out sometime?"

"Well, we're hanging out now."

"This is forced hanging out. I meant hang out voluntarily."

Erinn could feel herself tensing.

"Oh, no!" she said. "I'm not the hanging-out type."

"Come on. We'll go find some tall building and hock loogies over the side for old times' sake."

"Thanks for the offer, but really, Jude, I'm a solitary creature. I truly am. I sometimes wonder, did I become a writer because I'm solitary, or am I solitary because I'm a writer?"

"Who cares? Besides, you're a producer now. You've got to mix it up."

Erinn stood up and walked to the fire. She still held her precious camera against her body with one hand, but reached her other hand toward the flames, hoping that Jude would think she was looking for some additional warmth, rather than that she was feeling self-conscious sitting next to him.

"Do you think we're going to die here?" Erinn asked, not looking away from the fire.

Jude got up and added another small log to the fire.

"I don't know," he said.

Jude was standing next to her looking into the fire.

"I guess one of us will have to stay awake and keep the fire going," Erinn said.

"Well," Jude said, "we can definitely get through tonight, so try and look on the bright side."

Erinn felt light-headed and was uncomfortably aware of Jude beside her. She grasped for something to say.

"Try *to* look . . . try *and* look is a vulgarism."

"You got something to say for every occasion, don't you?"

Erinn's confidence returned now that they were back on common ground.

"Words don't often fail me, no," she said.

Jude spun her around and looked into her eyes.

"So what do you say to this?"

Jude put his arms around her and kissed her passionately. The camera was crushed awkwardly against her. She stepped back and looked at him in the shadowy light cast by the fire.

"Shit!" she said.

"May I quote you?"

"I *knew* this would happen."

"You knew I was going to kiss you? How? *I* didn't even know I was going to kiss you."

"I hadn't fully envisioned the conclusion, but I knew that the consequences of sharing a tight space in a . . . tense situation . . . with a . . . another human being, somehow, all things being equal, would be dire."

"Is there a reason, backward, you always say everything?" Jude said. "Hey, look, I'm sorry if I invaded your space. I don't even know what I was thinking. You just . . ."

Erinn tried not to care. But she had to ask.

"I just what?"

"I don't know," Jude said, walking away from her. "I mean, we're stuck here . . . we might die here. I felt like we were . . . you know, getting along. And . . . and you look really beautiful in this light."

"Spoken like a true director," she said, smiling.

She didn't believe for one minute that he thought they might die here—worst-case scenario, the snow would melt in a day or two and they'd simply walk out . . . but she chose to believe he really did think she was beautiful.

"Anyway," Jude said. "I didn't mean to freak you out."

"You didn't freak me out. I've just momentarily lost my composure."

"That is freaking out. Besides, what was so terrible about it anyway?"

"It wasn't terrible."

"Careful, now. A compliment like that might go to my head."

"A gentleman does not go up to a lady and overwhelm her—"

"I overwhelmed you?"

Erinn turned around to face Jude.

"All I'm saying is that the element of surprise doesn't always work in matters of the heart," she said. "A gentleman should ask a lady for permission to kiss her."

Jude was silent. Erinn felt foolish and turned back toward the fire. She heard him walking quietly across the room until he was standing behind her.

"Hey, lady." Jude touched her shoulders gently and turned her toward him. He tilted up her face until she was looking at him. "Can I kiss you?"

Their lips touched softly at first and then more insistently.

"May I kiss you?" Erinn corrected breathlessly, in a final attempt to avoid surrender.

"Whatever," said Jude, and he picked Erinn up and carried her to the bales of hay. He put her down and looked at her.

"You good with this?" he asked.

"I'm . . . I'm good with this."

Jude reached down and opened her coat.

He put the camera gently on the floor.

CHAPTER 13

Erinn was dreaming. A young man was walking by the Tiber River in Rome. He was looking at the massive stone steps leading two stories up to street level. He spoke to everyone who went by.

"Posso aiutarla!" he would say. If he thought the person walking by spoke English, he would say, "Please help me." Everyone ignored him. When Erinn walked by, he spoke to her in Italian. This made her proud . . . even in her dream. It seemed he needed help getting up the steps.

"I can't walk anymore," he said.

Erinn looked up. She told him she didn't know what she could do.

"You can carry me," he said. "I'll help you."

With this, he stiffened and turned into papier-mache. Erinn picked him up and easily carted him up the stairs. As she climbed, she wondered if he planned on reverting to flesh and blood when they reached the top. As long as he stayed a paper man, she wasn't too concerned, because she realized he wouldn't be any trouble to take care of. When she got to the top, she put him down in the middle of the street. Cars started honking furiously. The cars honked and honked. Drivers yelled. Erinn stood beside the papier-mache man and regarded him thoughtfully. She wondered if she should bring him back to the sidewalk. She was surprised that the people in the cars were all speaking English.

Erinn shook herself awake to the sound of honking horns and

people yelling . . . in English. She sat up, pulling her down parka over her naked frame. She ran a hand through her hair, which had hay sticking out of it. Reflecting on the events of last night would have to wait, she thought. Those voices were getting closer. She deduced that she didn't have time to dress completely and quickly zipped up the jacket and yanked on her pants. She stuffed her bra and panties into her pockets as quickly as she could.

She headed to the door, pulling straw out of her hair, when she noticed the camera sitting on the damp dirt floor. Her heart almost stopped. How could she have forgotten about the camera?

She picked it up and carefully dusted it off. She gently pushed the Power button. The camera hummed. Erinn realized she had been holding her breath. She looked through the viewfinder and tried the zoom. Everything seemed fine.

But where was Jude?

She stole a quick look at the fireplace. Embers were still glowing. Jude must have gotten up during the night to keep the flames going. She smiled. Suddenly, the door burst open, and a camera, much like her own but not as new, entered the room, followed by a cameraman. She glanced at the front of the camera for the telltale red light. It was on. This jerk was taping her!

Erinn jumped up and knocked the lens downward. The cameraman almost lost his grip on the camera and swore under his breath. He looked at Erinn. It was Carlos!

"What the hell?" Carlos said.

"I could ask you the same thing!" Erinn said.

"Dude! When you guys didn't come back to the hotel, we were scared shitless. We came out here as soon as the roads cleared. Once we saw the SUV on its side and figured out you guys had spent the night out here, we . . ."

Carlos stopped and gave a little cough.

". . . you called the police," Erinn said. She always had a knack for finishing the story. "I know. I would have done the same thing."

"Well . . . we didn't actually call the police." Carlos looked embarrassed. Erinn was puzzled. But then she realized what he had been about to say.

"You figured that this would make a great story and you could sell it to the papers."

"The papers?" Carlos asked. "Dude! You are so funny. This has YouTube written all over it."

Carlos almost lost his grip fumbling to shut the camera off.

"But we could have died out here," she said. "Did you stop to think of that?"

"Well, yeah. And I swear, Erinn, if you were dead we'd have called the police."

Erinn tried to stare him down and he broke eye contact first.

"OK, forget YouTube," Carlos continued. "What about the local news? The news will pay big bucks for this. Come on, Erinn."

Gilroi burst through the front door and grabbed Erinn in a bear hug. She tried to pull away from him, but he refused to let go. He buried his head in her shoulder dramatically. She noticed he snuck a fleeting look at Carlos's camera.

"He's not shooting," Erinn said. "You can knock off the theatrics."

"Oh," Gilroi said, letting go of her.

"So," said Carlos. "What happened?"

Erinn changed the subject.

"Where's Jude?"

"He's helping with your SUV. They're trying to pull it out of the ditch."

"What time is it?" Erinn asked.

"Almost nine," Gilroi said. "They cleared the roads about seven, and we've been looking for you ever since. We saw the smoke from the fireplace and ran into Jude on the way. He was trying to dig out the SUV with his hands. We called the tow truck, and once it got here, we came to talk to you."

"If one of the traffic helicopters sees this from the air, we're going to get scooped," Carlos said.

"Yeah," added Gilroi. "So could we please have an interview before this story gets out?"

"What story?" Erinn asked.

Gilroi led Erinn to the fireplace and positioned her, pulling hay from her hair and smoothing her eyebrows with his fingertips. He studied her.

"Well, you've looked better. But when you've survived a night in a storm like that, it probably works that you look like shit."

"Thank you, Gilroi."

Gilroi reached for Erinn's camera, but she clung to it.

"You're right," he said. "The camera is a nice touch. Keep it."

Carlos peered over the camera.

"Gilroi, get out of frame."

"No," Gilroi said. "I'm going to interview her." He turned to Erinn. "Don't worry, I have TV experience."

Carlos sighed and switched on the camera. Gilroi put his arm around her and turned his best concerned look toward the lens.

"Hello. I'm Gilroi Rose. Philadelphia held its breath last night, waiting for word of the two brave newspeople who went to Valley Forge to cover the worst storm in Pennsylvania history."

"Philadelphia held its breath"? For heaven's sake, a city can't hold its breath any more than a phone can be dead. And these are communications professionals!

"I'm here with one of those heroes now. Erinn Elizabeth Wolf. Erinn, can you tell me why you decided you felt you had to get personally involved in this storm of the century?"

"No, Gilroi. I really can't."

This version was certainly news to her. Gilroi raised his eyebrows, apparently trying to will her into saying something.

"It was a cold and stormy night," she said.

"Tell us about yesterday, Erinn," Gilroi prodded.

Erinn replayed the events of the previous night and felt herself blush. Why couldn't they have perished? she wondered. It would have been such a superior ending. Now she just had a sordid fling to deal with. Or maybe not. Maybe last night . . . meant something. But what?

She looked past Carlos's camera at the door, just as Jude walked in. The sun streamed through the opened door. He was in shadow, so it was impossible to read him. Her stomach tightened. Gilroi motioned for Jude to come forward, while still focusing his gaze in the camera's lens.

"Our other hero has just shown up. He's single-handedly been digging out the overturned vehicle that stranded these probing journalists. Jude Raphael, come on down."

Erinn thought Gilroi's on-camera experience must be limited to that of a game-show host. She tried to catch Jude's eye as he fell easily into line with Gilroi. She noticed he stood on Gilroi's left side, opposite Erinn, not next to her. Was this significant? Or just his best side?

"Jude, Erinn seems to be in shock about your ordeal here in Valley Forge. Maybe we can get a better sense of what happened from you."

"Well, Gilroi," said Jude. "As a probing journalist, I feel I did my duty last night."

"In other words, you did what you had to do?" Gilroi asked.

"Absolutely."

Erinn's mouth fell open in disbelief. Was he making fun of her? Well, if he thought he could get the best of her in a war of words, he was sadly mistaken.

"The storm was terrible," Erinn said. "Luckily, I managed to find this cabin and saved us from certain death."

Jude looked past Gilroi and stared at her.

"Oh! So it was a pity save," Jude said.

"What else would it have been? We would have frozen otherwise."

"I got a fire going," Jude said to Gilroi. "It took quite a while to thaw this lady out."

Gilroi looked from one to the other, like a deer caught in the headlights. The interview was cut short when a man in a Hertz jacket poked his head in the door.

"We'll take the SUV from here. Can you get a ride into town?" the man said to Jude.

Jude opened his mouth to respond, but Erinn was out the door in a flash. She was happy to escape Gilroi's intrusive questions, but she was more focused on getting the gear out of the truck. She strode toward the tow truck, camera protectively clenched under her arm.

Carlos, Gilroi, Jude, and Erinn rode back to the hotel in the Focus. The trunk was crammed with the camera equipment from the Explorer. The Hertz tow truck driver told Jude that a new SUV would be delivered to the hotel later in the day. Why was he talking to Jude? Erinn wondered. She was the producer. She was the one who had signed for the car in the first place. And the one who had gotten an SUV instead of a cramped little saltshaker of a car like this Focus.

Erinn was working up quite a head of steam and was just about ready to direct their attention to this when she stopped. She was also the one who was so pigheaded that they had almost got themselves killed, she thought, ashamedly. Perhaps it might be prudent if she kept a low profile just now.

"Well, at least we got this straightened out before the police got involved," Gilroi said. "APE would not be happy that you guys caused such a stink."

"They'd be cool," Carlos said. "As long as you're not dead and this didn't cost them any money. We're still flying under the radar, so it's all good."

"Yeah," Jude said. "Thanks for not calling the police. That would have sucked."

"Dude," Carlos said, shrugging his shoulders.

"Lucy, you have some 'splainin' to do," Gilroi said, mimicking Ricky Ricardo.

"You're thanking them for not calling the police and leaving us to freeze?" Erinn asked.

"Our permits are not . . . how do they put it . . . always in order," Jude said. "We buy the cheapest shooting permits possible and hope for the best. So we try to stay as far away as possible from the city fathers."

"Right on," Carlos said. Erinn watched from the backseat as Carlos and Jude did an elaborate fist bump—that ubiquitous social custom made *de rigueur* by the Obamas. "Besides, these two knew I'd handle everything," Jude said.

Jude and Carlos laughed and high-fived. Erinn looked out the window.

"Seriously," Carlos said. "If the park rangers had found you in that cabin, I wonder if you'd have been fined or something."

"Fined? Why would we possibly have been fined?" Erinn asked.

"I dunno," Carlos said. "Breaking and entering?"

Jude let out a snort. Erinn decided she had had enough of this conversation and resolutely stared out at the snow-covered park. This was exactly the scenery she had been looking for yesterday. She itched to get out of the car and shoot the incredibly beautiful landscape. But she knew she didn't have the collateral just now to ask that they stop. She sighed deeply. Gilroi, who was sitting in the backseat with her, patted her knee.

"That was some sigh. What are you thinking about there, lady?" he asked.

" 'But Mousie,' " Erinn said, quoting Robert Burns,

> "thou are no thy-lane, In proving foresight may be vain:
> The best laid schemes o' Mice an' Men, Gang aft agley,
> An' lea'e us nought but grief an' pain, For promis'd joy!' "

"What-ever," Gilroi said, removing his hand.

"And watch who you're calling Mousie," said Jude.

CHAPTER 14

Using the remote, Erinn shut off the television. She'd been watching the evening news in her hotel room, and luckily, it appeared that her little escapade in Valley Forge had gone unnoticed by the local media. She reasoned that the real story was when they were lost. Now that they'd been found, there wasn't anything of interest to report—who cared about good news?—so she was probably safe from any exposure. Carlos and Gilroi might be unhappy that they had nothing worth selling to any media outlet, but at least the higher-ups at APE would never have to hear about their near-death experience. The company would surely blame Erinn's irresponsibility and recklessness. She would have no defense. She blamed herself.

And speaking of irresponsibility and recklessness, they don't have to hear about anything else.

Erinn, who prided herself on always having a quote available, could only manage: *What happens in Valley Forge stays in Valley Forge.*

Her cell phone, plugged into its battery charger for the last two hours, sounded. She picked it up and saw that it was Massimo. Waves of guilt flooded her. She closed her eyes. After her night with Jude, was she ready to talk to Massimo, of all people? Not that she was romantically involved with Massimo, but still.

"*Pronto*," Erinn said into the phone.

"Ah! Erinn! I am lonely. I think about you during the last night."

Erinn winced. She couldn't very well say she'd been thinking of him during the last night.

"That's nice," she said. "How is Caro?"

"Caro is *bellisimo*. But he, too, is lonely."

"I'm sure Caro is more than happy with you as a companion."

"*Sì*. I move into the house to keep him company."

Erinn took the cell from her ear and looked at it as if the phone were going to translate this incomprehensible statement. Perhaps it was his interesting take on English that was the problem. Perhaps he was asking if he could move into the house rather than stating that he had moved into her house. When clarity was not forthcoming, she spoke again.

"What was that?"

"The cat, he is so alone. I am so alone. So, I move into the house. Now. We are not so lonely as before."

"Oh . . . I see."

"This is good?"

"I . . . well, I have to admit, I'm a bit taken aback."

"*Che cosa?* I do not understand. You have . . . how do you say . . . you have doubt?"

"Well . . . perhaps a little."

There was silence. Erinn felt herself panicking. She did not want to offend Massimo, who, after all, was only thinking of her cat.

"Oh, what difference does it make?" she said. "Doubt is uncomfortable but certainty is ridiculous," Erinn said.

"Ah! Voltaire!" Massimo said.

Erinn smiled.

"I have no doubts," she said. "By the way, have you gotten your head shots yet? You won't get anywhere without head shots."

"I have had no time," Massimo said. "The restaurant, she is very busy. And new head shots, they are very expensive, no?"

"Yes, they are. But I'm sure there are students around who would photograph you for less," Erinn tried to speak simply. "Maybe you could find somebody inexpensive on craigslist.

"What is it . . . this craigslist?"

Erinn smiled again. You had to love a man who knew Voltaire but not craigslist. He was a treasure. And she was keeping him—if long distance. The phone clicked in her ear—it was that infernal "call waiting" contrivance. She looked at it . . . her sister was calling."I have to go," Erinn said into the phone. "Have fun with the cat."

Erinn pushed the Call button on her phone. She could hear her sister screeching into the earpiece immediately.

"That . . . that . . . Italian . . . is sleeping in your house!"

"I know," Erinn said.

"You know?"

"Well, of course I know! Do you think Massimo would just move into my house without my OK?"

Erinn settled back on the bed. She loved getting the better of her sister, even if it meant stretching the truth—or out-and-out lying.

"I tried calling you last night. Did you check your messages? I must have called a thousand times."

"Three times, Suzanna. You called three times."

"Well, why didn't you call me back?"

"I . . . I've been really busy getting ready for the shoot. I haven't had a minute," Erinn said, reddening.

The truth was, Erinn was undecided as to whether or not she should confess her indiscretion with Jude. As much as Suzanna annoyed her, she was Erinn's sister and the person in whom Erinn confided in those rare moments when Erinn was in a confidential frame of mind. When they were younger, Suzanna had been the one running to Erinn, her big sister, with breathy confessions of infatuations and dreams of the future. It had been years since Erinn had anything personal she wanted to share with her sister—confessions now felt indulgent and weak—but part of her wanted to shock her sister, part of her wanted to brag "I'm still in the game." But now that Suzanna was ranting about Massimo, the urge to tell her had waned.

"Is everything going OK?" Suzanna asked.

"Yes!" Erinn said, perhaps a bit emphatically. "Do you remember Lamont Langley? He was sort of in my circle way back when?"

" 'Back in the day,' Erinn. Nobody says 'way back when' anymore. You're on a shoot with people half your age. You need to keep up!"

"Fine. Do you remember Lamont Langley, who used to be in my circle back in the day? He's going to play George Washington in *BATTLEready!*"

"Oh? Is he still alive? He must be a million."

"Why does everyone keep harping on Lamont's age? He's not even fifty!"

"Well, fifty is the new million. Say hi from me. OK, now that I know you're not dead or fired, I gotta go."

"You've got to relax," Erinn said. "All this stressing about me isn't good for the baby."

" 'Stressing about me,' " Suzanna said. "Good choice of words! Very up-to-the-minute, Erinn."

Erinn couldn't help smiling as she hung up. She leaned back against the headboard. Her laptop was sitting on the bed beside her and she pulled up her e-mail. She clicked on a recent message from Carlos, asking if she wanted to have dinner with "the boys" before the big shoot at the Betsy Ross House tomorrow. Erinn wavered. On one hand, she didn't want to see Jude or the other producers. On the other hand, she would have to face them all sooner or later, and if she went, she might be able to do some damage control if Jude started blabbing—a word Erinn did not use lightly. If she didn't go, Jude would think she was hiding. Just the thought of him smirking at her while she stayed in her room made her furious. She'd show him. She'd go! She dashed off a quick note saying she'd meet them in the lobby in half an hour.

Erinn pulled on a pair of black wool slacks and a red sweater. She brushed her hair and put on the lipstick that Suzanna had bought her. She picked up her purse and headed for the door, but turned around. She wanted to make absolutely sure that the camera and batteries were all charging. She unplugged them all and re-plugged them one at a time securely into the various chargers. She picked up her camera and regarded it thoughtfully. She was still uneasy about any possible damage sustained from a night on the frozen earth. She powered up the camera and rewound the tape. She watched the viewfinder and saw only the white glare of snow whipping past the lens. Sound was suddenly audible on the tape. Jude's voice could be heard saying, ". . . making sure the camera microphone is on. I want witnesses for how annoying you are. . . ." Erinn tried not to smile. As a woman, she was mortified by the events that had transpired, but as a writer . . . well, who would have guessed? Not she, and she was a damn good writer! *Deus ex machina*, indeed.

The video froze on the screen. Erinn looked at the viewfinder. The camera made a whining sound that squeezed Erinn's heart.

This is where the camera froze.

The whining sound continued.

Something IS wrong with the camera!

Erinn sat down at the desk, glued to the viewfinder. The screen was dark, but there was still sound—muffled, but audible. Then, there were some murky visuals. The cabin ceiling came into frame, then the wall, then the fireplace. Erinn squinted, trying to determine what she was seeing. She caught her breath as she realized what the camera had captured. While they were in the cabin, and the camera was under Erinn's coat, the camera had unfrozen and started shooting again. She was looking at what it had recorded when Jude lifted it out of her coat and set it on the floor. Mercifully, the camera was pointed at the fire, not at the bed . . . not at the hay. But the audio . . .

The sound was faint, and Erinn turned up the volume as loud as it would go. She could just determine the sounds of lovemaking coming from across the room. She sat mesmerized and mortified as she listened.

Erinn practically jumped out the window when the phone rang. She took a few settling breaths and answered it. It was Gilroi. They were in the lobby waiting for her. Erinn stammered an apology, and, losing her nerve, made excuses for the evening.

She couldn't face Jude right now.

She hung up the phone and put her finger on the Erase button, but stopped herself. She hit Rewind instead—and listened a second time. If the camera had been able to talk, Erinn would have asked it: *Could that enthusiastic woman possibly have been me?*

She sat, staring at the camera as if it were capable of providing some answers.

Snapping back to reality, and realizing that her camera might have sustained some serious damage, she took out the tape and replaced it with a new one. She hit the Rewind button, then the Forward button. She concentrated on the mechanics at hand—not on her romantic interlude. The camera seemed to be fine.

That's the only thing that's important.

Erinn spent a fitful night. She got out of bed a dozen times and paced the floor. She looked at the clock and watched the minutes tick by—or, more precisely, click by. There was no analog clock for miles, it seemed. Even this hotel, dedicated to its historic, colonial feel, had digital clocks in its rooms.

Erinn was not looking forward to seeing Jude, but there was a part of her that just wanted to get that scenario out of the way. Had she taken the coward's way out by not having dinner with the team? Was it going to be more awkward now, not less? She both anticipated and dreaded the morning light, which was now climbing murkily into her room—eastern exposure be damned.

Fortunately, the crew had an early call. They were to meet in the lobby at six a.m. sharp and be at the Betsy Ross House, ready to shoot, by seven. Erinn gathered her camera, lights, notebooks, phone, coat, and her wits and braced herself for the morning.

She picked up her notebook and opened it to double-check everything. It was filled with permits, timetables, and notes about the shoot. They would meet Lamont Langley and several other actors at the Betsy Ross House, along with a makeup-and-wardrobe person. If Erinn could stay focused on her work, she might be able to get through the initial awkwardness with Jude.When Cary had been assigning which producer would be in charge of which scenes, the segment of *BATTLEready!* that featured Betsy Ross was pretty much up for grabs. At first, Cary was inclined to assign the segment to Carlos, since the flag was featured so prominently in the Emanuel Leutze painting. Cary planned on using the painting—imprecise as it was—as the springboard for the "Washington Crosses the Delaware" show. Erinn remembered looking with astonishment at Cary. Hadn't Erinn pointed out the immense inaccuracies of the painting?

"People relate to the painting, Erinn," Cary had said. "That's the important thing. Who cares if it's accurate?"

"Who cares if history is *accurate*?"

Erinn felt it was her mission to set Cary straight. She pointed out that aside from the immense incorrectness she had already told them about, the flag that was featured in the painting was also wrong. Yes, it featured Betsy Ross's "stars and stripes" flag, but the reality was, while the flag was designed in May or June of 1776, it wasn't used until the Second Continental Congress flew it for the first time in September 1777. Washington crossed the Delaware on Christmas 1776—a full eight months before.

"OK, Erinn," Cary had said. "Was the flag in use by the time Washington was at Valley Forge?"

Erinn's heart started to beat a little faster. She had done her research and here was a perfect opportunity to show her stuff.

"Yes . . . Washington was in Valley Forge the following winter!"

"Fine," Cary said, typing something into her computer and shutting it down. "Then you can be the producer in charge of the Betsy Ross shoot."

With that, Cary had left the room. Erinn could feel herself glowing. Maybe she was going to be good at this job after all. She looked at the Revolutionary War timeline she had on her own computer. Technically, the flag would have been available to the soldiers at the Battle of Brandywine, which would mean Gilroi should be running the Betsy Ross episode. She was disappointed, but realized she should give the shoot to Gilroi. She looked around the building to find him. She would let him know that she didn't mean to usurp the Betsy Ross shoot and she would gladly hand it over. She didn't want any professional jealousy on the road. *Been there, done that,* she thought.

Erinn had run into Carlos and Gilroi at the bottom of the stairs. Carlos high-fived her.

"Dude," he said. "Thanks for taking the Betsy Ross shoot. I owe you one!"

Erinn was confused. She decided to ignore Carlos.

"Gilroi, the Betsy Ross shoot is yours, if you want it."

Gilroi looked at her, a small, sweet smile on his face. Then he burst into braying laughter. Carlos joined him. Doubled over, the two men—boys, as she now thought of them—headed off to parts unknown . . . without her . . . gasping for breath.

Well, at least I get to keep Betsy Ross.

Erinn continued to flip through the notebook. She was happy she had done all the extra research on Betsy Ross. It had always given her confidence to know all the facts . . . she felt it gave her an edge. She stared down at the pages. Although she knew the facts by heart, she read through them again. Betsy Ross was born Elizabeth Griscom into a Quaker household in Philadelphia on January 1, 1752. She was the eighth of seventeen children. When she finished her schooling, her father secured her an apprenticeship with an upholsterer. At this job, she fell in love with fellow apprentice John Ross, who was an Episcopalian. They eloped. The interdenominational marriage caused a split from Betsy's family and meant her expulsion from the Quaker congregation. The young couple soon started their own upholstery business and possibly had two children—although Erinn found some historical dispute about that.

Erinn's research revealed that Betsy Ross might or might not have actually made the first flag and probably didn't make it in the house in which they were about to shoot. Moreover, Betsy might or might not have ever lived in "the Betsy Ross House," although it was one of the most visited historic places in the city. She closed the notebook and gathered her gear. She lumbered, laden with equipment, toward the stairs. She told herself that she should not clutter up her mind with regrets and humiliation. She had to be on top of her game today. This would be her first day of being in control of a shoot, and she had a lot to prove.

CHAPTER 15

Gilroi and Carlos were already in the lobby when Erinn made her ungainly entrance. She did her best to make her trip down the stairs look easy—as if shouldering a load of equipment that would have felled a football team was the most natural thing in the world. Gilroi leaped up when he saw her and grabbed a bag.

"Let me help you with that," he said.

Erinn just nodded. She wasn't sure if she could speak. Her lungs felt as if they were about to burst. In days gone by (*back in the day,* she reminded herself), she would have insisted on carrying everything herself. Clearly, Carlos was trained by an old-time feminist, as he sat, trying to feign casualness. But today, she was grateful to the Gilrois of the world, who insisted that men were stronger than women and, therefore, should carry heavy things. Erinn knew that Massimo certainly had that old-world gentility and would have carried all her gear if she'd let him. *I wonder what Jude would do?* she thought.

Caring what Jude would or would not do in a given situation was not a good sign. She had to stop thinking about him!

Erinn dropped her gear and collapsed on the sofa with the other two producers. Sturdy blue boxes were piled high around them, since no good producer would ever let even a box of tape out of his or her sight. It was as if they'd built a little fortress in the middle of the well-appointed lobby.

Erinn looked at her watch.

"Jude will be here any minute," Carlos said, apparently reading her thoughts. "He's at the gym down the street. He always works out before we start shooting."

Erinn thought about her morning, filled with details and lists and strategies. She silently begrudged Jude his leisurely morning at the gym. Not that she would have gone to a gym if she'd had a leisurely morning at her disposal, but that wasn't the point.

"Jude will show up and say 'Ready when you are,' like we've been keeping him waiting. Happens every time," Carlos said, shrugging his shoulders.

Erinn was surprised that neither Gilroi nor Carlos seemed to have any problem with this.

At that moment, Jude burst through the front door, sweating copiously and wearing a ripped T-shirt, threadbare sweatpants, and orange Nikes.

"OK, guys, ready when you are," he said. "Let's bounce."

"You can't go to the Betsy Ross House like that!" Erinn said.

Jude looked down at himself as if he'd just noticed he had a body.

"Like what?" he asked, sweat dripping into his eyes.

"You're disgusting."

"Disgusting is in the eyes of the beholder."

"You are part of a production company with a stellar reputation. Do you really think they'd appreciate you showing up as their representative in your workout clothes?"

"Do you think a production company whose slogan is 'Go APE' gives a shit?"

"Look, we don't really have time to argue. We've got to go," Gilroi said, putting his arm around Erinn. "Don't worry, he'll dry."

"OK, let's do it," Jude said. "I've already asked the parking guy to call a couple cabs."

"Cabs?" Erinn asked. "Oh my gosh, I forgot to follow up with Hertz about the accident."

"No worries," said Jude. "I took care of it last night. There's a new SUV in the garage."

Erinn opened her mouth to speak. She wanted to say that the car was her responsibility, and who did he think he was usurping her job? But before she could formulate her words, Jude continued.

"I felt like you'd been through enough."

The guys, working like a well-oiled machine, started gathering up gear. She joined in, lifting as many boxes as she could carry without staggering. She contemplated Jude's thoughtfulness.

Or was it a power play?

Or was he thinking that she couldn't have casual sex and be absolutely fine with it?

She tried to focus on the business at hand."But, Jude," Erinn said. "If we have cars, why are we taking cabs?"

"It's cheaper to take cabs in the city than to park the cars. Plus, who knows if there is even parking anywhere near the location?"

Erinn reddened. She realized that she, as the producer of this shoot, probably should have checked that out. Another lesson learned. Another lesson that neither Jude, nor the other men, were throwing in her face.

She followed the men toward the cars. When she got outside, she was relieved to see the sky was clear. At least the weather was on her side. She looked over at Jude, who was sniffing his armpits. Carlos pretended to be bowled over by the smell. "Heterosexual men," Gilroi said to Erinn, shaking his head. "You can't live with them and you can't turn them."

Luckily, the trip to 239 Arch Street was uneventful. Gilroi was quiet, and Erinn used the few minutes in the cab to gather her thoughts. She was paying the cab driver and pulling her gear out of the cab when a tall woman in a shocking-pink down parka loomed over her.

"You the producer?" the woman asked.

"I am," Erinn said.

Gilroi took the camera bag from Erinn as the unsmiling woman introduced herself as Rita, the makeup-and-wardrobe person. She had a clipboard full of questions to discuss with Erinn. With that, the woman turned and climbed into a small trailer with a hand-lettered sign that read *BATTLEready!* Erinn turned to Gilroi, who kissed her on the cheek, told her that he'd start getting the equipment set up, and gave her a little shove in the direction of the trailer.

Erinn stood in front of the trailer, staring at the two metal steps, and swallowed hard. What could this Rita possibly want with her? Hadn't Erinn made sure the trailer was there? She looked back at the boys, who were easily joking among themselves as they set up equipment. Why couldn't she be working with the camera right now, instead of having to deal with . . . a person? People were just not her strong suit. Rita stuck her head out of the trailer door and stared at

Erinn. Erinn climbed the stairs, feeling as if she were on her way to the guillotine.

Once inside, Erinn caught sight of a tall man in a Revolutionary War costume adjusting a ratty-looking wig in the mirror. The man was Lamont Langley, whose face split into a grin when he saw her.

"It's you!" he said, picking Erinn up and spinning her around in the confined space. "I saw the name Erinn Wolf on the call sheet last night, but I figured it had to be another Erinn Wolf."

"No . . . one and the same," Erinn said.

Rita stared stonily at them as Erinn regained her footing. Lamont went back to fitting his wig.

"How the mighty have fallen, eh, Erinn? How the mighty have fallen."

Erinn wasn't sure if he meant her or himself. He was the one trying to get a hideous old wig to sit on his head. But he was an actor. As long as he was in front of the camera, he was probably happy. So he must mean she was the fallen one! She was the producer of a History Network show about the Revolutionary War, she said to herself . . . nothing to be ashamed of. Or, she admonished herself, nothing of which to be ashamed. She was getting sloppy around these kids. Erinn didn't have time to dwell on it. She turned to Rita, trying to appear authoritative for Lamont's sake.

"You have a question, I believe?" she asked her.

"Yeah," Rita said. "Where's Betsy Ross?"

Erinn stared blankly. She looked frantically around the trailer.

"She's not *here*," Rita said.

"Then . . . where is she?" Erinn asked.

"You're the producer," Rita said. "You tell me."

Erinn tried not to panic. She dimly remembered that the actress's name was Mary O'Donahue, but could remember little else.

"Well, where are the other actors?" Erinn asked.

"Don't *you* know?" Rita said. "They're all in the second trailer. I only work with the principal actors, George Washington and Betsy Ross. And I've already checked the other trailer. She isn't there."

There was a short knock on the door and Jude stepped in.

"Everything going OK in here?" he asked.

He gave Rita a kiss—obviously they had worked together before—and shook hands with Lamont.

"Betsy Ross is MIA," Rita said."What did she say when you talked to her last night?" Jude asked Erinn.

Erinn felt her stomach flip. She was supposed to call all the actors and check in with them the day before the shoot, and she had forgotten.

"I . . . I . . ." Erinn stammered.

Her cell phone jangled in her pocket. She looked at it, and saw it was a local Philadelphia number. Perhaps it was the missing Betsy. She indicated that she had to take the call and snapped open the phone.

"Erinn Wolf here," she said. "Oh, yes, Mary! We were just wondering where you were! Oh . . . oh? . . . oh . . . I see. Well, thank you for calling again."

Erinn pressed the End button and saw the "missed call" icon at the bottom of her phone. Apparently, not only had Erinn forgotten to call Mary O'Donahue, but Mary had called her and she'd missed it.

"So what's the deal?" Jude asked, reclining against the wall.

"It appears Mary burst her appendix. She won't be joining us."

Sensing that Lamont was her only possible ally, she tried to make eye contact with him in the mirror. She was alarmed to see him taking a nip out of an old-fashioned flask, before quickly stowing it in his lace cuff.

Rita rolled her eyes.

"Now what?" she asked.

Jude looked at Erinn.

"I'd rather not call the company about this," he said to Erinn. "They'll be pissed. You're the producer. Got any ideas?"

"I wouldn't ask her, if I were you," Rita said.

"You're the director," Erinn said to Jude. "Don't you have any ideas?"

Jude strode over to the clothes rack and looked through the dresses. He pulled one out and examined it.

"You have a corset around here?" he asked Rita.

"Of course I do," she said. Then, looking at Erinn: "I know how to do *my* job."

Jude walked over to Erinn, handing her the dress.

"Here," he said. "Stuff yourself into this. You're our new Betsy Ross."

He turned and left the trailer. Erinn, costume in hand, flew after him. She grabbed him by the shoulder and spun him around.

"I can't play Betsy Ross!" she said. "Who will produce this if I don't?"

"Dude, we're in a big mess. You get that, don't you? The way I see it, Gilroi or Carlos can produce this. Neither one of them can play Betsy Ross."

"Gilroi would love to play Betsy Ross."

"If we f-up this shoot, we're in serious, serious trouble. Somebody could get fired. So, let's just do what has to be done."

"But I'm not an actress."

"Erinn, you know as well as I do that there are no lines. This is just a reenactment."

"But—"

"Dude. You're doing this."

"Do your duty today and repent tomorrow," Erinn said. "Mark Twain."

"I'm always willing to endure humiliation on behalf of my characters," Jude said. "Ben Stiller."

He walked away. Erinn hugged the costume to her chest, praying for deliverance. When none came, she turned around and went back to the trailer.

Lamont, sprawled out in the makeup chair, looked blearily at Erinn and gave her a lopsided smile. He saluted her with his flask. Erinn turned and looked at Rita, who was holding an eighteenth-century-style corset. She tossed it to Erinn.

"Go put this on in the back room. I'll help you with the stays."

Erinn undressed, berating herself. *How could I have forgotten to call the principal actors last night?* she asked herself as she tried to figure out the corset. Rita came into the back room uninvited and silently went to work cinching Erinn into the stiff undergarment.

"I know you must feel terrible about screwing up this shoot," Rita said. "Is this your first gig or something?"

"I've . . . I've just changed careers," Erinn said.

"That makes sense," Rita said, while lacing the corset tightly up the back. "You seemed a little long in the tooth for somebody just getting started."

Erinn was too humiliated by the events of the morning to think of anything to say to defend herself.

"This isn't really the right corset for Betsy Ross," Rita said. "But then you're not the right Betsy Ross, so who cares, right?"

"What's wrong with it?"

"Working-class women had corsets that opened in front because they had no servants to help them dress. We've only got a corset that laces up the back."

"Betsy Ross wasn't working class," Erinn said.

"Give me a break. If she was sewing for a bunch of soldiers, she was working class. She was probably a low-life whore."

Erinn was shocked! Who was this woman defaming one of the greatest names in American history?

"As a matter of fact, she was part of a huge middle class that was flourishing during that period," Erinn said.

"Oh, yeah, right," Rita said, giving the corset a sharp tug, which dug the steel boning into Erinn's rib cage. "All those middle-class women, hanging out, having fun. Just like we do today."

Erinn reached for the dress, but Rita stopped her.

"Oh, no you don't," Rita said. "You've still got to put these things on."

She held up a pile of billowing undergarments.

"Miles of underwear to go before I sleep," Erinn said, submitting to Rita.

Rita helped Erinn into the rest of her costume. In addition to the corset, Erinn also donned a hoop petticoat. The hoops had pockets in them—eighteenth-century ladies used them as the "pocket books" of their day. Small books, sewing kits, handkerchiefs, and the like could be discreetly stuffed inside the petticoat. Erinn slipped her cell phone and some info from her clipboard into hers.

She also was forced into a "bum roll," as Rita called it. Bum rolls were padded rolls used to make a woman's butt stick out somewhat, defining it so it wouldn't get lost in the burgeoning gown. Erinn felt the last thing she needed was another roll, but she held her tongue.

Finally, Rita appeared to be satisfied and Erinn looked at herself in the mirror. Her posture, aided by the corset, was perfect. Her dress, a blue-and-cream cotton with a fitted waist, delicate lace sleeves, and yards of skirt, swished with the slightest step. Rita came up behind Erinn and fitted her with a curly wig and delicate cap. Erinn felt transformed.

And ridiculous.

CHAPTER 16

Swallowing what was left of her pride, Erinn threaded her way to the front of the trailer—not an easy task, given the volume of her skirt. Lamont, still admiring himself in the mirror, stopped and assessed Erinn.

"Ah, Erinn, how the mighty have—" Lamont started again.

"Yes, Lamont, I know. I am stingingly well aware of how the mighty have fallen. Let's go."

Erinn tried to escape the trailer, but Rita stopped her long enough to slap some makeup on her. At last, Erinn and Lamont descended the stairs. Mercifully, the crew was still busy and was paying no attention to the comings and goings of the makeup trailer. Erinn saw two costumed actors and she made her way over to them, Lamont in inebriated tow. She approached a tall man in a perfectly cut replica of colonial garb.

"Hello, I'm Erinn Elizabeth Wolf," she said, offering her hand. "I'm the producer of this shoot."

The man looked puzzled, so Erinn added, ". . . and Betsy Ross."

The man shook her hand, but was clearly playing to Lamont and the other costumed man.

"And we thought things were tight on Broadway! These production companies are getting cheaper and cheaper. First the producers had to be able to shoot cameras, and now they have to be the cast."

Erinn ignored the comment. She fished around in her petticoat pocket and pulled out her paperwork. She noted that the two men standing before her must be Ernest Martin and Paul Arnold, the two actors hired to play Washington's companions.

"And you are Ernest . . . or Paul?"

"Paul," the man said, and made an elaborate bow, evocative of the early and middle 1770s, bending one knee and sweeping his hat toward the ground in an arc. Once the Revolution was a thing of the past, such bowing would go out of fashion. But for now, he had it right.

Normally, Erinn would be impressed by an actor who had done his homework. She was currently not in the mood for pleasantries, but then, when was she?

"All right," she said, then looked at the smaller man. "You must be Ernest."

"Yes, ma'am," he said, twisting his tricornered hat. "I'm playing Robert Morris."

Erinn looked at him critically. APE had hired a local casting company, and from what Erinn could see, they had made a mess of things. Robert Morris had been perhaps the wealthiest man in the colonies. This Ernest Martin didn't convey wealth. He had no bearing whatsoever. On the other hand, Erinn thought, Bill Gates had no bearing, either. Besides which, she reminded herself as she stepped on her petticoat, she had no right to complain about how anyone else was doing his or her job.

Paul flung an arm around Erinn.

"So, I guess you've figured out I'm playing your uncle, George Ross."

Erinn shrugged off his ham-handed caress.

"George would have been Betsy's late husband's uncle, not hers," she said. "*Late* being the operative word. They would have been no relation whatsoever when Washington and Ross came about the flag."

". . . and Robert Morris," Ernest said. "Washington, Ross, and Morris came about the flag."

Erinn opened her mouth, but was horrified to realize that she was about to utter the word *whatever*. She shook her head and started again. She smoothed out the papers in her hands and held them flat so the men could all see them.

"Just so we know what we're doing," Erinn said. "We're going to be shooting two different scenes. In the first one, you three will enter and discuss the making of the flag. Silently. This will all be covered with a voice-over. So don't say anything—and don't overact."

She saw the men exchange a look. Actors had a private nonverbal language—a series of eyebrow arches, tics, and lip pursings, which they assumed no one could understand but themselves. From her Broadway days, she interpreted this look to mean, "Can you believe this woman thinks we don't know we should not overact?"

"The second scene will have the three of you coming back and looking at the flag."

"Can we overact when we see the flag?" Lamont asked.

They were interrupted by Jude, and Erinn introduced him as the director. As Jude made small talk with the men in their colonial costumes, she felt at loose ends. Normally, she would have turned over leadership of the shoot to the director at this point and gracefully retreated into the background with her camera, ready to shoot with Carlos and Gilroi. She looked down at her hoop skirt and realized there would be no graceful retreating. She tried to focus back on the conversation.

". . . so the whole thing is pretty straightforward," Erinn heard Jude concluding.

"Why do we have to do both scenes in the same room?" asked Lamont.

Erinn bit her tongue. Lamont knew better than to question the director. It was just another reminder that he had no respect for the genre in which they now found themselves working. She waited patiently for Jude to put him in his place.

"Not a bad idea," Jude said. "Maybe we could shoot you guys coming out of a coach or something."

Erinn tried not to let out a gasp, but it escaped her.

"Betsy?" Jude said. "You have a problem with that?"

"Well," Erinn said, "as a matter of fact, I do. Not as Betsy, of course, but as the producer in charge of this shoot."

Erinn reddened as Jude looked at her silently—and then winked.

"OK," Jude said. "As producer of this shoot, what's your problem?"

"There is, of course, the obvious fact that we don't have a coach—or horses—or other actors or other costumes budgeted for this scene.

Then there is the fact that the men came to see Betsy Ross in the summer of 1776, not the winter, which would make this landscape all wrong."

"That's why we pay her the big bucks," Jude said, tugging Erinn's lacy cap into place. Erinn grimly swatted his hand away. Jude spoke to the actors. "But you guys keep thinking. I run a collaborative set. I'm open to all ideas."

Erinn watched him walk back to the crew. Was he out of his mind? What director was open to *any* ideas . . . let alone *all* ideas?

"Lights are all set up," Carlos called from the doorway to the Betsy Ross House. "Let's get rolling."

"Hang on one second," Jude said, eyebrows furrowed as he looked at his notes.

He looked at Erinn so seriously that she held her breath. He was reading the production notes she had painstakingly made . . . had she done something wrong? Overlooked something important?

Jude came over to her and stood beside her, shoulder to shoulder, so they could read the notes together. His hair grazed her cap, and she tried to steady her breathing. He pointed to a paragraph. His close proximity made the words dance in front of her eyes, and she tried to make them come into focus. The words were just not making sense to her. Giving up, she stalled for time.

"What seems to be the problem?" she asked.

"We're supposed to show Betsy Ross cutting out a five-pointed star with just one cut," he said. "What the fuck?"

Erinn relaxed. She smiled at Jude.

"Yes, that's part of the myth . . . or history . . . of Betsy Ross. Washington apparently wanted to use the European six-pointed star, but Betsy showed them that she could cut a five-pointed star with just one snip of the scissors. This would be a time-saver and would be easy to teach other seamstresses. I thought it would be incredibly cinematic. That's why I added it to the shot list."

"Well, since you're now our Betsy Ross, can *you* do it?"

Erinn beamed. When she had read about the star and how it was cut, she was confused. As with everything Erinn encountered that made no sense to her, she did some Internet research and learned how to do it. She thought, ruefully, that she originally had planned on showing the woman who played Betsy Ross how to cut the star, but now, as fate would have it, all she had to do was rely on herself.

This was familiar ground.

"Don't worry," Erinn said. "I know how to do it, and I brought the props."

"That's my girl," Jude said, and kissed her on the top of her head.

Jude led the actors into the house, which was now a well-organized museum. Thankfully, the production company had managed to secure the museum on a Monday when it was closed to the public—therefore saving APE a lot of money. Closing down any establishment was a pricey endeavor and one the production company steered around whenever possible. APE had gotten permission to shoot for the day, but Erinn had made sure the crew was aware of the fact that they were shooting in a piece of history and to take extra care prepping and striking the set.

The house itself was styled on the colonial "bandbox" design, with one room on each floor and a winding staircase stretching from the cellar to the upper levels. The building's large first-floor window faced the street to display merchandise. Betsy used the first-floor front room as her workshop, and it was into this room that Erinn led her costumed troop.

The room was small and seemed even tighter, thanks to all the equipment and men. Erinn silently signaled Carlos and Gilroi that there would be hell to pay if they so much as raised an eyebrow over her costume. She hoped she looked threatening, but with the little lace cap perched atop her wig, she wasn't sure.

Erinn watched Jude as he checked lighting, audio levels, and furniture placement. He called the crew over to give final instructions. Instinctively, she started over, but Lamont stepped on her skirt.

"I don't think he means you, Betsy."

Erinn was irritated at Lamont's impertinence and annoyed that he was right. She glanced at a young man standing with Jude whom she had not seen before. He seemed very young and distracted. In alarm, she realized that he was holding her camera. Picking up her skirts, she swished over to the group of men.

"What's shaking, Betsy?" Jude asked.

"I . . . I . . . ," Erinn said. "I haven't met this young man who has my camera."

"Oh," Jude said. "This is Oliver."

Oliver nodded, but didn't take his eyes off the floor.

"May I speak to you in private?" Erinn said to Jude, pulling him aside.

"Erinn, we're falling behind schedule. What is it?"

"Why does that boy have my camera?"

"He was the local P.A.," Jude said. "But since we're a producer short, he's been promoted to cameraman."

"But he's so young."

"He's not that young."

"He's a fetus."

"Chill, Erinn. He'll be fine. Your camera will be fine. You'll be fine. It's the magic of television."

Jude finished his preparations and escorted Erinn to the chair where she would receive her visitors as Betsy Ross. Erinn felt her pulse race when he touched the small of her back. She wondered how Jude remained so calm. Did the fact that they had had a romantic interlude mean nothing? Was this the way it was between men and women now? She remembered the free-wheeling sexual energy of New York in the eighties, before the AIDS epidemic brought it to a screeching halt. But she had never been one for casual sex even then. She realized that there was no possibility of any sort of real relationship between the two of them, and she would be foolish to romanticize one night of passion.

She sat down, trying to stay focused on the business at hand. Jude handed her some needlepoint. *Needlepoint?*

"What am I doing with this? Betsy Ross was an upholsterer," Erinn said.

"I needed a prop, and I couldn't find a staple gun," Jude said. Carlos snickered in the background. "I got that sewing thing from the gift shop. Just deal with it."

Erinn tired to settle into her chair, a near impossibility considering all the stiff undergarments she was wearing.

Jude assembled everyone and ran through the scene.

"OK, guys, here's what we're going to do. Betsy Ross will be doing whatever. Gilroi, I want you to get all the medium shots. Carlos, grab close-ups . . . hand-held, you know what I want. But don't go nuts. The History Network doesn't want us to go crazy."

"What should I do?" asked Oliver.

"You just keep the camera on sticks and get the wide shots."

Erinn tried to catch Jude's eye, but he was busy getting the final details nailed down. She realized that he was doing her a favor by keeping her camera in the safest possible spot—locked down on a tripod.

Within minutes, they were ready to shoot. Erinn started pretending to needlepoint, and the actors were stationed just outside the door, waiting for Jude's signal.

"OK," Jude called. "Everybody quiet. And. . . . whenever you're ready, Erinn."

Erinn lifted her needle up and down in what she hoped was a realistic approximation of needlepointing. She tried not to be irritated with Jude. After all, he was keeping her camera out of the fray. But, she had to admit, she was annoyed when these young directors said, "Whenever you're ready." What was wrong with the clean and precise "Action"?

"OK, hang on," Jude said.

I guess that means "Cut."

"I think a rocking chair would be better," Jude said, looking at Erinn. "Can we get a rocking chair?"

Carlos and Gilroi groaned and Jude good-naturedly flipped them off. Normally, this would be a fair question to ask the producer, Erinn thought, but she was pretty confined in her costume.

"No," Erinn said. "We can't get a rocking chair."

Erinn saw Carlos and Gilroi exchange an appreciative glance. Apparently, most producers didn't stand up to their directors. Jude knelt down by Erinn's chair and looked up at her. She tried not to look into his eyes and busied herself arranging her skirt.

"Erinn," Jude said. "I know I'm a pain in the ass, but a rocking chair would really add dimensionality to this scene. This museum seems to have a ton of furniture. Don't you think you could find a rocking chair?"

Erinn let out a sigh and stood up.

Well, it is my job as a producer to help the director realize his vision.

She quickly looked at Carlos and Gilroi, who looked back at her with blank expressions. They were clearly waiting to see what she was going to do. As she got up from her chair and headed off the set, she passed Carlos, who whispered, "Wussy."

"Bite me," Erinn whispered back.

Erinn smiled to herself as she gathered her skirts. She knew that, far from being angered by this unpleasant exchange, Carlos would actually take great delight in Erinn's bad manners.

I'm learning. And that's never a bad thing.

As she moved through the closed museum, she saw the perfect rocking chair in a room that was cordoned off with a black velvet rope. She looked around. The entire museum was deserted. She took a deep breath, unlatched the velvet rope, and went into the forbidden territory. She grabbed the rocker and flipped it over. Examining the bottom of it, she sighed in relief. This was a replica, not a valuable antique.

Not the point, exactly . . .

In her Broadway days, she was always breaking the rules. And misbehaving always gave her a rush. As Erinn walked back to the set with the rocking chair, she realized that she was humming. Jude had a habit of making her feel young and restless. She should know better. But, as Hemingway would say—*the hell with it.*

CHAPTER 17

Erinn found herself enjoying the rest of the day. Jude had some inspired moments as a director, the fetus running her camera didn't break it, and Erinn cut five-pointed stars one after another without a hitch. The only problem seemed to be Lamont Langley. By the time Jude called for the crew to wrap, Lamont literally staggered back to the trailer, wig perched precariously on his head. Erinn followed his weaving with her eyes, pity welling up inside her. She realized that she wasn't the only one from those halcyon New York days who felt lost. Jude came up beside her and watched Lamont disappear into the trailer.

"Dude," Jude said. "Your friend drinks too much."

"I know," Erinn said.

"He really sucked today . . . even without any dialogue. I'd like to fire his ass, but I can't. We *need* a George Washington . . . and one who fits into that costume."

"I'll talk to him."

"OK."

Erinn was surprised that Jude relented so quickly.

"Thank you."

"Don't thank me. You do good work, Erinn. I respect your judgment and I know you'll handle it."

Jude walked away. She looked after him, a lump forming in her throat. It had been a long time since someone had praised her work.

She walked to the trailer, turned her full skirt sideways so she could fit through the door, and went inside.

Rita was waiting sullenly to help Erinn out of her stays, but Erinn indicated that that would have to wait. She settled next to Lamont, who was draining his flask, boots on the counter, head, sans wig, tilted back. His eyes were closed.

"Lamont, listen," Erinn said. "Let's have a chat."

"A chat, dear Erinn?"

"Yes. About your . . . your . . . well . . . about your . . ."

Lamont opened one bloodshot eye and looked at her.

"Is this the great Erinn Elizabeth Wolf, beating around the bush?" he said, waving his flask at her.

Erinn took off her own wig, stole a quick glance at herself to make sure she didn't have wig hair, and plunged in. She had internalized enough about drama to understand that you can't present yourself as a figure of authority with pathetic-looking flat hair. She steeled herself.

"No, this is the incredibly humbled Erinn Elizabeth Wolf trying to hang on to her job—and trying to help you hold on to yours, Lamont."

Erinn saw Rita perk up at this turn in the conversation. She busied herself with steaming the costumes as Erinn continued."OK, Lamont, let's face facts. We're not who we used to be. Nobody is going to give us the best tables or the best tickets or the best jobs anymore. But we still have our talent and our dignity, and it's our duty to bring them to this show. You need to rethink your behavior."

"What exactly are you saying?"

"I'm saying, I'll cover for you this time, old friend, but that's all. . . . You can thank me later."

"Gratitude opens a crack in consciousness that lets grace in," Lamont said.

"Don't you quote at me," Erinn said.

"I wouldn't dream of it," Lamont said.

"Good. And you'll stop drinking . . . at least on my company's time?"

Lamont stood up.

"No, my dear Erinn. I will not. You accept me as I am, or not at all."

"Lamont. Those days are over. We don't get to call the shots anymore. You stop drinking on the set or . . ."

"Or what?"

"Or you're fired."

"That sounds suspiciously like you're still calling the shots."

"All right, let me correct myself. *You* don't get to call the shots anymore."

"Oh, really?" Lamont said, weaving dangerously. "Well, then, go ahead and fire me."

Lamont struggled out of his costume, flinging the coat, britches, and boots around the trailer. He put his hands on his hips and struck what he must have assumed was a majestic pose, his middle-aged gut hanging over his jockey shorts. Erinn, though livid, tried not to laugh. She noticed Rita furiously steaming a blouse in the background, feigning nonchalance.

"Lamont, I'm warning you. You are on thin ice."

Lamont grabbed his coat and put it on over his undershorts. He then flung a scarf around his neck, preparing for a dramatic exit.

"I am prepared to give you a second chance," he said to Erinn.

"You're fired."

Lamont opened the door and stepped out. Rita and Erinn looked at each other when they heard a horrible crash. Erinn, slowed by her costume, hurried to the open doorway. She looked down. Lamont was sprawled in a heap at the bottom of the stairs, having misjudged the steps. Luckily, he had the Jell-O-like constitution of the pickled, and he stood up, unharmed, and wandered away, muttering. Jude came running over and looked up at Erinn.

"Reader, I fired him," Erinn said.

"What?" Jude said, following her back inside the trailer. "I told you we needed a George Washington. Get him back."

"Jude, you said you trusted me. I had no choice."

"This is Friday! We're shooting Valley Forge on Monday!"

"Then I'll get us a George Washington . . . who will fit our costume . . . by Monday."

"How?"

"I'm the producer, and I'll take care of it."

"OK. This whole thing is in your hands, then."

Jude jumped out of the trailer without using the metal steps. Erinn was once again impressed with his agility. She bit her lip, wondering what she was going to do next.

When the group got back to the hotel, the boys, all rubbing their sore shoulders and lower backs, went off to the gym around the corner. Erinn realized that she would have to get herself in better shape if she was going to compete in the boys' club on a physical level. She felt badly that they had to trudge into the cold evening to relieve their aches and pains. Erinn looked around the lobby. She still loved the fact that while the hotel might not be full of conveniences, it positively reeked of atmosphere. She now wondered, though, if that was enough. There were so many lessons she would need to mull over when she got home.

But for now, Erinn shouldered her heavy gear box and trudged upstairs. When she finally let herself into her room, she was gasping for breath.

Erinn looked out her window at her brick view. Sunset had settled over the city, but she just stood looking out. What would happen if she couldn't find a new George Washington by Monday? She realized that, while she would certainly be horrified to let the company down, she was most afraid of disappointing Jude. Was he right to have trusted her judgment?

Was Jude right and she wrong?

Could that be possible?

When it was clear that the wall across the back alley was not going to solve her problems, Erinn flopped down on the bed in defeat. She didn't have an after-hours number for the local casting office. There was no way they would be able to settle this crisis by Monday morning. She closed her eyes.

Her cell phone, silenced for the shoot, vibrated in her pocket. She fished it out and looked at the blinking number. It was her mother. Erinn flipped open the phone.

"Hello, Mother."

"Hello, dear. How is Philadelphia?"

"Colonial. How is New York?"

"Fabulous, as always. I still can't believe you left this city."

She knew her mother wasn't exactly rubbing it in, but she still found herself annoyed by the accusation that she didn't live in New

York. The entire family, save Suzanna—who was born and raised entirely in California—had bounced between New York and California their whole lives. Erinn and Suzanna's parents, Virginia and Martin Wolf, had been big believers that dramatic change was good for the soul. They had met in college—in Philadelphia, ironically—gotten married, and moved to New York, where they had Erinn. Deciding that Manhattan was no place to raise a baby, they bought and remodeled a dilapidated old barn in Napa Valley, took jobs as college professors, and raised their girls.

When the girls went off to live their own lives and Martin died, Virginia retired and moved back to New York, just as Erinn was settling (in defeat) in Santa Monica. But as soon as she could, she planned on getting back to NYC.

In reality, Erinn was much more like her father than her mother. Although her father had been dead for nearly ten years, Erinn still missed him. An introspective intellectual, Martin Wolf had always wanted to live in the heart of New York City. When he and a pregnant Virginia went looking for their first apartment, Manhattan was the only place they looked. No other boroughs, no suburbs, no *Connecticut* for his family. He believed in the city the way other people might believe in a new love. Even when the family had uprooted itself to California, his attachment to New York was an infatuation that lasted until he died . . . and one that he had passed on to Erinn.

When they were younger, Martin took Erinn and Suzanna to museums, libraries, lectures, and concerts. Erinn loved these outings with her father, while Suzanna moaned and complained and begged to go shopping. Suzanna favored their mother both in looks and in her outgoing persona. Virginia was an intellectual in her own right, but had more of a well-rounded personality. Although it was never stated, the family came to understand that social outings would as often as not be divided, with Erinn and their father going one way, Suzanna and their mother going another. Over the years, Erinn and her mother had made a mutual effort to get closer, but there always seemed to be a barrier between them. Sometimes it was just a veil, sometimes a brick wall."How are you getting along with . . . everyone?" her mother asked.

"I'm getting along with everyone just fine."

"That's nice to hear. I know how you can be."

"Oh? How can I be?"

"Prickly, dear."

"Prickly?"

"I don't think I'm telling you something you don't already know. I don't believe anyone has ever accused you of becoming the next Miss Congeniality."

"Very true," Erinn said. She had to admire her mother's biting wit—perhaps this was where Erinn got her "snarky" attitude.

And she did have to admit to "prickly."

"No problems with that young director person? Suzanna tells me he's very handsome."

"No, Mother, there are no problems with the young director person. And yes, he is very handsome." Erinn wondered, *Was he very handsome or just handsome?* She would have to dwell on that . . . but not now.

"Are sparks flying? Good sparks, I mean."

For a fleeting second, she pictured herself in the throes of . . . Valley Forge, but it made her blush just imagining it.

"No, Mother. He is much too young for me."

"Nonsense, dear. Didn't you see *Sunset Boulevard*?"

"Yes, well, the woman in *Sunset Boulevard* turned out to be crazy and the young man ended up dead in a pool. But thanks for thinking of me."

"And what about your fabulous renter? How is he?"

Suzanna was certainly keeping their mother abreast of Erinn's life. She had to give her sister credit for that.

"He's wonderful," Erinn said, thinking of Massimo with his regal bearing and broad shoulders. "As a matter of fact, he's perfect."

CHAPTER 18

Erinn, with the help of her GPS, had managed to find her way back to the Philadelphia airport. Traffic had been terrible, and she arrived with just moments to spare. She parked quickly in the parking lot designated ARRIVALS and vaulted into the terminal. She was relieved to find that the passengers from the Los Angeles flight had yet to arrive at baggage claim.

Erinn had a habit of playing out scenes in her head before they happened. Ever since she was a child, she would try to figure out how a particular event would occur. When she was in grade school, she used to get her report card and, on the way home, create the scene of domestic bliss that would certainly transpire when her parents saw yet another semester of straight As. As she got older, Erinn added subplots. On the way home from high school, she would write her parents' dialogue not only praising her accomplishments but also the speeches required to admonish Suzanna, who had only just started grade school, for her less-than-stellar performances.

Sometimes, she would write a scene so convincingly that if it didn't happen exactly as she had planned, she was at a loss for how to deal with the reality. When she wrote the dialogue that was to serve for breaking up with her first boyfriend, she was speechless when the boy didn't follow the script and broke up with her first.

Erinn loved Henry Miller's statement that "We create our fate every day we live," and she did that literally—she wrote her fate every day.

The problem was, she didn't edit. She often thought about how a given situation might play out and wrote the scene, but then didn't like the outcome she had devised. Instead of rewriting, Erinn would often just avoid the situation. When she thought about how an editor would react to the fact that Erinn hadn't finished whatever play she was working on, she was so hurt by the words the editor was uttering in her head that she just moved to California rather than deal with it.

Mimi, who knew all about this little quirk of Erinn's, pointed out that the editor's command of the English language was no match for Erinn's and that she should stop putting disapproving words in people's mouths—nobody but Erinn would ever come up with this stuff on their own. In reality, Mimi said, the editor would "just ream you a new one" and everyone could just move on. But Erinn had never mastered that. Once she had written the script and it had played out in her brain, it became her reality.

As she watched passengers straggle toward the luggage carousel, she reflected on her current situation. She knew her mission had been to find a new George Washington—someone who would look good in uniform and know how to act from his soul, since there was no dialogue. She knew Mimi would not be happy with how she was handling the problem, but as hard as she tried, she couldn't envision anyone from the production company caring how she solved this—as long as she solved it. Once she settled on that, Erinn put her plan in motion and never looked back.

Then why am I so nervous?

One second, he was nowhere in sight, and then there he was, smiling at her. Massimo, wearing a light-blue dress shirt and dark-blue trousers, looked fresh and overdressed among the bleary-eyed travelers staggering toward their bags. He had his jacket slung over his shoulder, dangling from two crooked fingers, in that classic continental way that Erinn found disturbingly attractive.

As he continued toward her, Erinn wondered if she should confess to her dalliance in Valley Forge. She had, of course, taken this into account when she wrote the scene in her head involving Jude meeting Massimo. But Jude was maddeningly unmoved (in her head), which annoyed Erinn so much that she threw caution to the wind, called Massimo, and offered him the job of George Washington.

Erinn was so proud of herself for thinking of Massimo, it didn't occur to her until after she'd hired him that the production company might not be thrilled that they were importing an actor from Los Angeles, when there must be thousands of perfectly serviceable George Washingtons in New York or Philadelphia. But Erinn would have to deal with that question when it came up. She'd written the script in her head and she was powerless to stop herself from hiring Massimo.

"Bella," Massimo said as he approached Erinn, kissing her on both cheeks.

"Come andò il vostro volo?"

"Molto bene, grazie."

"You spoke with Suzanna about watching the cat?"

"*Sì*. She is fine with the cat."

Erinn nodded. She knew she was a coward for pushing that conversation off on Massimo, but ever since Valley Forge, she had been keeping a low profile with Suzanna. Some sisters ran to the telephone whenever they had even the least interesting news to share, but that was not the relationship between the Wolf sisters. Erinn felt it was her duty to be a role model for Suzanna, so even at this stage in their lives, she didn't think it would do any good for Suzanna to know her sister had fallen—if not head over heels, at least ass over teakettle—into temptation.

Erinn retrieved the new Explorer from the parking lot while Massimo waited for his bag. She pulled up to the curb, and he shoved an enormous suitcase into the back of the SUV. Erinn smiled to herself. In her mind's eye, when she envisioned Massimo's arrival, she intuited a large suitcase. She had made his room reservation on the first floor of the hotel, so he wouldn't have to lug it up several flights of stairs.

A light snow was falling as Erinn pulled the SUV into traffic. Massimo looked out the window.

"Prevedono freddo?" he asked.

"*Sì*. The forecast says snow today and tomorrow, but cold the entire week."

"We shoot outside?"

"Yes. All week. But the costume is very warm."

"Well, we die for our art, no?"

"I hope not," Erinn said under her breath.

While Massimo got himself settled in the hotel, Erinn busied herself in her room. She had wrestled the Washington costume from Rita, who did not want it out of her sight. Erinn promised to guard it with her life, but she thought that the fact that Rita (who was a local hire) would have had to come out to the hotel on a snowy evening to fit the thing was what persuaded her to leave everything in Erinn's hands. Erinn wanted control of as much of this process as possible. She knew this was a house of cards she was building, and every step was . . . delicate.

Erinn second-guessed herself. Erinn knew that she was going to have to answer to Cary, who not only might wonder at the cost of bringing in an actor from out of town but might correctly think that Erinn was rash in casting Massimo—since Erinn really had no idea if he was any good or not. Jude might not like it because Erinn would have an alliance with the lead actor and that would shift the balance of power.

Erinn shook off her doubts. She had faith in her abilities as a producer. When she was working on Broadway, she was often called "The Lone Ranger," which was not usually meant as a compliment. Erinn had to admit, she never really got the hang of "collaboration." Why should she? She knew what she wanted and, after playing out any scene in her head, usually determined that she was right.

She tried to push away any fears that she might have overstepped her bounds. She had been given the responsibility to take care of business, and that was exactly what she had done. There was a knock on the door. She opened it and caught her breath as Massimo filled the doorway. She stood aside, and he walked in as if he owned the space.

He'll make a perfect George Washington.

Massimo, having slipped into his costume's waistcoat and breeches, stood in front of the full-length mirror as Erinn slid General Washington's blue wool coat onto his shoulders. The coat had a light-tan wool collar, lapel, and cuffs. Gilded buttons trimmed the length of the lapel. Erinn smoothed out the lines on the coat. She pressed her spread fingers along his broad back and they both admired him in the mirror.

The uniform looked as if it had been tailored for him. Erinn retrieved the wig from the wig stand on the desk and went to place it on Massimo's head. Realizing the height difference between them was too large a span for wig adjustment, she dragged her desk chair over to the mirror and jumped on it. She looked at the wig critically and stood in position to place it on Massimo's head.

Massimo put up his hand.

"No wig," he said.

Erinn caught a glimpse of herself in the mirror, balanced precariously on a hotel chair, with the wig poised as if she were about to complete a coronation. She realized she carried no authority in this position, so she stepped off the chair.

"Massimo," Erinn said. "It's true that George Washington didn't wear a wig and just powdered his own hair . . . and I'm proud and touched that you did your research. But your hair is not like Washington's. You'll have to wear a wig."

"No wig," Massimo said. "It will . . . how do you say? . . . make my hair not quite wonderful."

"Oh! Well, I see your point. OK, let's not worry about the wig tonight. But tomorrow, at Valley Forge, you'll have to wear it."

Massimo scowled.

"We die for our art, no?" Erinn said. "And we wear wigs."

"Sì."

Once she was sure Massimo was safely back in his room, and she knew that the costume would fit, she sent an e-mail to everyone involved.

Due to unforeseen circumstances, the e-mail said, *Lamont Langley will no longer be featured as General Washington. Massimo Minecozzi, an accomplished actor, will play George Washington in all further scenes. If you have any questions, please don't hesitate to ask.*

She snapped the computer shut and went to bed. She tossed around the queen-sized bed, getting herself so tangled in the sheets, she was afraid the circulation would be cut off in her legs. She tried to will herself to sleep. It was always after the fact that Erinn started second-guessing herself. Was she making the right decisions? She had cast Massimo and sent the e-mail. She knew that they might have to reshoot a few scenes where George Washington was in close-ups, but she was sure most of the footage could be saved. Now it was up to fate . . . or destiny. Erinn remembered one of her favorite quotes by the poet James Russell Lowell: “Fate loves the fearless.”

And she fell asleep.

The alarm rattled Erinn awake. She leaped to the computer and signed on to her e-mail account. She knew that, technically, the people on the West Coast shouldn’t be opening her e-mail about Massimo for another couple of hours, but she also knew that the whole lot of them—those on both the East and West coasts—tended to be night owls and compulsive e-mail checkers. She had no doubt everyone involved had probably read it during the night.

She sighed in relief as she read the e-mail from Cary, which said:

> Crisis averted. Good work.

From Jude, she got a curt:

> Whatever.

From Gilroi:

> Is he straight?

And from Mimi, to whom she hadn’t written, but who had obviously heard about it from Cary:

> What the fuck??????

CHAPTER 19

Erinn sharply stopped the SUV and just stared in amazement. Chills pricked her spine and she shivered involuntarily. She was on the crest of a small hill, and below her the Valley Forge of 1777 had come to life in the crisp early-morning light. Several extras, already in costume, were milling around the snow-covered location, stacking guns, starting small campfires, and drinking coffee out of tin cups. Erinn knew that APE had hired a group of reenactors to be in the recreation, but she never expected anything as breathtaking as this. And on their budget! She could already see the footage they would be able to capture and she had to hold back her tears.

If it had not been for the two large mobile homes, a smattering of late-model cars, and the presence of down-clad crew members, she would have thought she'd somehow been thrown back in time.

Several of the log cabins stood with their doors open. The huge masses of snow that covered the park on her last trip to Valley Forge had melted, so there was no way of knowing if any one of these cabins might be . . . *might be what?*

My cabin? Our cabin? The scene of the crime? The scene of the crime of passion?

"It is a magnificent sight, no?" Massimo asked from the passenger seat. Erinn snapped back to reality. She had almost forgotten she had company. Erinn had whisked Massimo off to the Explorer as the rest of the crew got organized at the hotel. She did wonder if Jude might have some deep, visceral reaction to the sight of another man with Erinn. She was well aware that Jude was playing the whole thing off as a casual encounter, but men were men after all. *Best to keep things professional and not take any chances.*

Erinn guided Massimo to the makeup-and-wardrobe trailer. Massimo carried the general's costume over one arm. Erinn, carrying the wig and boots, struggled up the metal steps of the trailer. Rita was already inside, and Erinn was relieved that the trailer had heat. She realized she was a little defensive about their working conditions, now that she had Massimo in tow. Not that she wanted to show off, but still . . .

Rita was studying what appeared to be a mason jar full of brass eyeballs swimming in an amber liquid.

She looked at Erinn as they entered, but completely ignored Massimo.

"What the hell is this?" asked Rita, brandishing the jar.

"I'm sure I have no idea," Erinn said.

"Then I'll tell you what it is," Rita said.

"If you know, why are you asking me?"

Rita unscrewed the jar lid and thrust it under Erinn's nose. Erinn sniffed delicately, then recoiled. Urine!

"Somebody cut the brass buttons off all the uniforms and peed on them!" Rita said.

"Who would do something like that?" Erinn asked, noticing that Massimo had pulled his button-heavy costume close to his chest protectively, in case some urine-streaming madman was lurking nearby.

"You're the producer, you tell me," Rita said.

There was a quick rap on the door, and the production assistant Erinn now thought of as "Fetus" stepped almost apologetically into the trailer. He blinked at Erinn.

"Do you want me to get the gear out of your truck?" he asked.

Rita pounced.

"Do you know anything about this?" she asked.

Fetus studied the jar.

"Yes," he said. "The reenactors did it. They're hardcore and refuse to wear any clothing that doesn't look authentic. They break into wardrobe the night before a shoot and pee all over the brass buttons."

"Why?" Erinn asked.

"To age them."

"I'm calling the police," Rita said, snapping open her cell phone.

Erinn tried not to knock the phone from Rita's hand. Diplomacy was never Erinn's strong suit, but she couldn't have three-fourths of her cast arrested. She placed her hand on Rita's wrist. Rita tried to stare Erinn down, but while diplomacy might not be Erinn's strong suit, stubbornness was.

"I'm not sewing a bunch of pee-soaked buttons back on those coats," Rita said.

"Why don't you get a cup of coffee?" Erinn suggested, steering Rita toward the door. "I'll take care of this."

Rita handed Erinn the jar and left. Fetus, wasting no time, followed at her heels. Even Massimo deserted the ship, quickly hanging up his costume and leaving the trailer without a word. Erinn was alone with the mason jar. She held it up to the light. She had to admit, the buttons looked much more authentic.

She found a pair of rubber gloves under the sink and went to work. She had a sense of déjà vu and realized that it was because she was sewing once again. First Betsy Ross and now this. Since the Continental Army was a ragtag group, there was no set pattern to the heap of jackets in front of her. There were a few uniforms and some old coats and shirts. She held up one jacket much like General Washington's, which should have buttons up and down both sides. Erinn sighed. It would take forever to sew on sixteen buttons. She sewed on a button and carefully cut the thread with scissors—reminding herself, under the urine-circumstances—not to break the thread with her teeth. She could just hear her mother's warnings about germs.

"You don't know where those buttons have been," her mother would have said.

But in this case, knowing where they'd been was even worse!

Erinn looked up from her sewing as the door rattled open. Jude bounced into the room and sat across from her.

"Hey, Erinn!"

"Hey . . . Jude."

"How long do you think this will take?" he asked. "I'm not sure the light will hold all day. The clouds are pretty unstable."

Erinn gestured at the stack of coats and beautifully patina-ed buttons and shrugged.

Jude held up another coat that would require a multitude of buttons. He studied it with a critical eye. The cuffs were frayed, the collar worn. One sleeve was so faded that it appeared to be made from a different fabric.

"You know," he said, "I think that the owner of this jacket would never have had a full set of buttons at this point in the jacket's life."

Erinn smiled as Jude put the jacket in the finished pile and picked up a needle and thread.

"Let me give you a hand. It'll speed this up."

Erinn could feel herself getting warmer and hoped she was not turning pink. She tried to follow Jude's casual lead, but it was hard for her not to think of their night together, especially here!

"Thanks for helping," Erinn said.

"Gets me out of the snow," he said. "Besides, we haven't had much of a chance to talk since . . ."

"Since . . ."

"Since we got back from Valley Forge last time."

"Well"—Erinn feigned a casualness she did not feel—"is there anything to say?"

"I don't know," Jude replied. "I figured if there was anything to say, you'd say it."

"Things like that happen," she said.

"Yeah, but you have to admit . . . it's surprising that it happened . . . you know . . . with us."

What did he mean by that? Is it impossible to think that he would . . . what did the kids call it now? . . . hook up . . . with an old bird like me?

Erinn had felt herself opening up, but Jude's comment caught her by surprise and she slammed the iron door.

"Are you satisfied with our new General Washington?" Erinn asked, changing the conversation. The new subject put her on higher ground, she felt.

Jude shrugged.

"I guess. How well do you know him?"

"Not well," Erinn said. "He rents my guesthouse."

Jude looked up with a start. Erinn flushed. She had completely forgotten that she had rejected Jude as a possible tenant. Whatever heated emotion she thought she saw flickering in Jude's eyes faded and he smiled.

"Well," he said, "he must be something then. I know it isn't easy to pass the guesthouse test."

Erinn racked her brain for something to say. The problem was, Jude was right. Massimo had passed the guesthouse . . . "test" . . . and Jude had not.

Erinn let out a yelp. She had pricked her finger. She and Jude both stood at the same time.

"It's fine, it's fine," she said.

Jude took her hand and looked at it.

"It's bleeding a little."

Erinn could feel her heart racing. She was always shocked when words failed her, but she could think of nothing to say as she stared into Jude's eyes. They seemed to be suspended in time, but the door suddenly crashed open and Carlos stuck his head in.

"Dudes," he said. "We gotta start shooting."

Erinn and Jude both stared at him mutely, Erinn's bleeding finger still clutched in Jude's hand.

"Like . . . now . . ." Carlos continued.

Erinn pulled her hand away.

"It's only a flesh wound," she said, as lightly as she could.

She and Jude stared at the pile of coats.

"There's still a shitload to do," Jude said.

"I have an idea," Erinn said. "We'll take all the coats and buttons outside and record the reenactors sewing them on while they sit around the campfire."

Jude grinned.

"You rock, Tin Lizzy."

Jude followed Carlos out the door. Erinn felt thrilled by the compliment. She insisted to herself that it was the fact that she, the producer, had pleased Jude, the director, who was making her spine turn to jelly.

Once everything was in order, the three camera operators, Erinn, Carlos, and Gilroi, prepared to start their day. They loaded tape into their cameras and checked light and sound levels. As a group, they wandered over to Jude, who was leaning over a large table studying a map. Erinn had wondered exactly how this sort of shoot happened, but now that all was being revealed, she found the process brilliant.

The reenactors were to go about their business and the camera ops would shoot little vignettes. Jude would give them a general sense of what he wanted, but there was an incredible amount of personal artistic freedom involved. Erinn couldn't wait to get started. Jude pointed to various spots on the map, indicating where the action would be taking place and what he wanted each camera person to cover. Erinn tried to follow what he was saying and not concentrate on the muscle in his forearm that contracted when he moved his hand from one position on the map to another.

Carlos would follow the freezing, starving soldiers, Gilroi would be attached to the soldiers who were making bullets and sewing on buttons (Jude glanced up at Erinn and gave her a wink), and Erinn would be assigned to General Washington, who would stroll among the dispirited soldiers.

"Is there something you want me to capture in particular with General Washington?" Erinn asked.

"Nah," Jude said. "Just show him giving them . . . you know . . . some hope and general inspiration."

Erinn looked at him. She could never tell if he was being sarcastic—"snarky," he called it—or sincere. Sensing that he was in work mode, she took this comment at face value. She vowed that she would get General Inspiration like Jude had never seen! She shot a glance over at Massimo, glorious in his Revolutionary War attire. She was relieved to see that he was wearing his wig. Erinn realized that Massimo, already in character as General Washington, was leaning over a table of his own, poring over an old map with a couple of reed-thin reenactors. It was almost a perfect replica of the crew's tableau.

Jude gave a few final instructions and the crew dispersed. As Erinn threaded her way among the reenactors, she felt like a ghost who was floating among the dedicated troops of the Revolutionary War. Erinn had been aware of reenactors, of course, but always regarded them with a benign amusement. Now, watching them in action, with their ill-fitting boots and threadbare coats, she found she had a newfound respect for these people, who were keeping history alive. She noticed there were a few women milling about the camp in eighteenth-century costumes. She was pleased to see them, because they added to the authenticity of the shoot. While very little was known about the women at Valley Forge, there apparently were some women in the camp. Erinn's research showed that, while officers' wives probably never made it to Valley Forge, enlisted men's wives often lived among the troops, some as paid housekeepers, cooks, nurses, and laundresses.

Erinn looked through her lens finder, setting up her first shot, when Rita appeared on her screen. She was fussing with General Washington's wig. Erinn felt herself boil! Massimo already looked a little out of place, she noted, with his pristine uniform. There was no need to add insult to injury. Erinn had learned that Washington had admonished Congress in no uncertain terms for their callous disregard of the freezing patriots. He staunchly refused to rest during the war, even at times when he was only a few hundred miles from home. He certainly wouldn't have been wondering how his hair looked!

Erinn approached Rita, who was adding a tiny black ribbon to Massimo's wig.

"Thanks, Rita, I think we're ready to go," Erinn said.

Rita gave Massimo's cheek a quick swipe with her makeup pad and beamed at him. *She* can *smile,* thought Erinn, trying to punch down her jealousy.

Massimo pointed the lens of Erinn's camera his way and flipped the LCD screen so he could see himself. In amazement, Erinn watched him preen. She had heard tales of actors having the audacity to touch a producer's camera, but she hadn't believed it. And Massimo, at that!

Massimo straightened up and looked at Erinn. He was tall and filled out the uniform nicely. Technically, he was perfect, and she knew no one would fault her choice.

CHAPTER 20

By lunchtime, the crew knew they were getting some really good footage. Erinn was thrilled that everything was going so smoothly. She admitted to herself that while she had gotten off to a rocky start, now she had much to be proud of.

When Jude called "Lunch," Erinn headed toward the crew, but then saw Massimo, cape flapping in the breeze, heading to the buffet line. She was torn: Should she follow Massimo, since she felt that she was the reason he was here, or should she sit with Jude—and the crew—which is where she finally felt she belonged? She looked back and forth between the two men. Clearly, the night with Jude had been folly, but she had to admit she couldn't quite let it go. Jude had some very wonderful qualities. He was patient, kind, loyal to the crew, and had some good instincts.

Massimo, on the other hand, was the right age, worldly, interested in the arts. He had watched the cat without complaint. And hadn't he dropped everything to come be her George Washington? He was, perhaps, a little self-absorbed, but everyone had flaws.

Then why couldn't she shake Jude from her thoughts? She knew it was impossible, but when she let herself go, she thought about them . . . hanging out. She watched as a young woman in costume approached Jude. The woman had long corn-silk hair, a turned-up nose, freckles, and that overbite that men seemed to find so attractive. Erinn never understood that, but she had never met a man who couldn't be undone by a toothy girl. Jude leaned in to hear something the girl had to say. Then he laughed. The girl's hair glinted in the sun. Her curls shook as she laughed and she squeezed Jude's arm. The two of them headed to the buffet line. Erinn took a quick look at her cast list. The girl's name was Giselle.

Of course it was.

Erinn felt her self-confidence fading and decided to go with Massimo. She stood beside him in line and he took her hand and kissed it.

"This day, she goes well, no?"

"Yes. Very well. You are doing a great job."

Erinn knew that Massimo wouldn't be interested in the technical aspects of the day. She would have to wait until she was with the boys to go over that sort of thing.

The line was moving slowly and there was plenty of food. Too much food, it turned out—many of the hardcore reenactors refused to eat. Some of them had brought beef jerky to gnaw on, but there were several who just continued to melt lead, so they could make more bullets. Erinn tried to stay focused on Massimo, but she couldn't keep her eyes off Jude and the small-waisted Giselle, who were standing right in front of them in line.

Rita suddenly appeared, carrying a large bathrobe. She butted in and held out the bathrobe to Massimo.

"You need to put this on," she said. "You can't risk getting your costume dirty."

Massimo held up his hand.

"No, Rita, I cannot," he said. "I am George Washington. George Washington does not worry about this, and so I do not worry about this."

"Christ, who knew they had method actors in Italy?" Rita said. "He's as bad as the reenactors. Next thing you know, he'll be pissing on his buttons."

Jude, who was watching this exchange, turned to the girl.

"I'm not a real fan of method acting. I mean, you might end up doing your best work at the craft services table, and then where are ya?"

Giselle laughed and squeezed Jude's bicep. Erinn could barely hear them, but she did her best.

"Jude, you crack me up, I swear! I'm going to put that on Facebook."

"I'll be here all week, Gazelle," Jude said in some sort of bodacious borsch-belt accent.

Giselle burst into another round of titters. Erinn felt a tweak of jealousy at Giselle's nickname. Gazelle. Lithe, quick, keeping up with the herd. Clearly not an old relic like Tin Lizzy.

Erinn thought they seemed very young and . . . perfect together. She was just an old fool! She shot a glance at Massimo, magnificent in his uniform. He was smiling at her and handing her a plate. *Gallant,* Erinn said to herself as she took the plate. She stole another quick look over at Jude, who was carrying his plate to a table, his BlackBerry between his teeth and a can of Coke tucked under his chin. *Massimo is gallant.*

Erinn kept an eye on her watch and called the group back to work after a half hour. The sky was starting to darken and there was no time to lose. She took up her position with her camera and again followed Massimo as he talked, soothingly, to wounded soldiers. He helped the "nurse" Giselle bandage a young soldier's eye. Erinn forced herself to get close-ups of Giselle's perfect profile. Since the eighties, Erinn had made it a one-woman crusade to smash the stereotype of women not being able to get along in the workplace. But panning across Giselle's ethereal features was cruel and unusual punishment.

Jude called "Cut" and summoned all the cameras—and Massimo—to his side.

"We need a little more movement, guys," Jude said. "I think we need Washington to ride in on a horse and scan the camp. Massimo, can you ride a horse?"

"*Sì,* yes," Massimo said.

"Bueno," Jude said.

"Dude, that's Spanish," Carlos said.

"Whatever," Jude said. "Carlos, you'll be the wide shots; Gilroi, medium; and Erinn, Washington's POV."

Massimo looked at Erinn.

"That means point of view. My camera will see what your eyes see."

"Ah, sì," Massimo said. "I know this POV. I did not understand the English word."

Erinn's mind reeled.

"But . . . if I'm Washington's point of view, don't I have to be on horseback, too?"

"*Sì* . . . yes," Jude said. "You know how to ride, don't you?"

"Of course I do," Erinn said, although it had probably been twenty years since she'd been on a horse.

Fetus appeared with two saddled horses. The horses had strained the budget, but they were beautiful and worth every penny, Erinn had thought when she first laid eyes on them. Now she was sorry to see them. Massimo mounted as if he were born in the saddle. Erinn looked around her. The cast of reenactors continued about their business, but the entire crew was standing around, arms folded, smirking. Erinn was not a religious woman, but she sent up a prayer. *Please God, give me the courage and strength to get up on this horse. Don't let me fail . . . or flail.*

This reminded her of a quote from Winston Churchill, and she threw it in for good measure: "Courage is going from failure to failure without losing enthusiasm."

She knew she would have no enthusiasm if she fell off the horse, but failing Winston Churchill was the least of her worries.

Massimo reached down and extended an elegant hand toward her camera. She surrendered it and closed her eyes. She visualized riding through the Tuscan hills, one of her favorite memories. She rode up and down sloping vineyards and guided her horse along a placid riverbank. At one point, as the river got deeper and deeper, she felt the horse's footing soften and realized that he was swimming. Erinn inhaled, strengthened by the reminiscence, and climbed effortlessly into the saddle. She opened her eyes to applause. The crew was grinning, clapping, and whistling. She tried to hide a smile, but sent up a silent thank-you to heaven . . . and Winston. Massimo handed Erinn her camera and bowed deeply. Erinn hoped that Giselle was watching and looked over to the campfire that she was tending. Giselle gave her a toothy smile and waved. The fact that Giselle didn't see Erinn as even the tiniest threat could not dampen Erinn's mood.

She was, literally, back on the horse! Jude told her to get some footage of Massimo riding in the woods, then, when he came into the camp, switch to the POV position and try to shoot around the other cameras whenever possible. Erinn nodded and off she went with Massimo and their two horses.

Massimo and Erinn trotted out to a crest just out of sight of the set. Massimo turned out to be a fantastic horseman, and Erinn got some great shots of him riding majestically through the snow, cape snapping behind him. The temperature continued to drop, but Erinn didn't feel the cold. All the professional cobwebs of the last ten years were shaking loose. She felt as if she had been waiting her whole life to do this kind of shoot.

After she was sure she had enough footage of Massimo looking courageous and heroic, she instructed him to head slowly into camp. She would stay alongside him, shooting a close-up of his profile until he crested the hill. At that point, she would shoot slightly behind his shoulder.

"Ah! The POV," Massimo said.

Erinn followed Massimo closely into camp, shooting down at the faces of the reenactors as they reacted to Washington's presence. Everything was quiet, and Erinn was aware that the only sound she heard was horses' footsteps and the very slight whisper of her camera. She had goose bumps and had to wipe her eyes a few times. It all felt so real.

"OK," Jude called out. "I think we got it. Good work, everybody."

Whatever spell had been thrown over the set snapped. Erinn dismounted, turned over her horse to Fetus, and everything returned to the twenty-first century.

Snow started to fall midafternoon, and Jude, who had had his eyes glued to the monitor all day, looked and signaled Erinn to walk with him. She tucked the camera under her arm and followed Jude toward the outskirts of the shoot.

"Well?" Jude asked.

"Well, what?"

"It's snowing."

"Yes."

"And?"

"Is this some sort of code?"

"It's snowing. You're the producer. It's your call whether we wrap the shoot or not."

Erinn almost staggered under the weight of such a decision. She had no idea the producer would have such enormous responsibility.

"Well," Erinn said, "as the director, do you have everything you want?"

"No. But then, I'll never have everything I want. Do I have everything I need? Probably."

She thought quickly. Her gut told her that they should keep shooting.

"Let's wrap," Erinn said.

Her gut had told her to come to Valley Forge in a snowstorm the first time and look what had happened. She could only hope she'd made the right decision this time. She watched as Jude walked back to the set, where cast and crew were all looking at him. Erinn couldn't tell if he approved of this choice or not.

"That's a wrap," Jude said.

Everyone clapped and shook hands. Erinn was comforted by this show of approval, until she realized that everyone else was just happy to get off work early.

"Good call," Fetus said. "Thanks!"

Fetus joined the rest of the crew, busily striking the set. The boys moved fast, pulling down lights and wrapping the gear as quickly as they could. Snow was no friend to production equipment. Gilroi raced by Erinn, who was also packing gear. Erinn announced to the reenactors that they would be contacted for the next shoot. She looked at her clipboard. The next time they convened, it would be for the "Washington Crossing the Delaware" shoot. Carlos would be the lead producer, and she would be the backup camera op—along with Gilroi. Normally, Erinn relished being in charge, but she had to admit the fact that all responsibility would not be resting on her shoulders came as a relief.

Relief? She felt herself flush at the admission. Relief at abandoning responsibility struck her as absolutely plebeian. Maybe she was getting old.

She caught a quick glimpse of Jude and Giselle busily punching their phone numbers into each other's BlackBerries. Erinn tried not to give in to temptation, but she couldn't resist. She checked out the cast list for the "Washington Crossing the Delaware" shoot and looked for Giselle's name. It wasn't there.

Of course there would not be a woman's role in the crossing scene. There were no women in the boat.

Erinn chuckled at her own insecurity and stupidity. She finished stowing the camera and tape and, staggering under the weight of the camera box, headed to the wardrobe trailer to collect Massimo, who was just coming out in his civilian clothes. He smiled when he saw her and she forced Jude out of her thoughts. Massimo took the camera bag from her and headed to the SUV. Erinn swiveled her head around, hoping nobody saw her relinquishing the bag. She was never comfortable with men carrying her gear, but after a day shooting, her back ached and her arms throbbed.

Our next hotel will have a gym. Atmosphere be damned.

The snow continued to fall as Erinn maneuvered the SUV back to the hotel. Massimo was chatty, pumped from the day's shooting. He relived every scene, and Erinn tried to tune in once in a while to murmur an "um-hum." She remembered this reaction from her Broadway days. Everyone behind the scenes was exhausted at the end of a performance, but the actors were coiled tight as wires, enough energy emanating from them that they could almost light up the street by themselves.

Back in the hotel lobby, Erinn wondered vaguely if she should wait for the boys to arrive but decided that she could connect with them later. Massimo insisted on carrying her gear to her room, but once there, he seemed content to leave it at the door—*Both literally and figuratively*, Erinn thought.

Her laptop sat on the desk, the Apple insignia practically winking at her, luring her to check her e-mails, but she was exhausted. She hopped into the shower, her head against the cool wall. It had been years since she had felt such physical fatigue. She smiled to herself.

Better get used to it. This looks like it's going to be your new life!

After the shower, she lay down on the bed. Her lower back hurt so much, she knew she wouldn't sleep. Tomorrow was Saturday, thank God, so they wouldn't be shooting. She could just sleep late.

She sat up, glowering at the beckoning computer.

OK, you win.

She clicked open her e-mail.

CHAPTER 21

"We've been canceled," Erinn said.

The boys—including Massimo—were having breakfast when she dropped the bomb. As soon as she read the e-mail from Cary, Erinn had sent them all a nebulous message, instructing them to meet in the lobby at nine sharp. They greeted her cheerfully, but there was a hint of apprehension. They had to know something was up. Even a go-getter like Erinn wouldn't call a meeting on a Saturday morning unless it was important.

Oatmeal, fried eggs, potatoes were all pushed aside and they stared at her. Carlos put his BlackBerry on silent, which as far as Erinn knew, was unheard of.

"That's impossible," Jude said. "We haven't even been on the air yet."

"We haven't even finished shooting," Gilroi added.

For a moment, Carlos said nothing. He just turned the BlackBerry around in his hands as if he'd never seen it before. Erinn looked at him and he waved the device at her.

"Guess I'll be returning this," he said.

"So . . . ," Gilroi said. "Dish."

Erinn sat. She had told them. At least the worst was over. She had printed out copies of Cary's e-mail for everyone—thank God for that portable printer she'd bought just before the trip.

Suzanna had thought the printer was an extravagance for a freelance producer.

But now, it has proven itself invaluable, Erinn thought as she passed out the dreaded e-mail. *Of course, if I could choose between keeping my job and Suzanna being right, I'd choose Suzanna being right . . . maybe.*

A waiter brought Erinn a cup of coffee and she busied herself with cream and sugar while the boys read. She had printed a copy for herself, but she didn't need it—she had read it so many times, she had it memorized.

> Dear Erinn: Sorry to be the bearer of bad news, but we just got word that our sponsor for *BATTLEready!* has pulled out. We put out feelers—trying to scrounge up some emergency funding—but came up empty-handed. With the economy being what it is, we're not sure when or where we'll get the cash to finish the first episode—let alone a full season. Please pass the information on to the crew. I wasn't sure who I should write to, since there are three producers out there, but we got the news on your watch, so I picked you. We'll fly the entire crew—and your friend Massimo—back to Los Angeles tomorrow. Start packing! We'll put our heads together when you guys get home. Thanks for all the hard work.—Cary

Erinn had resisted the urge to edit Cary's memo, and decided to print it just the way Cary wrote it. Bad news didn't really get any better just because it was grammatically correct.

The boys sat quietly—digesting the news, if not their toast. Massimo finally broke the silence.

"I am no longer George Washington?" he asked.

"Nope," Jude said. "And I'm no longer a director, and these guys are no longer producers. Like you guys say, *'Que sera, sera.'* "

"Dude. That's French," Carlos said.

"We're now just passengers on the Unemployment Train," Gilroi said.

"Well, I guess we sit tight and wait for the plane tickets," Erinn said.

"Fuck that!" Jude said. "We're having a wrap party tonight!"

She was relieved that the news had settled as well as it did. The group made plans to meet again that evening, and they all went their separate ways. Massimo stood in the lobby looking lost. Erinn walked up to him.

"Bene?" Erinn asked.

"Sì," Massimo answered. *"Sono deluso."*

"I know," Erinn said. "We're all disappointed. Do you want to see the city today? That might make you happy."

"No, I will buy a new suit. That will make me happy."

Erinn turned to go, but Massimo took her arm and spun her toward him. Erinn had no time to react as Massimo kissed her on the lips. *"Fino a stá sera,"* he said.

"Yes, I'll see you this evening."

Erinn watched Massimo glide out the hotel door. What was that all about? She turned around and saw Jude looking at her. He was standing at the front desk, and when she caught his eye, he turned back to the clerk.

Erinn wasn't close enough to see what Jude's reaction to the kiss had been.

Probably nothing. She wondered what *she* thought of the kiss? It was obviously more than friendly. But she was his landlady! Erinn decided she couldn't add the intrigue to her brain or it would explode. But it did make the idea of a wrap party more interesting.

She pushed the kiss aside and wondered what she would do with her day. Even in her heyday, there was a lot of downtime in her professional life—it was the nature of show business, no matter what branch you swung from. She knew she needed to keep busy. There would be enough time over the next few days and weeks to go over all the "what ifs" of losing a job. Every muscle in her body ached, and it only took a few steps up the stairs until it came to her. What she really needed was a massage. She checked with the concierge and was pleased to hear that not only could she get an appointment, but the masseuse would come to her room. Erinn checked her watch. She realized that since becoming a producer, she checked her watch compulsively. Time was money. She wondered if that habit would continue, or if time would go back to being just time.

She'd answer a few e-mails, get a massage, see a few sights, and take a nap before the impromptu wrap party.

Not a bad way to spend the day, considering I just got . . .

Fired? Erinn wondered if she'd be fired. Or was she laid off? Or, merely, was she no longer employed? She headed up to her room—these were the very thoughts she wanted to avoid.

Erinn settled down at her computer. Last night, after she had opened Cary's e-mail, she just didn't have it in her to read anything else. She looked at the time . . . she knew she'd have several panic-stricken missives from her sister by now. Erinn was sure they would all be variations of Mimi's favorite, all-purpose, "What the fuck?"

Erinn clicked on the latest communiqué from Mimi. It was indeed full of breathless hysteria about "dodging a bullet" when she hired Massimo to her concern about the show's abrupt demise. Erinn put her head in her hands. Mimi was three thousand miles away and she was still exhausting. What happened to the concept of agents being hard to find when you needed them?

A knock on the door made her jump. Surprised with the speed with which the masseuse had arrived, she clicked out of e-mail and gave herself a once-over in the mirror on the way to the door. She looked as worn-out as she felt. Erinn hoped the massage would help with that as well as with her aching limbs. She hated to admit it, but she was looking forward to the wrap party.

Erinn wondered if she was supposed to be naked under one of the hotel's plush robes; she was still completely dressed. As she swung open the door, she said, "Sorry I haven't taken off my clothes yet."

Erinn froze. Jude was standing on the other side of the door. He breezed past her.

"I'm thinking you're expecting someone else," he said.

"I was going to get a massage."

"Oh." Jude seemed to hesitate. "Well, then . . . I guess I'll talk to you later. After you're naked . . . I mean, relaxed . . . I mean . . . I'll talk to you later."

He headed to the door, but Erinn stopped him.

"You can talk to me now." She wasn't quite sure why she was detaining him. She had always prided herself on her self-awareness, but she'd be damned if she was going to wonder about this now.

Jude came back into the room and sat on the bed. Then he jumped up as if it were covered in hot coals and took a chair instead. Erinn sat on the bed and they stared at each other.

"I really liked working with you," Jude said.

"And I you."

"Listen, Erinn, I've been thinking about the wrap party, and I know I'm probably going to get shit-faced, and I . . . I want to talk about something and I think I should be sober. I don't want to be a puss . . . I mean, I don't want to be a little bitch about it."

"God forbid."

"So, I was wondering . . . are you with that Italian poser dude?"

"Italian poser dude? Massimo? You think he's posing as an Italian?"

"No! But he's a little too perfect, don't you think?"

"You mean, do I think he is refined, educated, handsome, and industrious?"

"Yeah."

"Well, yes, I do. Do you have a problem with that?"

"A huge problem! Don't you think he's just a little on the nose for you?"

Erinn looked at the ceiling. She wasn't sure what to make of this comment, let alone the conversation. Erinn started to think that it had been a long time since she'd been in this sort of situation, but blushed when she realized it had been less than a week—and with this man. Jude got up and started pacing. He avoided looking at her.

"Don't get me wrong, I get what you see in him, but . . ."

Jude looked out the window at the brick wall. Erinn waited, but he said nothing.

"But what, Jude?"

"Are you with him or not?"

"No, Jude, I am not with the Italian poser dude."

Jude turned to face her.

"I can't get Valley Forge out of my mind," he said.

"It was a great shoot," Erinn said. "Everything went very well."

"You know that's not what I'm talking about," he said. "Don't you think about it?"

Jude sat on the bed beside her and took her hands in his. Erinn tried to control her breathing.

"Jude," Erinn said. "I'm not a simpleton. Of course I've thought about . . . Valley Forge."

"It was good, Erinn. We were good. I know you have a lot of shit you think about, but . . ."

"But?"

"But couldn't we give this a chance . . . you and me . . . you and I . . . you and me?"

"You and me . . . and no, Jude. We couldn't."

"Why?"

"Because of Giselle."

Jude stared at her blankly.

"OK . . . I'll bite," he said. "Who is Giselle?"

"That pretty girl who was playing the nurse on our shoot. You exchanged phone numbers with her."

"I exchange phone numbers with a lot of pretty girls."

"Exactly."

"This isn't going to turn into some psycho jealousy thing, is it?"

"Of course not! It's just that . . . when I looked at the two of you talking and laughing, I thought, he should be with her. You two looked perfect together."

"I look perfect with a lot of people."

"Jude," Erinn said, "I'm too ol . . . I'm too tired to deal with an avalanche of emotions."

"But that's not fair! I'm in that avalanche with you. I'm . . . I'm bombarded with really frozen . . . white . . . passion."

"You're bombarded with really frozen white passion?"

"I thought we were doing an avalanche metaphor thing," Jude said. "Erinn, look, I've always dated the prettiest thing that would date me. Then I met you."

"I'm sure there's a compliment in there somewhere."

"The point is, it doesn't matter how young and beautiful that . . . that Giselle was . . . she was a girl on a shoot. All I know is—our connection was amazing. You've got me thinking."

"About what?"

"Stuff."

Erinn nodded slowly.

"Could you be a little more specific?"

"Usually, when I'm on a shoot, I couldn't care less what it's about. But since I met you, I mean, I've been all over this Revolutionary War. You know . . . like Helen Keller."

"I hadn't realized Helen Keller was interested in the Revolutionary War," Erinn teased him.

"No, dude. In the movie. She suddenly wants to know stuff. I'm like that."

"There's a quote that haunts me—"

"And I have a feeling you're going to share."

"At eighteen, our convictions are hills from which we look. At fifty, they are caves in which we hide."

"Well, I'm not eighteen and you're not fifty, so maybe we can meet in the middle."

Jude kissed her. Erinn could think of a million reasons why this was a terrible idea, but she could not bring herself to stop. Jude tipped her back onto the bed, never breaking their kiss.

He's very practiced, Erinn thought. Then she ordered herself to stop thinking.

"Besides," Jude said, looking into her eyes. "I wouldn't mind following you into a cave. . . ."

A knock on the door startled them both. Erinn pushed Jude, who landed sideways on the floor. Erinn straightened her clothes and headed for the door.

"My masseuse is here."

"OK," Jude said. "But will you think about it?"

They stared at each other. They were only a foot apart, but neither of them reached out to the other. The knocking continued.

"I'll think about it. Please go. I'll see you tonight at the party."

Jude grinned and gave her a fist bump. Erinn stared at her fist as Jude vanished into the hallway. He was replaced by a Viking of a female masseuse.

She'll pound some sense into me, Erinn thought.

CHAPTER 22

The wrap party was going to be held at the Black Sheep. Erinn tried to stay relaxed—after all, she had paid good money for that massage. But every time she thought of Jude, she could feel herself tense. She tried to write the script for the party, but her mind seized. There were too many possible subplots to even contemplate.

A month ago, she was happy, living in her solitary world.

Well, happy *might be too strong a word.*

But she had had nothing to worry about but the bills. Now, she was reeling from the complications of juggling two men—if only for this evening.

And I have to worry about the bills all over again. She thought sadly about the abrupt cancellation. Massimo was still her tenant and his rent check would help until the next production job came along. *What if the next production job doesn't come along?* she wondered.

She told herself that now was not the time to complicate the situation on the home front.

During the afternoon, instead of dozing after the massage, she'd hit the town. She took in a few historic sites, but couldn't keep her mind on anything the docents had to say, so she threw in the towel and went to Macy's. While Erinn was not one for shopping, she excused herself because this Macy's was a historic landmark.

Founded in 1866, John Wanamaker pioneered a shopping concept that would morph into our present-day idea of a "department store."

In 1911, he opened Wanamaker's in downtown Philadelphia to huge success. Throughout the decades, the store had seen some rough days. It used to break Erinn's heart in the eighties, on excursions from New York, to see such a grand building in decline, but Macy's had swooped in several years ago and the structure now shined.

Erinn was flooded with nostalgia as she ran her hand over the huge bronze statue of an eagle that was the centerpiece of the Grand Court. This famous feature, which John Wanamaker had purchased at the St. Louis World's Fair in 1904, had become an immediate meeting spot for the locals. Generations of Philadelphians rendezvoused in Center City with the saying, "Meet me at the Eagle." Erinn was glad to see the eagle had weathered the storm, and while she had no one to "meet at the Eagle," she thought fondly back to the days when she had.

Erinn looked through racks of clothes, having no idea what she was looking for. It took her a while just to figure out what size she was. Where was Suzanna when she needed her? She pulled out a black turtleneck in a size ten and held it up to her body. She was contemplating the fabric, when a slim young woman, clearly another shopper, stood beside her.

"That's really cool," the young woman said. "Do you think they have it in a size zero?"

"That-a-way," Erinn pointed to the other end of the rack.

Size zero? Erinn couldn't imagine such a thing. In her day, size five was considered about as small as a woman could be and still stand upright.

I bet Giselle is a size zero.

Her cell phone rang. Erinn put on her half-moons and looked at the phone—it was Mimi.

"Hello?" Erinn said.

"Hey, sweetie. Just checking in. You doing OK with the cancellation?"

Erinn caught a glimpse of herself with her recently toned body from weeks of camera work. She was wearing her new Victoria's Secret bra and boy-cut panties under her clothes and knew, just like the mythic Victoria, she was looking good!

"Holding up magnificently, if I do say so myself."

"You OK? This doesn't sound like you."

"Gotta go, Mimi," Erinn said. "I'm going to a party and I'm not ready."

"What? All right, who is this, and what have you done with my client?"

Erinn laughed and snapped the phone shut. Mimi—and the world—would just have to get used to the "new" Erinn. Or the return of the "old" Erinn from long ago. It depended on how you looked at it.

Erinn couldn't remember when she'd spent so much time preparing for a party. She couldn't remember the last time she had even *attended* a party! She pulled the black turtleneck out of its Macy's bag, wiggled into her jeans, and added her new heeled shoes and some dangling earrings. She knew not to go overboard with the makeup. She gathered the nice clothes were already going to come as a shock to her co-workers. Better not to go nuts. She fluffed her hair and added the lipstick that Suzanna had bought her.

She studied herself. She looked pretty good for forty-three. But she didn't look twenty-three or even thirty-three. She was no Giselle—she knew that. Now that she was back in the world, Erinn wondered if this insecurity came with the territory. She grabbed her coat and keys and headed down to the Black Sheep.

Carlos and Gilroi were already in the bar. Erinn let out her breath—she realized she had been holding it in anticipation of seeing either Massimo or Jude. The boys made appreciative noises at the change in Erinn's appearance, but not to the point that she felt self-conscious. Erinn spotted a familiar-looking woman buying a glass of white wine at the bar and tried to place her. Then she realized who it was.

Cary!

Cary caught Erinn's eye and threaded her way toward the group.

"Surprise!" Cary said.

The boys had already seen her, and they laughed that extra-hearty laugh underlings dredge up when their superior is around.

"What are you doing here?" Erinn asked.

"Well, I just felt so bad that we got canceled. So I flew in to be with my team on the last day."

"I guess that means the company is going to pay for the wrap party," Gilroi said.

"Have you met us?" Cary said. "The party is Dutch—as usual."

"Whatever," Carlos said. "They can take away our show, but they can't take away our wrap party."

Gilroi jumped up, pulling Erinn to her feet. She found herself dancing cheek to cheek with Gilroi while he crooned along to the Gershwin tune "They Can't Take That Away from Me."

The music abruptly changed to "El Pollo de Lamontitos," an easy salsa number, and Carlos cut in. It only took Erinn a minute to remember the steps and even throw in a dance embellishment here and there, much to everyone's delight.

Erinn thought back to an evening a little over a year ago. Before Eric had finally announced his feelings for Suzanna, her sister had decided to take salsa lessons, in a desperate bid for independence; fifteen years of holding still, longing for Eric, was enough. She had developed a monstrous crush on her dance instructor and threw herself—in Erinn's opinion—shamelessly at him. Suzanna thought nobody was the wiser, but Erinn's sisterly intuition was in high gear and she knew something was up. And she knew in her bones that the dance instructor had no real interest in her sister.

On Suzanna's birthday, a group of her closest friends were going to have a surprise party for her. Erinn knew that Suzanna was going dancing before the party. While Erinn was brushing her teeth, she conjured up various scenarios for the evening—a habit many writers shared. In one vivid scenario, Suzanna and the dance instructor wound up looking for a place to carry out their passion. Erinn stopped brushing her teeth mid-stroke.

Suzanna knows I never lock the guesthouse!

Erinn made sure the guesthouse was locked before she left for the party. She couldn't be sure it had made any difference, but it didn't matter now—Suzanna was with the love of her life.

As the song ended, Carlos dipped Erinn dramatically to the floor and back. Suzanna looked around the room for Jude, secretly hoping he'd seen her great dance moves. He was nowhere to be found, but Erinn was extremely optimistic about the future. She hoped he showed up in time to dance.

Maybe salsa will turn my romantic life around, too.

Breathless, Erinn returned to the table, and Cary handed her the hard cider that had magically appeared.

"You really seem to have come into your own," Cary said. "The crew loves you."

Erinn nodded. "It's been a great experience. I'm sorry it's over."

"Well . . . we have something coming up in about a month—" Cary started, but was interrupted by Massimo.

Cary and Massimo exchanged a European double-cheek kiss, which surprised Erinn. She hadn't realized the two of them had met. But Cary had been reviewing the footage, and she probably now felt she knew Massimo. He had been a fantastic General Washington! Massimo turned to Erinn.

"May I have this dance?" he asked.

Erinn listened. They were playing "Innamorata," sung by Dean Martin. Erinn looked at Cary, who shrugged.

"I'm not going anyplace," Cary said. "Go dance. We'll talk later."

Massimo led Erinn to the dance floor. He was wearing a beautifully cut new suit and wore it well. He pulled Erinn close. She quickly looked toward the door. If Jude came in now, she'd be hard pressed to convince him that she wasn't with the Italian poser dude. She tried to relax into the dance, but as they swayed, she caught Gilroi's eye. He wiggled his eyebrows lasciviously. She pointed to him accusingly and mouthed *Not helping.* Gilroi laughed.

"Bella mia," Massimo breathed into her ear. "This is good, yes?"

"*Sì* . . . yes," Erinn said, distracted.

"I will tell you the truth, Erinn," Massimo said, pulling her closer. "I owe you my life. George Washington was my greatest role."

"Oh, well, a simple thank-you would do."

Massimo stopped dancing.

"No! My life!"

Erinn got their feet going again. She was actually glad Massimo had presented this opening.

"Well, when I get another job, I'll try to get you another great role. But in the meantime, I'll go back to . . . well, something . . . and you'll go back to the restaurant . . . and the guesthouse."

"*Cara mia,* it breaks my heart to tell you this, but I must. To be George Washington, I . . . *come si dice?* . . . I leave the restaurant."

"You left the restaurant? You mean, you have no job?"

"I did this for you!"

Erinn could see the hurt in his eyes. And she realized that if he had asked if he should quit, she would have supported the decision. After all, she had needed a General Washington.

"OK. It's OK . . . we'll work it out," she said.

"And I will stay in the house with you and we can rent the guesthouse to someone new, yes?"

Erinn was having a hard time focusing. If there was no Jude, she might just say yes to this. But there was Jude. She shot another look at the door. Or was there?

The song ended, and Massimo escorted Erinn graciously back to the table. He bowed to Erinn, then to Cary, and then melted into the crowd.

"Damn, he's hot," Cary said, toasting Erinn. "You seem to have all the boys at your feet."

Erinn flushed. It wasn't true, she knew, but as Mimi always said, façade was everything, so she demurred. Erinn was anxious to get back to Cary's conversation. She took a sip of cider.

"You mentioned you might have a new show coming up?"

"Yes," Cary said. "It's really exciting—and something very different for the History Network. It's a challenge show. And it takes place . . . drum roll please . . . in a lighthouse."

Erinn froze. All sound and movement stopped.

"Like *Survivor*?" she whispered.

"Just like *Survivor*!" Cary said. "Isn't it divine?"

"Extremely divine," Erinn said, trying to control the tremor in her hand. "Where did you find such a . . . divine . . . concept?"

"Well, I can't say—confidentiality and all that crap." Cary winked at Erinn. "But I can tell you we got the idea from someone we all know and love."

Erinn pushed the cider away. Jude was the only one who knew about the lighthouse. The room started to spin. There had to be some reasonable explanation.

"I . . . need to talk to Jude," Erinn said suddenly.

"Well, good luck—I haven't seen him in the last hour."

"He was here?"

"Before you arrived, yes. As a matter of fact, we were talking about the lighthouse idea. Wink, wink, nudge, nudge."

The room started folding in on Erinn. Cary looked alarmed.

"Erinn? Are you OK?"

"I will be," Erinn said. "I'm just feeling a little light-headed. I must have had too much to drink."

"You've had half a cider."

"I'm going to go back to the hotel. I'll be fine."

She started toward the door, but Massimo stopped her.

"Erinn!" he said. "I will walk with you, no?"

"No," Erinn said. "I . . . Massimo, I need you to go back to Los Angeles with the team. Take care of Caro."

"Where will you be?"

"I'll be . . . I'm taking a vacation. Please go back and take care of the cat."

Erinn staggered out of the pub and gulped the night air. She commanded herself not to cry. *How could I be so foolish?* she asked herself as she made her way blindly toward the hotel. *He was just trying to charm me so he could steal my idea.*

All the way home, Erinn tried to think of possibilities that would leave Jude in the clear.

I'm a writer. I just need to think. There have to be a hundred scenarios. There has to be another explanation.

As she entered her room, she stepped on the speedy checkout notice, which had been slid under the door. She picked it up to put it on the desk, when she noticed another, smaller piece of paper underneath.

It was a note, written on hotel stationery. It read:

> *Erinn: I need to talk to you about LET IT SHINE. There's been a development, and I don't want you to hear about this from anybody else. Come by my room when you get back from the party.*
>
> *—Jude*

Erinn sank onto the bed. Well, all right then—it was the old adage, "All's fair in love and war."

She saw herself in the mirror. She felt foolish in her new shoes and silly earrings. She took them all off and threw them in the trash. She quickly packed her suitcase as she stuffed her feelings back into the metal locker from which they had somehow escaped. She took a breath and felt oddly centered. She was used to this hollowness.

It fit better than the shoes.

CHAPTER 23

"OK, Erinn, that's enough," Erinn's mother, Virginia, said, pulling back the drapes so that sunlight flooded the tiny guestroom of her Greenwich Village apartment. "Come on now, let's greet the day!"

"I'm not ready to greet the goddamned day," Erinn said, putting her head under the pillow.

"I swear, dear, you're worse than that Carrie in that *Sex and the City* movie."

Erinn peeked out from under the pillow and opened one eye.

"Say again?"

"You know, when Big stood Carrie up at the altar and she went on her honeymoon with her girlfriends and just . . . pouted . . . the whole time. It was most unbecoming."

Erinn sat up. Suzanna and their mother shared a love of all things *Sex and the City*, and in retirement, her mother's passion for the characters seemed to have escalated.

"Well, this is hardly the same situation. I was not left at the altar. This is professional."

"Ah! Professional pouting. I see."

Erinn and her mother stared at each other, Erinn scowling, Virginia smiling benignly.

"OK, you win. I'll get up," Erinn said with a shrug.

Virginia patted her daughter's knee and left the room before Erinn could beg her to draw the drapes. Erinn sat back against the ornately carved headboard and noticed that her mother had left a glass of orange juice on the nightstand. In her head, Erinn could hear her mother saying, "There's no better way to start the morning than with a great big glass of orange juice." She'd been saying it since Erinn was a child.

Erinn drank the juice, and hated to admit that she was starting to feel slightly more human. The drink turned sour in her mouth as the events of Philadelphia started playing again in her brain. Erinn put the glass down with a thud. She wondered: *How long have I been at my mother's, anyway?*

And then: *How long did Carrie pout over Mr. Big?*

Erinn dragged herself out of bed and into the shower. As in many old New York apartments, Virginia's plumbing led a life of its own. One wrong turn of the ancient handle and the water would turn so cold or so hot that it could shoot you involuntarily out of the shower. Luckily, the shower seemed to understand that Erinn was in no mood for games. Washing her hair turned out to be blessedly noneventful.

Erinn emerged from the bathroom, wrapped in one of her mother's silk kimonos. Virginia was in the kitchen, the morning paper in front of her, looking out onto the bleak landscape of her tiny garden. The barren sticks of last year's plants stuck up through the snow.

"I've always imagined this is what the Phantom of the Opera's garden would have looked like," Virginia said without turning to look at Erinn. "Bleak, bleak, bleak."

Erinn poured herself some tea. She caught a glimpse of herself in the mirror and expertly pulled her hair into its tousled do. She sat down with her mother and regarded the garden.

"Last year, I went on a tour of the Los Angeles Arboretum before the flowers bloomed," Erinn said. "We were riding on a long open-air cart and the driver was pointing out all the various roses, but there was nothing to see but branches. I thought . . . what if aliens saw us right now? What would they think?"

"I always wonder what aliens would think if they saw us at a movie theater before the show begins," Virginia said. "All these people staring at a blank screen."

"Interesting," Erinn said, and sipped her tea.

"Dear, may I ask you something?"

Erinn nodded, sipping her tea and musing about aliens.

"When did you stop combing your hair?" Virginia asked, gazing at Erinn's updo.

Erinn fell into the familiar rabbit hole that was childhood and instinctively planned on blaming her sister for the unfortunate hairdo. But she stopped herself. She had to admit she really liked the softer look. She touched her hair and pulled a curl over her forehead.

"I've made a lot of changes lately," she said.

Erinn noticed her mother had scooted the *New York Times* closer to her. It was open to an advertisement for holistic eardrops made from garlic and olive oil. She looked at her mother, who sat innocently sipping her tea. But Erinn wasn't fooled for one minute. This was Virginia's oddly passive way of telling Erinn she needed to buck up, get out into the world again. She needed to listen.

Erinn went back to bed.

The following morning, Erinn got out of bed without her mother's pressure, craving orange juice. She opened the bedroom door, planning on tiptoeing to the kitchen, when she saw a large glass of orange juice sitting on the floor right outside her room. When she was growing up, this unnerving radar of her mother's used to annoy Erinn. Now she was grateful for it. Erinn started to take the drink into her room, but she could hear her mother puttering in the kitchen and carried the glass in there instead.

"I see you've decided to join the living." Erinn's mother poured a cup of tea for her as she made her way to the table. "Look at this magazine, dear. You're in it!"

Erinn snapped awake and looked at the magazine in front of her. Under the headline *Whatever Became Of*... was a short paragraph about Erinn Elizabeth Wolf returning to the city of her early triumph. Erinn let out a sigh of relief. That was all the information given.

Virginia sat at the table and brought the phone with her.

"I'm listed, you know. I bet the phone is going to ring off the hook now that everybody knows you're back."

Erinn and her mother stared at the phone in silence. It did not ring.

"Oh, Mother, nobody cares that I'm back. This is silly!"

The phone rang so suddenly and so shrilly that both women jumped. Virginia answered it. She handed the phone to Erinn.

"It's for you."

"Erinn Wolf here."

"Really?" asked the voice on the other end of the phone. "Are you really her?"

"Am I really *she*?" Erinn corrected.

"Well, are you or aren't you?"

"Let's start again. I am she."

Erinn's mother put the call on speakerphone, so she could listen. Erinn always took a secret pleasure in her mother's pride. Virginia had practically glowed at the premiere of *The Family of Mann.*

"This is so exciting," said the voice. "You know, I saw *The Family of Mann* six times! I can't believe I'm talking to a celebrity."

"Well, that's very flattering," Erinn said.

"When I saw your name in *Celebrity Magazine,* it sure brought back memories," the voice said. "Even though it was in *Whatever Became Of.* I guess that means you're no longer a celebrity."

Erinn watched as her mother started to frown.

"No," Erinn said. "It means you are no longer flattering."

She hung up the phone. Her mother looked at her over her reading glasses.

"Erinn, dear," she said. "Was that nice?"

Erinn stared at the column again. Was the fact that she was mentioned in a magazine a coincidence? No one but her mother knew she was in town. No one had seen her—she hadn't been out of the house.

"Mother?"

"Yes, dear?"

"Do you think it was a coincidence that *Celebrity Magazine* wrote an article about me while I just happened to be in town?"

"Oh, I have no idea."

"You did this, didn't you?" Erinn said.

"I did not!" Virginia said.

"Then it must have been Suzanna."

Her mother snorted and waved her hand in dismissal.

"Then it was Mimi!"

"It was not Mimi. If Mimi wanted to expose you, she would have contacted *People* magazine, not *Celebrity*."

"I cannot imagine that *People* magazine would have any interest in my whereabouts."

"That's exactly what Suzanna said."

"So you *did* tell Suzanna I was here?"

"Well, of course I told her you were here. Suppose she went to your house and discovered that man was back with the cat—and no you. She would think you had been murdered. I couldn't have your sister frantic with worry."

Erinn decided to let her mother off the hook. Her mother was no match for Suzanna's badgering. Perhaps it was just serendipity that *Celebrity* should mention her. Perhaps they mentioned her all the time. Erinn wouldn't know if New Yorkers still cared about her, what with her living on the West Coast.

She made a mental note to order a subscription to *Celebrity* when she got back to California.

Erinn stood up to pour them both more tea—a secret family signal that a subject was closed. She could see the relief in Virginia's eyes. Erinn decided she should go easier on her mother.

"Are you intending to see any friends while you're here?" Virginia asked.

Erinn retracted her resolution. Her mother was relentless.

"I . . . I don't really have any plans."

"Well, I think it would do you good to get out. You've been sleeping for almost three days," Virginia said. "The city has changed a lot since you've been back."

Virginia prided herself on knowing the town—even though she'd only been back for fewer than two years. The fact that it had been nine years since Erinn had been back to New York went unspoken.

One for Mother.

Erinn knew it made no sense staying inside—that's what she did in Los Angeles. When she used to live in New York, she'd turned her kitchen into a closet since she was never home enough to use it. But she did not want to revisit the city right now, no matter how much it had changed.

"I'm not really interested in going out right now," Erinn said. "I thought I'd just stay inside with you."

"I have my own life, dear."

"I thought you and I could have lunch at Tavern on the Green."

"You loathe Tavern on the Green. Besides, it's closed."

Erinn's mother looked at her.

"Erinn, you can't pull the rug up every time something goes

wrong," Virginia said. "I let you hide the last time, and I regret it. Now, call someone—anyone—and leave the house."

"Mother, please, I know you mean well, but I'm an—"

Virginia held up her hand.

"I don't want to hear that you're an adult, dear. First of all, you aren't acting like one, and second, I'm your mother," Virginia said, putting a phone down on the table in front of Erinn. "Call someone—anyone—and make a lunch date."

"I don't have any phone numbers."

"What about Facebook?"

"Oh, Mother, please. I am not on Facebook."

"Dear, you can be such a caveperson."

"Even if I find someone with whom to have lunch . . . I don't know where to go."

"Everyone's going to the Chelsea Market these days," Virginia said, leaving the kitchen.

Erinn stood outside Chelsea Market, waiting for Lamont Langley to show up. She looked up at the gray sky and, for a moment, longed for the California sunshine. She jumped up and down trying to stay warm.

Erinn had not kept up with any of her New York friends or colleagues, but she had Lamont's number from the *BATTLEready!* call sheet. Erinn was surprised that Lamont had agreed to meet her after the George Washington debacle, but he seemed amenable to the idea of getting together. She saw him striding toward her and she squinted. He seemed to have some people with him. As they got closer, Erinn recognized at least two of the men—they were older now, but they were definitely two of the elusive "money people" who backed Broadway shows back in her own heyday. Memories of successful plays and of feeling as if the good times were never going to end flooded her as the men came closer. One of them took her hand and kissed her on the cheek.

"Hello, Erinn. It's been a long time."

CHAPTER 24

Erinn closed her eyes as her plane lightly touched down on the runway at Los Angeles International Airport.

After her lunch with Lamont, she had come back to her mother's to find Virginia had packed Erinn's suitcase and dragged it—and all of her camera gear—to the front door. Virginia had just come from a pottery class, where she had spun out Erinn's sad tale along with a lumpy serving tray. Apparently, "tough love" was the verdict handed down by her fellow artisans, and Virginia was throwing Erinn out.

"Go home, dear. I've gotten you a ticket," her mother said. "Here's your boarding pass and a little gift for the plane."

Ever since Erinn had been a little girl, her mother had always sent her girls off with small presents, prettily wrapped, to open during those endless hours in the middle of a trip. After reading everything in the in-flight magazine, Erinn dug into her carry-on and examined the gift bag from her mother. The gift bag was entombed in an airline-regulation plastic bag for liquids, and Erinn anticipated a bottle of French perfume—her mother's one weakness. She debated as to whether she should open it or not. After all, Virginia had tossed her out like an old boot! But Erinn knew she meant well. *Always the mother*, Erinn thought, carefully separating delicate ecru tissue paper. She pulled out a tiny green suede pouch. She could feel the tiny stopper through the bag. Her pulse quickened. Her mother's love of perfume had passed on to the next generation. Erinn tried to guess what it might be. Chanel No. 5? No, wrong shape. Shalimar? Ditto. Erinn gave up and opened the drawstrings. She lifted out the slim vial.

It was a bottle of eardrops.

Always *the mother.*

Erinn looked out the window of the taxi as it crawled through the congested traffic on Lincoln Boulevard, inching its way toward Santa Monica. Erinn tried to think positively, and was happy to see that her winter flowerbeds looked great—as a matter of fact, her garden could compete with the professionally tended landscaping across the street in the park. She had Massimo to thank for that, she supposed. Thank God for Massimo!

The taxi driver had no interest in helping her to the door with her gear, so Erinn pulled, pushed, and lugged until all the suitcases and equipment cases were in the front hallway. Erinn listened. The house was completely still. Perhaps Massimo had moved back to the guest-house after all.

Caro meowed a sullen hello from the top of the stairs and padded down to greet her. Erinn was surprised how much she had missed her pet. She picked Caro up and stroked the soft fur. She realized she was a sorry sight: a middle-aged woman, teary-eyed, stroking a huge cat, whose paws spilled lankily over Erinn's arms.

Still sniffling and cradling the enormous cat, Erinn went into the living room. On one hand, she felt as if she'd never been away, but on the other hand, she felt she'd left this room one person and returned another.

She had some emotional shoring up to do, that was for sure.

Erinn sat down at the computer and stared at the dark screen. She wasn't quite sure she was ready to dive back into e-mails—and she certainly didn't know what she wanted to do about her stolen light-house idea. She turned the computer on and absentmindedly opened Word. She listlessly looked at the most recently opened documents. *Let It Shine* had been opened while she was away.

Surprised, she dropped the cat unceremoniously to the floor and dug out her half-moon specs. Caro landed flat-pawed with a thud and stared at her accusingly. Erinn looked again at the list of newly opened documents. She was staring speechlessly at the screen when she heard footsteps in the hallway. Guiltily, she reached for the mouse, to shut down the page, but stopped herself.

This is my *computer!* she thought as Massimo breezed into the room.

"*Che sorpresa!* I saw your bags in the hall," he said, kissing her on both cheeks. "I was not expecting you."

Erinn tried to detect any hint of apprehension in Massimo's demeanor, but couldn't see any.

"I have been sleeping with Caro in your room," Massimo announced.

Erinn waited.

"I will move to another room?" he asked.

"Well, I think you should move back to the guesthouse . . . now that I'm home."

"But, *cara mia*, I thought in Philadelphia, you said we would rent the guesthouse to someone new."

"No, Massimo, in Philadelphia, *you* said we would rent the guesthouse to someone new."

Erinn was annoyed, but realized she had set herself up for this one. She could smell something fantastic coming from the kitchen and told Massimo that she would get settled and they would talk over dinner. Massimo seemed to relax. He headed quickly toward the kitchen, Caro following at his heels.

Traitor, Erinn thought—about the cat.

She went up to her room and unpacked. Erinn had planned to dump all her clothes in the hamper, but her mother had washed everything before packing them. Erinn sat on the bed. She realized that she had been looking forward to doing the laundry. It would be something to do, something to think about.

Dude, you are so lame, she thought as she caught a glimpse of herself in the oval mirror that attached to her antique dresser.

After emptying the suitcases, she headed downstairs. Massimo was setting the table in the dining room. He had spread a black-and-silver embroidered shawl over the table and used her hand-painted Italian china. He had obviously made himself at home, she observed. This stuff wasn't just lying around the house. He had to know where she kept everything.

What was that Carlos called me? Ms. Tight Sphincter? I need to relax.

Erinn smiled and took a seat while Massimo poured wine. She didn't recognize it as one of her own, so he must have bought it.

Or poached it from the restaurant . . . when he still worked there.

Massimo served them Portobello mushrooms with rice and tomato sauce. Erinn took a bite and was transported back to Italy. Maybe she was being too hard on Massimo. He took liberties, to be sure, but perhaps it was just cultural. The Italians were just more casual about this sort of thing, she told herself. Besides which, he cooked like an angel. She looked at him and they stared at each other in the flickering candlelight. His liquid-mercury eyes sent a shiver down her spine.

And he looks like an angel, too. Maybe I shouldn't send him to the guesthouse . . . or even out of my room.

Caro sat at Massimo's feet. Erinn was a little jealous of Caro's affection for Massimo, but at least she was sure Caro would approve of her new roommate.

Massimo continued to pour wine, offer second helpings, and set out small glasses for port (which *was* hers, Erinn noted) so seamlessly that she hadn't realized two hours had passed. Massimo started to clear the dishes, but Erinn insisted on helping.

Massimo demurred, but when Erinn said, "Massimo, it's my house. Let me help," a little too forcefully, he gave a small bow and followed her into the kitchen.

The Italian china had to be hand-washed and dried. Massimo rolled up his sleeves as he opened the taps. He handed Erinn a dishtowel and they set to work.

When Erinn had finished drying the large serving platter, she headed to the china cabinet, when Massimo stopped her.

"Cara mia," he said. "The china now lives in the cabinet beside the stove."

Erinn froze midstep.

"You . . . you rearranged my kitchen?"

"*Sì* . . . but you do not have to thank me. It was nothing."

"Oh, it was something," Erinn said, trying to keep her anger at bay.

Massimo had turned on the Vibiemme Domobar espresso machine, and the smell of dark, strong coffee filled the kitchen. Erinn punched down her hard feelings.

She would be insane to give this up because of a few—eccentricities.

Erinn and Massimo took their espressi into the living room. Massimo lit a fire, and Erinn mused that one never really needed a fire in Santa Monica . . . not like in Valley Forge, where they . . . She stopped herself and focused on the crackling logs. Massimo sat on the same couch as Erinn, but at a respectful distance, she was relieved to see. The cat, not usually a diplomat, curled up between them. They sipped in silence. When Erinn could stand it no longer, she asked, "Massimo, was my sister here while I was away?"

"*Sì* . . . I don't think Suzanna trusted me with Caro."

"Did she ever . . . go to my computer?"

"No."

"Was anyone else in the house?"

"*Sì*. A very loud woman. With the soul of a man. "

"Mimi?"

"*Sì!* Mimi. She disgraces the name. Puccini would roll in his grave if he would hear such screeching."

It often took a moment for Erinn to unscramble Massimo's conversation, but she understood that he felt that her agent, with her aggressive ways, did not live up to the tragic, waif-like heroine named Mimi in Giacomo Puccini's operatic masterpiece *La Bohème.*

"And what did she want?"

Massimo shrugged.

"She said she was your agent. I know in Hollywood agents rule the world, so I let her in. She went to the computer."

Erinn's stomach lurched. But why would Mimi steal her show? Did she want to sell it with a different writer attached? She thought back to Cary's remark that the show had been pitched by "someone we know and love," and she flipped between feeling betrayed by her agent and relieved that it wasn't Jude.

Or *was* it Jude? He'd made no attempt to contact her since leaving the note.

And the note! That implied guilt, didn't it? She realized she had been silent a long time.

"I'm sorry, Massimo," she said. "I was thinking."

Massimo moved closer. He played with a tendril that was curling on Erinn's neck.

"About me, I think?"

"No," Erinn said, moving a few inches away from him. "I think my agent might have . . ." She couldn't bring herself to say it.

"I am . . . what do you Americans say? . . . I am here for you. Talk to me."

Erinn took a deep breath.

"I'm afraid my agent may have stolen a show idea from me. It's about a lighthouse . . . and . . ."

"No!"

"I know it is hard to believe, but . . ."

"No!" Massimo said again. "Your agent did not take your idea."

Erinn started at Massimo. So it was Jude? But how would Massimo know?

"How do you know?"

"Cara mia," Massimo said. "Is not with your idea. I am with your idea."

Clearly, Massimo did not understand what Erinn was trying to say. She tried to think what the Italian words were for "back-stabbing agent" or even "lighthouse," but she was very tired and the words did not come.

"I don't think you . . ."

"Sì . . . sì . . . sì," Massimo said eagerly. "I wants to read your work, and I am lonely and bored in the house. I reads about the lighthouse, and I say to myself, 'Massimo, that is a good idea.' Before I got to Philadelphia, I meets Cary and I tell her about this great idea."

"Did you tell her it was *my* idea?"

"No, *cara mia*. Why make it . . . *complicato*?"

"You just can't . . . be . . . with someone else's idea," Erinn said, "when there is money involved."

My God, I sound like Mimi.

"Oh, no, Erinn, there is no money. I gives to them the idea."

OK, I am not like Mimi. Mimi would curl up and die at this point. I must remain cool.

She tried to think of a simple way to explain that this was just not done. This was America! This was commerce! Hearing Mimi's voice niggling in her ear, she thought, *This is a negotiation. I must remain breezy.*

Nothing came to mind.

"I have done a wrong thing?" Massimo asked.

"Well . . . uh . . . yes . . . being with someone else's idea and then selling it . . . for no money . . . to someone else is not a good idea," Erinn said, trying to keep her voice steady. Massimo's grasp of the English language seemed to come and go rather conveniently, she thought, but then reprimanded herself. Of course his English would slip during heated conversations. Her Italian was nonexistent at this point!

"But I will get another job with this new show now! Cary will make me a . . . *come si dice* . . . a person who plays . . ."

"A contestant . . ."

"*Sì.* And I can now pay rent. You can now be a producer. It is a good thing!"

"But can't you understand? It was my idea. . . . There is money involved."

"Money is like a pie. You eat it up a piece at a time and then . . . there is no more money. So, money, she is not important."

Could Massimo be so innocent? Erinn wondered. He really did not seem to understand that he had done anything wrong. And it did mean that he would be able to pay rent and that she would be a producer.

And it did mean that Mimi hadn't stolen her idea. Although why Mimi had been in her place at all remained a mystery.

And most of all, it meant that Jude was innocent. He hadn't called, but then she had not contacted him, either. *Well,* she thought, *I will rectify that!*

"You'll have to move back to the guesthouse," Erinn said.

She wasn't sure how she was going to sort through everything, but there had to be a cap on *breezy.*

CHAPTER 25

Erinn hadn't worried about contacting her sister. She knew their mother would be on the case and Suzanna would wait until she got an "all clear."

It was barely nine in the morning when Mimi barged into the house. Nine in the morning for Mimi was practically the middle of the night for anyone else. Erinn was returning the Italian plates to their rightful place in the china cabinet when Mimi plopped down at the kitchen table.

"I'm not speaking to you," Mimi said.

"You'd be amazed how remarkably at peace I am with that," Erinn said as she continued moving the china.

"Seriously, Erinn, you're pretty low on the professional food chain to pull a diva act," Mimi said.

"What diva act?"

"Disappearing like that," Mimi said. "This is not New York in the eighties."

"You know something, Meems? Your 'not speaking to me' needs work."

"I had to do some really fast damage control."

Alarms went off in Erinn's brain. This was not good—she just knew it. She looked out the kitchen window and could see the guest-house. The door was open, which meant Massimo was around. She stopped putting the dishes away, clipped a leash on Caro, and took Mimi's arm.

"Let's get some air," she said.

Mimi let herself be led out the door, but cautioned, "Fine, but these are new shoes and they are already killing my pinkie toes."

"We'll just go over to the park," Erinn said.

They settled themselves on a bench looking out at the Pacific. While the cat still wouldn't actually walk on the leash, it was a way to take him to the park and insure that he wouldn't get away. *Sometimes with cats,* Erinn thought, *you take what you can get.* She plopped Caro onto her lap, stroked his fur, and felt herself relaxing. She loved looking out at the waves. They were, indeed, pacific.

Erinn, my dear, you really can be pretentious.

Mimi sat with her arms folded across her surgically enhanced breasts, making an uncomfortable-looking shelf on her chest. Except for the excess boobage, Mimi looked remarkably like an angry child. Erinn wondered how Mimi ever got anyone to take her seriously as a hard-bitten agent. She was obviously such a kid at heart.

"So . . ." Erinn prompted. "Damage control."

Mimi's years as a paranoid industry insider kicked in, and she swiveled her head around to make sure no one was listening to them.

"Well," Mimi said in a husky whisper, "when you took off like that, everyone was frantic. I mean, Carlos and Gilroi didn't even get to say good-bye. And Cary was apoplectic. She wanted to talk to you about her new show. She thought you'd be a great addition."

Erinn had been so upset, that she didn't even think about how her retreat to New York might have looked. Perhaps she needed to be grateful to her agent. She had obviously gone the extra mile. But then she remembered . . . no one had tried to contact her. How upset could anyone have been? She posed the questions to Mimi, who looked at Erinn as if she'd gone simple.

"That was the damage control part. As soon as I heard, I came over to your house and got your e-mail contact list. I told everyone you'd gotten a last-minute assignment in Lapland."

"Lapland?"

"Yeah . . . it's way the hell north and freezing and—"

"I know where Lapland is."

"Of course you do. I forgot that you know everything. Anyway, it sounded like they probably didn't have e-mail or cell phone reception in at least parts of Lapland, so that's where you went. I sent a 'I'll contact you when I get back from my trip' mass e-mail . . . so if somebody e-mailed you, they wouldn't worry."

"Very enterprising," Erinn said.

"I knew you were not going to look at e-mail or answer your phone while taking one of your trips on the bipolar express."

"Am I that predictable?"

"I knew you'd ask me that. Anyway, just for insurance, I came by a couple times and did some troubleshooting. I made a file with all the correspondence in it. You're in the clear, and you can get back to people when you feel like it. I suggest you start with Cary, who seems to have a job for you."

"But what about *Celebrity*?"

"I hear they're in financial trouble," Mimi said.

"That's not what I meant and you know it. There was an article about me."

"Yeah, I got a copy of that at the agency. Well, I think it was just a big fat coincidence—somebody must have seen you on the street or something and thought it was worth reporting. Weirder things have happened."

"I suppose that's true."

"The good news is, it proves people are still thinking about you, and we can use that to get you more money next negotiation. The bad news is, that article almost blew your Lapland cover. Luckily, most TV people don't read *Celebrity*."

I do, thought Erinn. *And I'm . . . or I was . . . a TV person.*

Erinn looked out over the water. She knew Mimi was telling her the truth. It certainly explained why she hadn't heard from anyone. And it appeared she was going to have to straighten out some very important details with Cary. However, she was sure that could all be worked out—especially with her pit bull of an agent in the mix.

Now the only mystery left was Jude. Erinn was itching to get back and see if she had any e-mails from him. She did wonder why Jude hadn't set Cary straight about the lighthouse idea. As if she were reading her mind, Mimi said, "Jude was completely freaking out. He didn't believe for one minute that you went to Lapland."

"Why wouldn't he?" Erinn asked indignantly, but calmed down when she remembered she hadn't been, after all, in Lapland.

"Well . . . I guess he would have heard of any productions going on in Lapland . . . he's pretty clued in. But that isn't the point. The point is, he's called me a hundred times asking about you."

More alarms went off in Erinn's mind.

"Why would Jude be calling you?" she asked.

Mimi started twisting her hair around her finger. The gonging in Erinn's head was almost deafening.

"I *am* your agent, aren't I? Who else would he call?"

Erinn's writer's instinct kicked in. The agent-client bond might account for one phone call, but not hundreds. Erinn granted that Mimi was pretty theatrical in her own right and tended to exaggerate, but even so, it probably meant Jude had called at least three times. Erinn stared hard at Mimi, who was still twisting her hair, so Erinn knew she was right—Mimi was lying.

"Want to try again?" Erinn asked.

"Hey," Mimi said. "You're the one who disappeared into thin air! Why am I suddenly the one being cross-examined?"

She wondered how Mimi could possibly be successful at negotiating. The woman was so transparent. Erinn regarded her agent, who looked as if Erinn were about to pounce on her carefully constructed sand castle. For a moment, Erinn took pity on her, but then snapped back to reality. She pounced.

"I will give you to three to start talking," Erinn said.

"Oh, please! You sound like my mother."

"One . . . two . . ."

"OK, OK, I give."

Mimi stopped fiddling with her hair. Erinn shielded her eyes as the sun continued to climb.

"You are not going to like this, so brace yourself," Mimi said.

"Consider me braced."

"Jude's a client."

Caro sprang from Erinn's lap as she leaped to her feet. Mimi grabbed the leash as Caro started to formulate that he might be able to make a run for it.

"What?" Erinn said.

"I *said* you should brace yourself!"

"I was braced. This goes beyond bracing! When did that happen?"

"Well . . . he's been a client for a really long time."

Erinn sat back down. She stared at the sun-baked wood of the bench, which was beginning to show signs of wear. The wood had split in several places, and Erinn could see the pathway through the cracks.

"How long?"

"Long . . ."

"Mimi!"

"OK . . . OK . . ."

Erinn could hear the resignation in Mimi's voice. The whole story would now come out. She waited, adjusting her posterior over the fissures in the bench. She was resolved not to let any cracks show.

"I'm waiting," Erinn said.

"Jude has been a client for a couple years. He works fairly regularly, but he has some long periods of downtime—like everybody in town. Especially these days. He told us that he wasn't sure if he was going to stay in Los Angeles or not."

Erinn felt her pulse race. Jude might leave Los Angeles? *Stop acting like an adolescent,* she chided herself. Now that she knew Jude had not betrayed her with *Let It Shine*, she was hoping to speak with him. Then it struck her—that's what his note was about. Cary had told him about *Let It Shine,* and Jude wanted to warn Erinn that somehow her idea had been stolen! She chided herself. *Let's be honest,* she said to herself. *You're hoping to reconcile with him.* Although she wondered—to what end? Mimi did say that Jude had called a hundred times, though. Maybe Mimi wasn't exaggerating . . . and if she wasn't, well, a hundred times is a lot of phone calls. Erinn decided to think positively.

"So you got him a job on *BATTLEready*!" Erinn said, ready to forgive all. "You're his agent. You got him a job. That's what agents do."

"Well, actually," Mimi said, "it isn't that simple."

Erinn's eyebrows shot up. She knew she had to stay calm if she wanted to hear the unvarnished truth, so she tried to keep her face as impassive as possible.

"I'm listening," Erinn said.

"I don't know what I was thinking," Mimi said, putting her face in her hands.

"More important, *I* don't know what you were thinking, so why don't you tell me?"

"Jude was threatening to leave town. He was going to try his luck in . . . oh, Austin . . . or some godforsaken place that nobody has ever heard of. He had just gotten a notice that his rent was going to skyrocket and I . . . I . . ."

"*You* sent Jude to rent the guesthouse?"

"Well, you needed a tenant. I thought I'd kill two birds with one stone," Mimi said without looking at Erinn.

"Wait, wait," Erinn said, squeezing her head. "Suzanna said it was her idea to rent out the guesthouse."

"Well . . . we sort of came up with the idea together."

"When? How? Why?"

"Suzanna and I have gotten really close. I have a lot of meetings at the Bun, and we . . . you know . . . have sort of bonded on what a train wreck you are."

"I'm so happy for the two of you."

"So we came up with our plan to help you along. We figured that she should pitch the idea to you, since you have trouble with me being an authority figure and all."

"What about the ad in craigslist?"

"There was no ad."

"Mimi, that's insanity. What if I had checked?"

"You? Check craigslist? Ha!"

Erinn was thunderstruck. *Beyond thunderstruck*, she thought, but could not think of a word that conveyed such emotion.

"This makes no sense. What about the other people who came to look at the guesthouse?"

"They were just clients I knew were looking for a place, too. I'd made such a big deal about you needing a tenant, that once I sent Jude over, I figured I had to keep going, or you'd get suspicious," Mimi said. "Plus, your mother was really into the idea of getting you some extra income without hurting your pride."

"My *mother* knows about this?"

"Yes. And you want to hear something funny?"

"More than you can imagine."

"She said that Suzanna would never be able to keep this a secret. And here I am, blabbing and spilling my guts. So funny."

"Proditio!" Erinn said, walking to the edge of the cliff. She turned on her agent. "That means 'betrayal' in Latin."

"Would you mind following along in English? This is hard enough without you playing the martyr."

"Oh, so now *I'm* the one at fault."

"I'm not saying that. I'm only saying that if you weren't completely pigheaded about everything this situation would never have played out the way it did," Mimi said. "It was an intervention, only you weren't there."

"This is still a story without an ending," Erinn said, quoting Rick in *Casablanca*.

Erinn thought of Gilroi, who would catch the reference. She felt a pang of wistfulness and missed the shared camaraderie, but she forced herself to concentrate on Mimi.

"There isn't much else to tell," Mimi said.

"How did Jude and I end up together on *BATTLEready!*?"

"How the hell should I know?" Mimi said. "Cary hired him. You think I can just pick up the phone and get somebody a job? What do you think I am, a miracle worker?"

"No . . . I think you're an agent."

"Oh! Yeah," Mimi said, and giggled.

Erinn couldn't resist asking, "What is Jude doing now? Is he going to Austin now that *BATTLEready!* is over, or does APE have"—she tried not to think about it as "her show"—"something else for him?"

"He's not at APE."

"What?"

"He got a job at another company. Doing a show on cougars. You know—older women, younger men."

Erinn, you're an idiot, she thought. *You ran out and ignored him. How long did you expect him to care?*

Maybe she should just let Jude recede into the past. Perhaps that was best for everyone.

Another thought struck Erinn.

"And Massimo? Did you send him to the farmers' market? Was that a set-up, too?"

Mimi snorted. "No, sweetie. You found that gem on your own."

"What could you possibly have against Massimo?"

"I'm up to speed—Suzanna has told me all about him."

Oh, yes, my unbiased sister.

Erinn and Mimi were both silent as they watched Caro chase a leaf around the bench. Erinn looked back at her house and toyed with the idea of retreating—of not pushing the conversation any further.

But as hard as she tried, the past few weeks on *BATTLEready!* had changed her, reawakened her to the world. She didn't really want to return to her old ways, shuttered against life, but she knew there were some things she was going to have to face in order to move on.

Unfortunately, Mimi knew about those things, too.

"Put the damn cat back in the house and I'll treat you to lunch," Mimi said.

"That's OK," Erinn said. "I think I'm having lunch with my sister."

"Oh, really?" Mimi said. "I was just over there, and she didn't mention it."

"She doesn't know."

CHAPTER 26

Erinn and Suzanna looked over their menus at the Veranda, the beautifully appointed bar in the Casa del Mar Hotel by the sea. Erinn couldn't remember the last time she'd been in the hotel. Even though it was in her neighborhood, the prices had been out of her range for years. Erinn looked contentedly out the window at the Santa Monica Pier, which could be seen from the big picture window in the bar.

Sharing glasses of white wine, the sisters left each other to her own thoughts. Erinn looked around the room. The Casa del Mar Hotel was built in 1926 during Prohibition and catered to the glamorous Hollywood community. The hotel was rumored to have had a special relationship with the police, who would tip off customers to stash their booze before a raid. The hotel hung on to its glory through the thirties and early forties, but when it was commandeered by the U.S. Navy as a rec center for enlisted men, the property went into a nose-dive. By the late nineties, the hotel's history included a stint as a rehab center, and it had garnered a respectable if still down-at-the-heels reputation as a Pritikin Longevity Center. Erinn had always loved the building and was thrilled, at the turn of the twenty-first century, to find the hotel fully restored to its 1920s grandeur. It was just a shame that her money started to run out just as the hotel was reopening its doors.

Erinn tried not to think about those days. She thought about how she had slowly lost touch with the world—and created a sad, solitary life. She saw with complete clarity how she had almost repeated the same mistakes all over again. But Jude had not betrayed her, and while Massimo might have sold her series out from under her, it was an innocent mistake.

She had wasted enough time sulking in New York and was looking forward from now on.

Erinn realized it had been a while since they had spoken. Her sister seemed to be staring absentmindedly at the menu. Erinn broke the silence.

"What are you thinking about?" she asked.

"Thank God for Eric," Suzanna said, snapping her menu shut. "Since he got his business degree, he tells me meals like this one are deductible."

Erinn ordered a shrimp-and-crab Louie and Suzanna ordered a yellowtail roll.

The food was delicious, and the sisters enjoyed small talk throughout their meal. The Wolf women had a tradition that any intense conversations were to be had over coffee. Suzanna and Erinn could both hear their mother's admonishment that meals were not to be ruined by "high-running passion at the table."

Coffee—for Erinn; Suzanna was on a strict decaf green tea regimen during the pregnancy—finally arrived. Erinn realized that Suzanna knew nothing about Massimo's part in the still unresolved *Let It Shine* debacle, or her nerves would have gotten the better of her by now. There was no sign of her biting her lower lip. While Erinn studied her sister, she had to admit that she felt like she was leading a lamb to the slaughter. She was ready to attack.

Suzanna met her sister's gaze.

"So, Mimi told me you know all about our 'renting the guesthouse' thing."

Erinn's jaw dropped open.

"I can't believe Mimi told you! Is there no loyalty anywhere?"

"Eric said we'd never get away with it."

"You don't seem very contrite!"

"Well"—Suzanna rubbed her rounded belly—"I'm not. I thought it was for the best. And frankly, I think Mimi and I would have done a lot better than that Massimo."

She's trying to turn the tables.

In the past, Erinn would have just shut her sister off. But if Erinn were going to face the world with a new, more positive attitude, she felt it best to practice with someone who loved her.

"OK," Erinn said. "Let's talk about Massimo. I want to know why you dislike him so."

"It's not that I dislike him," Suzanna said. "Well, it is. But I have reasons."

"Which are?"

"In alphabetical order?"

Erinn raised her eyebrows over her coffee.

"OK," Suzanna continued, putting her coffee cup down. "I'm just going to lay my cards on the table. No more beating around the bush or sweeping things under the rug."

"Suzanna, please, I'm in cliché hell. Get to the point."

"He's a user."

"He is not!"

"Erinn, you let him move all his stuff into your guesthouse. Then he moves into your house. He takes advantage."

And you don't even know that he quit his job and gave my show idea to the production company, Erinn thought.

If she was going to defend Massimo, she decided, best not to bring any of that up.

"That's not fair. You decided you disliked him before you even met him," Erinn said.

"You're blind to his—many—faults," Suzanna said. "You don't see the truth because he's . . ."

"Because he's what?"

". . . Italian."

Erinn felt the coffee stick in her throat. She was afraid that this was what was prejudicing her sister. She refused to meet Suzanna's eye.

"You can't condemn a whole country, just because of . . ." Erinn said.

"Because of . . . ?" Suzanna asked.

Erinn knew her sister was calling her bluff. She had not mentioned his name in almost twenty years. But this was a new day.

"Because of Augustino," Erinn said.

There. I've said it. I've said his name. And I'm still breathing.

"Wow," said Suzanna, taking her sister's wrist gently. "I'm impressed. Well, if Massimo has brought you along like this, maybe I'm being too hard on him."

Erinn wondered. Had Massimo brought her along? Had Jude? Or could she give herself some of the credit? But Massimo was the subject at the table, so she continued.

"I don't think you can compare Massimo and Augustino."

"I'm not comparing them," Suzanna said. "And I'm not *blaming* Massimo for being Italian. I'm just afraid you've fallen for him *because* he's Italian."

"Surely you give me more credit than that. I mean, I've met other Italians in the last twenty years."

Suzanna sipped her tea. Erinn waited.

"Augustino was the love of your life," Suzanna said. "You were never the same afterwards."

"Afterward," Erinn corrected, absently. "And that's what's supposed to happen when the love of your life dies."

"I know," Suzanna said and squeezed Erinn's wrist again. Augustino had been dead all these years and this was the first time she had talked about him to anyone.

Augustino Artigiani had been an actor who ran in Erinn's Broadway crowd. Originally from Bari, Italy, Augustino led the same charmed life as Erinn. He moved to New York and got an agent within twenty-four hours and his first off-Broadway role in 1984. He met Erinn at a party in a cavernous loft in SoHo. She spoke a little Italian, which she had studied in school, and he was captivated.

In the following year, Erinn sold a play and Augustino got plum lead roles. When Erinn sold *The Family of Mann* in 1987, Augustino squired her to all the press conferences, television appearances, award shows, and soirées. They used to call each other "Fanny" and "Nicky"—although Augustino was a better sport than Nicky Arnstein any day.

But the world spun out of control in the late eighties, with the AIDS virus laying waste to everyone in its path. Nobody knew what had hit them. Augustino was one of the first casualties, but certainly not the last of Erinn's friends to die from that horrible, wasting disease. Erinn thought back to 1990, when the local hydrangea plants had picked up a fungus that was killing them all over the city. All the beautiful plants and all the beautiful young men—and women—

seemed to be dying. To this day, Erinn couldn't look at a hydrangea without feeling overwhelming sadness.

When Augustino was diagnosed, there were many questions and few answers. So many people in those days pointed fingers at AIDS victims—trying to keep the disaster from their own door—by calling it the "gay disease." But Augustino, who had the bad luck to have contracted the disease through a blood transfusion, refused to qualify his sexual orientation. He was no better or worse than any other unlucky person, among them so many of their mutual friends, who had been stricken. In Erinn's eyes, he died a hero.

As the months took their brutal toll, Erinn found out answers didn't really matter anyway. All that mattered was Augustino was dead.

Right after Augustino died, Erinn remembered sitting in front of a brand-new contraption called a "home computer" and just staring at the screen wondering, "Who is next?" She was diligent about getting tested for years afterward, always braced to be "next," and sometimes disappointed when she was given yet another clean bill of health. She found it ironic that HIV continued to be considered a gay disease, as all the women she knew diligently went for their screenings every six months.

Erinn's thoughts returned to the present as she watched a waiter pour more coffee and offer more hot water for Suzanna's tea. Erinn looked up as Suzanna handed her a tissue. Erinn rubbed at her eyes. She hadn't realized she'd been crying.

"So many people died," Erinn said.

"And you died with them."

"What was I supposed to do, carry on with my little Noel Coward existence by myself?"

"Erinn, it's time to move on. Get on with your life."

"I can't win with you," Erinn said. "You tell me I'm stuck in the past, but now I've let Massimo into my life and you think I'm pathetic."

"Not path—well, yes, I do think you're pathetic. But I'm willing to keep an open mind if you are."

"What does that mean?"

"I'll entertain the possibility that Massimo is a great guy who just happens to be a charming Italian and it's kismet or whatever, if you entertain the possibility that he's a con artist who's playing you like a violin."

"Ah! A musical con man. The worst kind."

Both sisters laughed, relieved to end the tension.

"I'm keeping an open mind about Massimo, I assure you," Erinn said, and was surprised to find that she meant it.

Erinn took a sip of water while Suzanna signaled the waiter and ordered a shot of Baileys Irish Cream to add to Erinn's coffee. Both sisters were inordinately fond of the spiked coffee, but Suzanna hadn't had one since she found out she was pregnant.

"Bottoms up," Suzanna said. "You're drinking for two. OK, now on to the big question," she said, her cheeks pink, even though Erinn was the one drinking alcohol. "You boinking Massimo?"

Erinn cringed. The sisters had never shared those kinds of intimacies. And clearly, Suzanna wasn't exactly comfortable with this conversation, reverting to her childhood word for sex.

"*Boinking*? Suzanna, please. We're grown women."

"OK . . . are you *fucking* Massimo?"

OK, that's worse.

"No," Erinn said quickly. "I have not been *boinking* Massimo. What do you think I am, a sex maniac? Do you really think I'd sleep with Jude and Massimo at the same time? What would Mother say?"

Suzanna sputtered, then coughed harshly.

"I think Mother would say you're a total slut!" Suzanna said, strangling on her words. "What are you talking about? Are you saying you had sex with Jude?"

Erinn's eyes widened. She assumed that Jude had told Mimi about their night of passion—and that Mimi had told Suzanna. She'd visualized the scenes very clearly in her head, and it never occurred to her that it hadn't happened.

"I thought you knew."

"Well, I didn't."

"You know now, so let's drop it."

"Fat chance! I introduced you . . . sort of . . . and I get to know. I can't believe he would have sex with you!"

"Why not?"

"You're so . . . mature."

"Why don't you come right out and say it? I'm old and he's young. You think it's unseemly."

"Are you kidding? I think it's *totally* seemly. We're just a couple of late bloomers, that's all."

Erinn looked at her sister, who seemed embarrassed but sincere.

"Maybe Mimi can get you a job on Jude's new show about cougars. No wonder he jumped at the chance to direct that show! Life imitating art."

"You are being extremely immature."

"Who seduced who?"

"Whom."

It was as if the floodgates had opened. Erinn filled her sister in on all the Jude details at Valley Forge. Suzanna seemed a bit more understanding, Erinn thinking she was near death and all that.

"Wow," said Suzanna. "That must have been intense."

"You have no idea."

"Was it weird afterwards? I mean . . . awkward?"

"In the extreme. And I haven't been able to forget about it—or him—no matter how much I pretend otherwise. Even after Valley Forge, as I watched him work, I realized he was a very special, talented person. And now I've thrown it all away, thinking he sold me out. I should have known he would never do that. Just as I should have known he would never tell Mimi about our . . . indiscretion."

"Oh my God!" Suzanna said. "You're in love with him."

"You always distort things," Erinn said. "I'm just saying I came to appreciate him on many levels."

Suzanna suddenly sat up straight.

"Sorry. The baby just kicked. This is too much excitement, I guess."

Leaning confidentially forward, Erinn said, "I've written him a thousand e-mails, but never sent them."

"You wrote him love letters?"

"They're e-mails!"

"I'll bet you have one on your cell phone somewhere, don't you?"

"What if I do?"

"Oh, Erinn. I bet they're amazing," Suzanna said. "I want to hear one!"

"Suzanna! It's personal!"

"Love letters . . . love e-mails . . . usually are. Now read me one," Suzanna said, signaling for another round of Baileys coffee for Erinn. "Please?"

Erinn scrolled through her cell phone. She, being fascinated by technology, had mastered all the extra functions in her phone, including the "notebook," where she could write notes to herself. The boys had almost convinced her that she needed an iPhone, but she hadn't quite been able to convince herself that she wanted or needed to spend that much time with an instrument that would keep her in constant communication with the human race. At this precise moment, she was also grateful that her phone didn't send and receive e-mails, or she might have sent something she'd have regretted.

She found what she was looking for and cleared her throat.

"OK, this is the latest one. I wanted him to know how sorry I was for doubting him."

She began to read.

"Dear Jude, Years ago, there was a song that reflects my feelings now. 'I came to realize, I lost a prize, the day I said good-bye to you.' These words are significant, because you are a prize. You're everything I hope to be but am not—brave, resilient, generous, and warm. . . ."

She looked at Suzanna. "That's as far as I've gotten."

"That was . . . that was beautiful."

"Of course it was beautiful. I'm a writer, for God's sake."

"Well, you've got to send it. Jude needs to know you feel this way."

"There is no point. I'm sure he has moved on. I'd just look like a sorry old woman."

"Well, you are a sorry old woman. Sending that e-mail might change things."

Erinn wasn't sure sisterly bonding was all it was cracked up to be. There was something to be said for Suzanna's hero worship of the old days.

"Suzanna, you need to be realistic. Jude is a fine . . . but unrefined . . . young man. He is not educated, sophisticated, or complex. We could never make a go of it."

"There you go with that superiority complex that is just so unappealing. I swear, Erinn, no wonder you're lonely."

"If loneliness is the price of superiority, then so be it."

"Oh, don't give me that 'loneliness is my destiny' bull. Take a chance. Get back in touch with the living. Go home and send that e-mail!"

"I'll think about it."

Suzanna and Erinn, swimming in coffee and tea, left the Veranda after a two-hour lunch. Suzanna signaled for the valet, and Erinn announced that she would walk home. Suzanna looked alternately hurt and worried, but Erinn assured her that she had had a lovely time, but she wanted to clear her head. She only lived about a mile from the hotel and the walk would do her good. Erinn hugged her sister goodbye.

"I know you're going to tell Mother about Jude," Erinn said. "But take it easy on me."

"I'll make the whole thing seem absolutely fabulous," Suzanna said. "Or as fabulous as I can make boinking on a bunch of scratchy hay sound."

Erinn started home, thinking about Jude. And Augustino.

And Massimo.

Could Suzanna be right? Could Erinn be blinded by Massimo's charm? *No,* she said to herself, *she is wrong. I'm smarter than that.*

Erinn walked through her front gate and headed up to the house. She stopped a few steps from the front porch and turned on the path that led to the backyard. Now that she was on a mission to confront her demons, she might as well talk to Massimo about her sister's misgivings. She wasn't sure what she was going to say, but Erinn was confident she could handle anything that came up. She was, after all, a writer.

Massimo's door was still open. She stopped in her tracks as she got close to the guesthouse. She could hear Massimo speaking on the phone. He was speaking in Italian, and he was speaking quickly, so she couldn't understand everything he was saying. But one thing was clear.

He was speaking to his wife.

Erinn spun around and walked quickly to her house. Caro was sitting on the back stoop, looking at her and swishing his tail. They stared at each other. Erinn sighed and went back to the guesthouse, making as much noise as she could, so Massimo would not think she was sneaking up on him.

He hung up the phone as she knocked on the opened door.

"Cara mia," he said.

"Caro mio," she said. "You have three hours to get out of here."

"I do not understand," Massimo said, his root-beer eyes taking on their most sorrowful expression.

"I think you do understand. You are to leave my house, and you are not going to be *a people* on *my* show. Start packing. *Capice*?"

Erinn walked back to the main house and scooped up the cat.

Maybe I'm not as smart as I think I am after all.

Erinn watched from the picture window as the cab carrying Massimo and his belongings drove out of sight. In the hours it took him to leave, Erinn found the folder Mimi had made on her desktop—*How could I have missed it?* she asked herself—and answered e-mails from Carlos, Gilroi, Fetus, and Rita, all of whom wanted to stay in touch. There was an e-mail from Lamont in New York, saying he hoped she'd be coming east sooner rather than later, and several e-mails from Cary, insisting that Erinn get hold of her as soon as she returned from Lapland.

"APE is not going to let you get away," she said. "Remember that great project on the lighthouse we talked about? We need you to be part of it."

Erinn wasn't sure exactly where APE would stand on *Let It Shine* when the truth came out, but she found she didn't really care. She had more important things to worry about.

There had been no e-mails from Jude. There was no way Erinn was going to send her . . . love manifesto now.

Well, I guess it's not a story without an ending after all.

Erinn headed down to the Rollicking Bun Tea Shoppe and Book Nook. She looked at her watch. The tea shop would be closed, but the bookstore would still be open, and she hoped to distract herself with a good novel.

Eric was standing on a ladder, adding books to a high shelf as Erinn walked in.

"Hey, Erinn, welcome home," he said, his long legs bringing him back down the ladder. "How were things in Philadelphia?"

"Always sunny," Erinn said, proud of her first current pop culture reference in twenty years. "How are you?"

"Glowing," he said. "I know they always say that expectant mothers glow—but I've got to tell you, I feel it, too."

Erinn smiled. *What a nice thought.*

"You looking for anything in particular?" Eric asked.

"No, I just thought I'd wander."

Eric smiled and gestured toward the meandering stacks of books.

While the tea shop was kept neat and orderly, there was a chaotic, mysterious feel to the bookstore. It sometimes seemed as if a tome might suddenly reach toward you from a darkened corner and beg, "Read me."

Erinn could feel her pulse calm as she strolled through the aisles, gently touching books she had read and loved. She knew that people found her odd—and thought she was lonely. But books had always kept her company and brought her solace. She was happy to be in their company now.

Erinn never read romances. She had no patience with the boy gets girl, boy loses girl, boy gets girl story lines. But she found herself, for the first time, gravitating toward the Romance section.

Get a grip on yourself.

Even though the tea shop was closed, Erinn wandered into it, hoping to see her sister. She knew she had to tell Suzanna that she'd thrown Massimo out—she was sure to find out anyway. One of the beautiful things about Suzanna was that she wasn't smug with the "I told you so's," which made it easier to actually tell her.

Suzanna was watering plants, and Erinn stood still and watched her. Her sister, who Erinn suddenly remembered was now eight and a half months' pregnant, was bathed in the warm, golden radiance of a Southern California afternoon. The soft shafts of sunlight caressed her hair. Erinn leaned against the door frame, wishing she had her camera with her. Suzanna looked up sharply and stared at Erinn. She didn't seem to recognize her.

"I'm sorry, Suzanna! Did I startle you?"

"Erinn!" she said, dropping the watering can and reaching toward her sister.

Erinn instinctively ran toward her. For a fleeting second, she thought the pool of water around Suzanna's feet was from the dropped watering can. But as her sister clutched her belly and howled, Erinn knew her water had broken.

Erinn grabbed Suzanna with all her strength and started walking her toward the back door.

"Eric!" Erinn called. "Get the car! It's showtime."

CHAPTER 27

Erinn circled Los Angeles International Airport, keeping an eye out for her mother. When she had called to let Virginia know that her granddaughter had arrived two weeks early, in good health and with striking lung power, the newly minted grandmother booked the next plane out of New York. Erinn saw her mother standing on the curb in front of the American Airlines terminal, and she cut off a Hertz van in her hurry to retrieve her.

Traffic was bumper to bumper as the women made their way back to Santa Monica. Erinn caught her mother up on all the details.

Suzanna's labor had been astonishingly quick. Luckily, the Rollicking Bun was only a few minutes from the hospital. Because everything had happened so fast, Erinn wasn't able to pick up her video camera, so there would be no permanent record of the blessed event. Erinn was disappointed, but Suzanna said she was perfectly happy not to relive the actual birth.

Suzanna and Eric wanted to name the baby Virginia Erinn Cooper, but Virginia, while wildly excited about the prospect of being a grandmother, had gently put her foot down.

"That's very sweet," she said. "But I have no interest in being called Old Virginia or Big Virginia. I think you should name the baby after Erinn."

Erinn never thought of herself as vain, but she was with her mother on this one—the idea of ever being referred to as "Big Erinn" or "Old Erinn" or even the more benign "Senior Erinn" was just too jarring. Better to nip this in the bud.

"I really am honored, but you know how those double family names can be so . . . confusing," Erinn said.

"Yeah . . . fine . . . forget it," Suzanna said, calling her sister out. "We can forget the whole thing, if you want."

"No!" Erinn said. "I love the idea! But maybe . . . maybe we could call her by her middle name, Elizabeth, or some nickname like Beth."

"Nickname?" Suzanna asked. "Who are you? You've always hated nicknames."

"God forbid I should ever change my mind about anything in this family."

"Liz," Suzanna said slowly. "What about Lizzy? Could you get used to Lizzy?"

Erinn's heart squeezed for a second and then she said, "Yeah. I think I could."

Erinn had to admit, if only to herself, that she'd grown rather fond of that particular nickname. She was happy to bequeath it to her precious niece. It would be her own private memento of all that had transpired over the last few months.

Erinn's guesthouse didn't stay vacant for long. Suzanna and Eric had remained very close with several of their Napa Valley childhood friends, and they all arrived within days of Lizzy's birth. Fernando, the Napa Valley High School buddy who had once been the pastry chef of the Rollicking Bun, left his new B and B in the hands of his business partner and headed down the coast from Washington. He had catered Suzanna and Eric's wedding in Erinn's backyard two years previous and was a big fan of the guesthouse, calling dibs on it within minutes of announcing his arrival.

Suzanna's childhood girlfriend Carla was a very busy architect in Northern California, but she canceled all her appointments and drove down as soon as she heard the news. She wanted to stay in the apartment over the tea shop with Suzanna, Eric, and Lizzy, but Virginia had already laid claim to the guestroom, and there was no overruling Grammy. Carla would be staying in Erinn's guestroom.

All the excitement should have kept Erinn's mind off Jude. He did manage to pop up in her thoughts from time to time, but Erinn was very practiced in the art of pushing things aside. She just immersed herself in all things Lizzy.

The Rollicking Bun was having a little get-together for the loyal friends, family, and patrons who wanted to be part of Baby Lizzy's arrival. Erinn realized that she was probably the one who should have planned a baby shower before the big event, but it honestly hadn't even crossed her mind. Since the baby had arrived early, no one seemed to have noticed the rather glaring sisterly omission.

Suzanna's pediatrician—and all the baby books and other mothers—said that newborns didn't have fully functioning immune systems and crowds were a bad idea. Suzanna was happy to have the party, but was determined to keep Baby Lizzy upstairs. Eric had bought several digital picture frames—the ones that rotate several pictures in one frame—and placed them around the room. Erinn stood in front of one of them and realized that she had taken every single one of the photos.

Maybe I've got the makings of a good aunt after all!

Fernando had shooed everyone out of the kitchen as soon as the party had been announced.

"Out, out, you damned spots," he said, waving everyone away. "Fernando the Fantasmo is ready to cast his magic spell *again*."

Erinn was determined to make up for not videotaping the birth—although all the main players assured her it was hardly her fault. She brought two full boxes of tape with her, although she made sure no one saw that all of it was recycled. In her mind, it wasn't professional to use old stock. In Philadelphia, the crew always shot take after take, reminding each other "Tape is cheap." But Erinn knew that tape was only cheap when somebody else was paying for it.

She had to admit that the time she spent in Philadelphia had sharpened her social skills. While she stayed behind her camera most of the time at the party, when she did have a conversation with someone she hardly knew, it wasn't painful.

All the regulars were there, including Mimi and Cary. Cary caught her eye and smiled. Erinn waved and ducked behind her camera, but she could see Cary threading her way toward her.

"Hi, Erinn!" Cary said. As a veteran television producer, Cary hardly noticed the camera between them. "How was Lapland?"

"Oh . . . well," Erinn stalled. "Does anything ever really change in Lapland?"

Mimi, sipping a girlie pink punch Fernando had whipped up, appeared instantly.

"Now, Cary, Erinn just became an aunt," she said, steering Cary away. "No business today."

Cary turned back to Erinn. "It's been too long," she said. "Stop by the office next week, and we'll chat."

Mimi directed Cary back to the appetizers, giving Erinn a thumbs-up that Erinn caught on tape.

Erinn heaved a great sigh of relief. With the birth of her niece, and the arrival of out-of-town guests, she managed to keep thoughts of her own life, *BATTLEready!,* her career, and Jude out of her mind. It appeared the universe was giving her a signal that it was time to step up to the plate again.

When Erinn got home, the house was bathed in the pinkish hues of sunset, which caught her eye. It had been over a month since she had been home from Philadelphia, and the season's light had changed. Winter—even California's sorry excuse for winter—was ebbing. Although she was pleasantly tired from the party, she knew she couldn't resist the sunset. She grabbed her camera and headed out to the park. The sunset would be perfect in about ten minutes, and shooting would relax her before her houseguests returned from the other end of town.

She headed over to the bluff. Seeing Cary had brought *BATTLE-ready!* back full force, and Erinn's mind was whirling with thoughts of Jude. She looked through the viewfinder, but it was cloudy with tears. She thought of the old saying, "Love begins with a smile, grows with a kiss, and ends with a teardrop."

That's not helpful.

She admonished herself, and she tried to focus on the spectacular colors stretching out over the water. Oranges, pinks, reds were all vying for attention and practically screaming, "Look at me! Look at me!"

Panning slowly, she turned the camera lens from the ocean to the park itself, adjusting the iris as the light changed. Erinn, like most serious professional videographers, had nothing but disdain for auto-focus, auto-iris, or auto-anything else. She concentrated on steadying her movements, while adjusting the various settings as she turned the lens one hundred and eighty degrees from the sunset. She was so absorbed with her camera work that it took her a minute to realize that someone had ridden into frame on a skateboard and ruined her shot.

She looked up, annoyed. It took her a few seconds to realize that the person standing there was Jude, smiling at her.

"Hey, Erinn! I thought that might be you."

Erinn shut off the camera and tried to steady her breathing. *I must remain cool*, she said to herself.

"How is the chick magnet working these days?" she said, nodding at the skateboard.

"Some women are attracted to it," he said, grinning. "Magnet . . . attracted . . . get it?"

As if the magnet joke wasn't reminder enough of the chasm between them, Jude suddenly stomped on the front of the board, which sent the back spinning into the air. Jude caught it expertly and tucked it under his arm. It was a practiced gesture, one he had probably been perfecting since high school. Erinn said a silent prayer of thanks giving that she had not sent her confessional e-mail to Jude.

What could I have been thinking? she said to herself as she looked at the impossibly young man in front of her.

"So . . . what's new?" he asked.

"My sister had a baby," she said.

"Oh, yeah," he said. "I heard something about that."

"They named her Erinn."

"After you?"

"I assume so, yes."

"How about a hug, then?" he said. "To celebrate the arrival of little Lizzy."

Erinn nervously extended one arm. She had the camera in the other arm and Jude was holding his skateboard, so it was awkward and uncomfortable.

"Did you know," Jude said, while embracing Erinn, "that hugging has health benefits? Seriously, studies have shown that hugs reduce blood pressure and increase levels of oxytocin."

Erinn thought Jude sounded as if he had memorized this little tidbit. Why would he learn by heart some obscure piece of scientific trivia? Would this actually work as a pickup line? she wondered.

"I did know that," she said. Jude continued to hold onto her, so she was speaking into his armpit. But she was grateful to have something to talk about beyond the obvious. "But it's still very interesting, isn't it?"

"Yeah. Even though I have no clue what oxytocin is."

"It's a mammalian hormone."

Erinn released herself. Jude stared at her.

"You're kidding me, right? You actually know this?"

"Oh, yes. It's fascinating! Oxytocin's biggest role comes into play during childbirth. I've been reading up on childbirth lately."

"Oh. Well, yeah. I guess you would be."

"Large amounts are released after the cervix and vagina have stretched during labor. Afterward, it helps facilitate breastfeeding by stimulating the nipples."

"Really?" Jude said.

He and Erinn both smiled at each other.

"Tell me less," they said in unison.

"Dude," Jude said, putting his arm around her. "Don't ever tell anybody that. Nobody will ever hug again . . . although that 'stimulating the nipple' action is pretty tight."

Erinn laughed. Jude visibly relaxed.

"I'm glad I ran into you," he said. "I've been really bummed that I couldn't get hold of you."

Erinn held up her hand.

"Let's not even get into that quagmire," she said. "I know you were trying to warn me that someone seemed to have stolen my show idea."

They started to walk along the path that threaded through the park.

"I freaked out when Cary told me about the show, but I really didn't know enough details to be sure you didn't have a partner who had pitched it or something like that. I mean, I thought you didn't . . . you don't seem like the partnering type . . . but you never know. I figured the best I could do was let you know what Cary said and back off."

"Well, thanks. You did your best."

"Did I?" Jude asked. He looked . . . haunted. "I kept wondering if there was anything else I could have done."

"No, Jude, you were great," Erinn said, squeezing his arm reassuringly. "And I'm sure Mimi will be able to straighten everything out. I'm not worried."

"Cool."

"Besides"—Erinn tried to make light of the situation—"money is like a pie. You eat it up a piece at a time and it's all gone. It's inevitable, so no real loss."

"Hmmm," Jude said. "I don't really think that's true. I think money is more like a river. You scoop some out, and more flows in. Enough for everybody. Fuck the pie idea. That's just lame."

Erinn thought about it. The river analogy *was* a much better way to think about it. And if money were like a pie, disappearing a slice at a time, than you'd guard it jealously. Massimo truly wasn't as innocent as she'd thought, on any level.

But Erinn was through thinking about Massimo.

The sun had completely set and a strong wind picked up over the ocean. Erinn looked at her watch. She probably had an hour or so before her houseguests descended. She invited Jude back to the house. They made their way into the kitchen. She set the camera down on the table and made coffee. Caro jumped into Jude's lap.

"Hey there, Truck!"

Erinn set out the coffee, and Jude caught Erinn up on the crew. Jude, Carlos, and Gilroi were all over at a rival production company working on a "new show"—Erinn noted that he left out the description.

"Even if APE gets going on *Let It Shine*, it will be a couple months before they're in production," Jude said. "You should come work with us. We'd have fun."

Erinn noticed that he said "come work with us," not "come work with me."

That says it all, doesn't it?

Erinn stirred her coffee and reached over to pat Caro. She didn't look at Jude and tried to keep her voice steady.

"I can't," she said. "I'm moving back to New York."

Jude almost lost hold of his cup, and set it down with a clatter. He put Caro on the floor and looked at Erinn.

"When?"

"Sooner rather than later," she said.

"Why?"

"Do you remember Lamont?"

"George Washington?"

"Yes, George Washington . . . well, George Washington the first. Or, the first George Washington. Either way, yes. George Washington."

"You hooked up with Lamont?"

"I'm not sure what you mean by 'hooking up' . . . I had *lunch* with

Lamont! If that qualifies as hooking up, then so be it. Just lunch. With some mutual friends from days gone by. With friends from back in the day, I suppose you'd say."

"OK . . ."

"When I was visiting my mother, an article ran about me in *Celebrity*. I didn't think anything of it, but apparently, it caused a bit of a sensation. Anyway, our friends—who back Broadway shows—decided that it would be feasible to do a revival of *The Family of Mann*. It looks as if it's going to happen."

"Oh," Jude said, not looking at her. He seemed to be fighting with himself, but Erinn couldn't decide what about. "Don't you want to stay in Santa Monica . . . now that you have a niece?"

Erinn was surprised at the tugging on her heart.

"Well," she said, "I'll miss seeing her grow up. . . ." Erinn wanted to say, "But my work has to take priority," but somehow the words wouldn't come.

Finally, he spoke again. "Oh."

"I thought you would be happy for me," Erinn said.

"Yeah, you'd think."

"But you're not?"

Jude stood up. He still wouldn't look at her.

"Does it matter what I think?"

It was Erinn's turn to stare at the table.

"Seriously, Erinn. I'm asking you. Does it matter what I think?"

"That depends."

"On what?"

"On what it is you think."

"Wow, you can dodge better than Bill Clinton," Jude said. "Now come on . . . would it matter to you . . . would you consider staying in Los Angeles if I told you that I . . ."

Jude stopped speaking. He absently picked up the camera and wouldn't meet her eye. Erinn wondered if he was stalling for time. He pushed the Rewind button and silently watched the video Erinn had just shot in the park.

The nerve!

She saw his expression change, and she looked over his shoulder to see what he was viewing.

The LCD screen showed the fire at the cabin in Valley Forge. She was sure she had deleted the footage! No, she hadn't! She'd just switched tapes! She couldn't believe she had left this evidence just lying around all these weeks. What if Baby Lizzy had seen it? She leaped for the camera, but Jude blocked her advance easily. He pushed the Play button, and the audio of their energetic lovemaking filled the kitchen.

Caro looked around the room, confused.

Erinn stared at her shoes for a moment, then took her seat. She willed herself to look at him. Jude was contemplating her in return. He shut off the camera. He stood up and started pacing, and Erinn grabbed the camera and pulled it to her as if it were an errant five-year-old throwing a tantrum in the center aisle of a grocery store.

"I think about you all the time, Erinn," he said quietly. "I think about us. You've changed me. I mean, I know I'm not the smartest tool in the shed. . . ."

"Sharpest tool . . . it's a simile."

Jude stopped pacing.

"Don't start."

Erinn held up both arms in surrender. Jude continued to pace.

"But I swear, Erinn, you've changed the way I look at . . . at everything. You've changed the way I think. I'm using the Internet to look stuff up, not just porn."

Erinn was startled by this admission, but merely shook her head sagely.

"I can't pull quotes out of my ass the way you do," Jude said. "But I found a quote I really liked."

Erinn waited. Jude seemed to have run out of steam. He stared out the back window.

"Do I get to hear it?" she asked.

Jude turned to face her.

"Oh, yeah. Sure," he said. He stared at his shoes. "In the arithmetic of love, one plus one equals everything, and two minus two equals nothing."

"But," Erinn said, "two minus two does equal nothing. That's not the arithmetic of love, that's just arithmetic."

"Aw, shit! I knew I'd blow it. Wait . . . it's one plus one equals . . ."

Erinn glimpsed the video on the LCD screen and memories flooded back. She thought about how alive she'd felt—and how easily she'd slipped back into her old habit of shutting out the world once she got home.

She made an instinctive decision . . . and went with it. She stood up and put her hands on Jude's cheeks.

"Before you venture into calculus," she said softly, "why don't you just kiss me?"

There was no hesitation. Both of them came to the kiss with an acute longing, as if they were saving each other from drowning. The kiss continued, until Caro, who had leaped up on the counter, roughly patted Jude's backside. Erinn and Jude broke apart and looked at the cat, who seemed to be glaring at Jude.

"Don't worry about him," Erinn said. "He's just hoping that 'This too shall pass.' "

"I hope he has to wait a long time."

They kissed again. Breathless, they stopped kissing long enough to embrace.

"I wasn't expecting that," Jude said.

"Nor I."

"I mean, I was hoping . . ."

"Go to the refrigerator and get some champagne," Erinn said, fearing words would ruin the moment. She was surprised by this. Words had always been her salvation. "I'll get the glasses. I guess we should celebrate!"

Jude popped the cork and poured the sparkling wine into the flutes in Erinn's hands.

"To what shall we toast?" Erinn asked.

"Dude . . . you're the one with the words."

"All right then," she said, raising her glass. "*Coincidence* is the word we use when we can't see the levers and pulleys. To coincidence."

"I don't know what the hell that means, but I'll drink to it." Jude kissed Erinn and headed toward the living room. "I'll start a fire—for old times' sake."

Jude started the fire, and Erinn curled up on the couch. It was dark, but she was loathe to turn on the light; the darkened room was much more evocative of the cabin.

"Just so you know," Erinn said, "I am smarter than the average bear. I did see the levers and pulleys."

"What does that mean?" Jude said, as he continued building the fire.

"Just that, unlike you, I was not born yesterday."

"As you've pointed out a zillion times."

Caro jumped onto Erinn's lap. She petted the cat contentedly, feeling the warmth of the fire on her face. She closed her eyes and sipped the champagne.

"I don't mean to brag, but I can see plot points when they are literally laid at my feet. I don't have all the pieces, of course, but I'd venture it goes something like this: I'm guessing that you've known I've been in town for a while, but have been lying low . . . until the time was right.

"And why now? Did my sister call you and tell you my defenses were probably down after the shower tonight? Was I supposed to think it was a *coincidence* that you showed up in the park this evening? I'll bet you memorized that little gem about the hugging at the same time you researched quotes on love. Am I right?"

"You're good. I'll give you that."

Erinn continued to stroke the purring Caro, who was kneading her lap.

"I was secretly hoping she would call you. But I couldn't be sure. I didn't know exactly where you stood, if you know what I mean. But I thought the best I could hope for was—you would let a day or two go by, just for show. I got nervous when I didn't hear from you. But—here you are!"

"You figured it out. Good for you."

"I wasn't positive at first. But then you mentioned that they called the baby *Lizzy*. Someone would have had to have told you that. So then, I knew I was right."

She toasted herself.

"And that's all that matters to you, isn't it? That you're right."

Erinn heard the shift in his tone. Alarmed, she opened her eyes. He was still kneeling by the fire, but he was looking at her. She met his gaze and was alarmed at what she saw.

"No!" she said. "Not at all! It's just that . . ."

"It's just that you have to rub my face in it for this to be truly perfect."

Jude stood up and headed toward the front door. Erinn jumped up, with Caro in her arms, and followed him to the door.

"No, Jude! My God!"

He reeled on her.

"You know what, Erinn? You *are* always right. You're right that this isn't going to work. What the fuck was I thinking?"

"No . . . I was wrong! I was very wrong. And I'll be wrong again, I promise."

"Save it. I'm out of here. Have a nice life in New York."

Jude slammed the door. Erinn tried to blink back tears. Why did she have to humiliate him? He was a wonderful, sensitive man and she'd driven him away. She was alone. She deserved to be alone. There would be no boy-gets-girl ending for her.

She put her head in Caro's fur and wept as the cat drooped sullenly in her arms.

Caro managed to leap out of Erinn's arms when the front door vibrated with a load banging.

"Erinn!" Jude shouted. "Open this door, goddamn it."

She opened the door.

"I am *not* going to let you drive me away."

Jude suddenly stopped and stared at her. Erinn drew herself up. She was not going to be confrontational but neither would she beg forgiveness. She had her pride.

God knows, she had her pride. She stared back at him.

"Yes?" she asked.

Jude tried to hide a smile.

"You have cat hair all over your face."

Erinn, mortified, ran to the mirror, wiping the cat hair away as fast as she could. Jude was howling in the background.

"Stop laughing," she said. "You've made me the fool."

"Oh, Erinn, knock it off. You've made your own goddamned self the fool."

As she finished wiping away her fur-encrusted tears, Erinn spotted her messenger bag. She took a deep breath and dug out her phone.

"Jude, I want to read you something," she said, quickly scrolling through the phone's functions. " 'Dear Jude, Years ago, there was a song that reflects my feelings now . . .' "

Jude put his hand over hers and snapped the phone shut.

"You don't have to read that to me."

"I really want you to hear how I feel," Erinn said, trying to pry the phone open.

"Then just tell me . . . just *talk* to me . . . don't read to me or quote at me."

Jude pulled her toward him and breathed in the scent of her hair. He took the phone out of her hand and threw it over his shoulder. Erinn heard the phone clatter on the Travertine tile.

"My phone . . ."

Jude's lips traveled the length of her neck.

"You needed a BlackBerry anyway."

Erinn melted into his embrace. She wasn't sure how much longer her legs would hold her. Jude suddenly pulled her away from him and held her at arm's length.

"Look, Erinn, I don't think you saved the footage from Valley Forge because you wanted to recycle tape. We both know that everything changed that night. You're a supreme pain in the ass, but we can have lots more nights like that."

"But not tape them."

"But not tape them," Jude said. "Well, actually, that tape was pretty hot."

Erinn looked alarmed, and Jude laughed.

"Chill, Erinn. I'm kidding," he said, then turned serious. "Listen, if you have your heart set on going to New York, I'll go with you. I'm sure I can get a stupid reality job there, no problem."

"I'm not going to New York," Erinn said.

"What? But you just said—"

"They don't need me there. They can start the revival without me. That's a closed chapter. My new life is here."

Jude brushed away a few of Caro's pewter-colored hairs and kissed Erinn lightly on both eyes.

"Dude," he said.

"Dude," she said.

They were jolted out of their kiss by banging in the kitchen. Erinn could make out the voices of Fernando and Carla.

"Yooo-hoooo," Fernando called.

"Anybody home?" Carla asked.

"I am," Erinn said, snuggling into Jude's embrace. "I'm home."

Celia Bonaduce is a producer on HGTV's *House Hunters*.
This is her second novel. She lives in Santa Monica, California,
with her husband in a beautiful "no-pets" building.
She wishes she could say she has a dog.
You can contact Celia at: www.celiab.name

PROLOGUE

Suzanna tended to cut herself a lot of slack, but to say she was thinking about stalking a dance instructor put her in a bad light—even to herself.

Her chance encounter with an amazing man who (it turned out) taught dancing definitely needed some spin. She decided to think of it as the universe's way of saying she needed to get into shape.

Suzanna was standing in line behind him at Wild Oats in Venice, California. The first thing she noticed about him was that he didn't have his own grocery bag with him. *Was he actually going to use a store bag*? Suzanna wondered.

He was a rebel—no doubt! She could tell he was gorgeous, even though she could only see him from the back. He had long black curly hair slicked back in a shiny ponytail. Suzanna didn't go for ponytails as a matter of course, but she could have written sonnets to this ponytail.

Except she couldn't write sonnets. But if she could have, she would have.

She tried to stand as close to him as possible, to judge his height. She guessed he was in the almost-six-feet category, and he had broad shoulders. Fernando, her best friend and co-worker, would have been smitten as well. He loved what he called "those lean, long-limbed gods." *Lean* was a good word, but to Suzanna's ear, it verged on *skinny,* which just wasn't sexy no matter what you called it. But this guy was not skinny. He was flawless. In the old days, she and Fernando would have spent hours giddily agreeing on the perfection of this man. They used to have the same taste in men. But their opinions about almost everything seemed to be going in different directions these days.

The man was wearing a white dress shirt—one that had been professionally laundered. You could have spread butter with the razor-sharp crease in the sleeve. He was also wearing black dress trousers . . . not pants, trousers. Suzanna was impressed. She always thought you could tell a lot about a man by his laundry. Eric, Suzanna's other best friend and other co-worker, probably would have said the guy was trying too hard and looked like Zorro. Suzanna could feel herself becoming irked with Eric for his snide comments, but she pushed the emotions back down. After all, he hadn't actually said that her fantasy man was trying too hard . . .she just figured he would.

What can you expect from a straight man?

There was a large, round security mirror in one corner of the store and Suzanna kept trying to angle herself so she could get a look at his face, but all she managed to do was knock over a display of organic oatmeal cookies. By the time she had finished paying for her groceries, he was gone. She sprinted, as casually as possible, into the parking lot, but he was nowhere to be found. Dejected, she hopped on her bicycle and headed out of the parking lot.

And that's where fate took a turn.

He hit Suzanna with his car.

Suzanna was sprawled on the ground, trying to catch her produce as it rolled by. She knew the man must be horrified by what had just transpired, even though he didn't get out of the car. He just opened his door and leaned out. Suzanna noted the BMW insignia on the hood. It was an older model, but very well-maintained, she noticed. She smiled at him to let him know that she was fine, but he didn't smile back.

He's just hit me with his car. Maybe he thinks it would be rude to look like he's taking the situation lightly.

Once Suzanna was on her feet, she realized he was as handsome as she'd imagined: deep-set, smoldering eyes and a slightly bored look. She was impressed that he could manage to look bored even though he had just hit somebody with his car.

Nerves of steel.

She walked over to the car window, showing off her hearty good health. By this time he had gotten fully back into the car, but he handed her his card and said in a mysterious accent:

"Call me if there is a problem."

And he drove off. She stared at the card. It had no name on it, just DIAGNOSIS: Dance! and the studio's address and telephone number.

Suzanna stared after the car.

She was shaken *and* stirred.

PART ONE

VENICE BEACH

CHAPTER 1

Suzanna knew she was out of her element as soon as she walked up to the dance studio. She couldn't help but compare the place to her own little run-down business on the other side of town. Her combination tea shop and bookstore was her pride and joy. Or the bane of her existence, depending on her mood. The place could have subbed as a location for *Fried Green Tomatoes: The Sequel.* A location scout had actually asked Suzanna about it. While the tea shop sat smack on the rundown boardwalk in Venice Beach, DIAGNOSIS:Dance! was on more ritzy Main Street—uptown in every sense of the word. Maybe not as uptown as Santa Monica, but Main Street was the best Venice had to offer.

As she walked into the dance studio, the wooden floors gleamed at her and the disco balls suspended from the ceiling threw off sparks of promise. The mirrors—the endless walls and walls of mirrors—showed nary a ghost of a fingerprint. Suzanna sneaked a peek at her reflection because, in all honesty, there was no escaping her reflection. She became instantly aware of the little muffin top peeking out between her T-shirt and jeans.

I look like someone who could use some dance lessons.

She hovered in the back of the studio and checked out the dancers as casually as she could. Some of them were clearly professionals, but Suzanna was relieved to see there were others who seemed like regular people . . .just ordinary folks who'd decided they needed to dance. Except even the regular people were beautiful. Everybody was in shape. Everybody had perfect hair. Even the janitor and the staff were fabulous. She could feel her nerve ebbing away.

Suzanna eyed the front door.

Too late for a graceful exit?

She started to leave, but caught sight of the gorgeous dance instructor from the Wild Oats entering through her escape route. He took her breath away, and she doubled her resolve to become a dancer as he glided past. She inhaled his exotic cologne, an intoxicating blend of lavender, peppermint, roasted coffee, tonka bean, and chocolate. Being raised in Napa Valley and running a tea shop gave Suzanna an edge when it came to identifying scents. She tried to focus, looked around, and located the front desk. She was determined to speak to a Beautiful Person in person.

This is going to be worse than signing up at a gym. That's not true. I don't think they are going to weigh me at the dance studio.

Dancers were swirling around in gaspingly ethereal pairs as she beat a path to the front desk. She felt like a colossus bushwhacking her way through gracefully swaying weeping willows.

The Beautiful Person looked up from her computer, looked at Suzanna, and screamed.

No, she didn't. But Suzanna was braced for it, and when it didn't happen, she was grateful for the woman's tiny benevolence. The Beautiful Person was so fragile, she appeared to be made out of lace. She looked like a faerie.

Suzanna started to swell.

"May I help you?" the faerie inquired in a whisper.

"I'm thinking of taking some dance lessons," Suzanna whispered back, trying to keep her feet on the ground. She was swelling so much, she was sure her feet wouldn't stay there for long.

"Private or group?"the faerie continued. Her voice was so wraithlike that Suzanna could barely hear her, even though Suzanna reckoned her ears might be clogged from the swelling. She didn't know which.

The faerie tactfully ignored the fact that Suzanna appeared to be ingesting several canisters of helium. The studio was a business, and Suzanna guessed the girl had seen all kinds. Suzanna knew about that. She owned a business herself.

Suzanna tried to keep her eyes from squeezing shut—the pressure was awful. She felt as if she were about to tip sideways and float to the ceiling, a bouncing, bloated gargoyle looking down on the Beautiful People below.

She hated when this happened. Eric and Fernando always insisted that she wasn't really bloating and floating, but Suzanna thought they were probably just being polite.

The first time she had what she referred to as a "panic swell," she was in junior high school and madly in love with a boy named J. Jay. They had a drama class together and were cast opposite each other as the leads in *Romeo and Juliet*. In rehearsal one day, Suzanna was standing on a ladder that was serving as the balcony and looking down at J. Jay, with his blond hair and blue eyes. She poured her heart into the dialogue, trying to convey that this was not just Shakespeare talking, but her—Suzanna. She infused adolescent passion into every syllable:

> My bounty is as boundless as the sea,
> My love as deep; the more I give to thee,
> The more I have, for both are infinite . . .
> I hear some noise within. Dear love, adieu!

Wildly in character, she turned on the ladder to determine what noise she was hearing from within, and *bammo,* she bumped down the ladder and fell to the floor in a heap. A gasp rose, in unison, from the other kids. As soon as it was clear that she was not dead, this being junior high the gasp turned into suppressed giggles and predictable guffaws. This was not the end of her humiliation, however. A collective gasp once again filled the auditorium as she picked herself up off the floor. She looked around at all the kids laughing and pointing, and that's when she started her first panic swell.

It started, as always, in her ears. She could no longer hear the kids laughing, making it doubly hard to determine what was so hilarious. Then, her body started to expand as the kids continued to point and the full weight of what was going on became clear. . .

The straps of her training bra had somehow come loose on her descent into hell, and her bra was circling her waist. At this point, she had liftoff. Her toes could no longer stay on the ground. She floated to the ceiling and bounced along the tiles until she managed to pull her shirt over the offending undergarment. To add insult to injury, J. Jay was leading the pack in their hilarity. Suzanna prayed that she would be able to stay on the ceiling forever, but suddenly, *pop!*—she was back on the ground, pretending to find the whole thing hysterically funny.

Suzanna pretended to laugh. Then she pretended to laugh harder. In the kill-or-be-killed world of junior high, Suzanna came up with one of her lifelong survival skills. In times of severe humiliation and mortification, she would laugh so hard it looked like she was crying. That way, when she *was* crying, no one could tell that her heart had been broken into a million pieces. It was really very effective, not to mention a great cover. It was something that she used many, many times in her life.

She recommended this approach to Fernando, who took it with a grain of salt—he had no problem weeping copiously when he was unhappy—and to Eric, who disregarded it. Suzanna thought grimly that she'd had to use this strategy when it came to Eric more than once in her life and that perhaps things would have turned out differently if he hadn't ignored it.

Through swollen eyes, she looked around the studio and saw that the dancers all seemed to be having private sessions. She thought of the hot dance instructor and how much fun it would be to have his entire focus. Even though she would, of course, have to pay for his complete focus.

Would it feel like going to a dancing prostitute?

But dancing was a wholesome, healthful activity . . . she wouldn't really be a "john," would she? Another possible plus: a private lesson would lower the risk of public humiliation.

"Private or group?" the faerie inquired again, sounding a little less serene.

Suzanna tried to steady her voice so that she sounded normal; the panic swell brought an elevated timbre to her voice.

"Private . . . I guess."

"Great! They are $120 a lesson."

The faerie beamed up at Suzanna, and *pop!*—she was back on the ground.

"Did I say private? I meant group."

What's a little more public humiliation anyway? I mean, after the bra incident, I'm a veteran.

"Groups are great, too," squeaked the faerie. "We have several different classes. Salsa, ballroom, tap . . ."

"Wow . . . so much to choose from."

"Level?" the faerie asked, switching gears.

Suzanna was momentarily stumped, but noticed a small anteroom at the studio, where a class was being taught by her handsome dance instructor. He didn't notice her staring as he whirled on assured feet and with his alluring hips.

'Who is . . . what is that class?" Suzanna asked.

"That's beginning salsa."

Watching the dance instructor in action, Suzanna felt remarkably . . . inspired.

"I'm a beginner," she said. "And I am going to start with salsa."

Suzanna rummaged through her purse and pulled out a credit card. She held it out to the faerie and then snatched it back. Her roommate, co-worker and co-best friend, Eric, in the midst of earning his business degree, had made their method of paying for things so elaborate that she could never keep her credit cards straight. She pulled out another card and handed it over. Suzanna took her receipt and looked at it with pride. She was signed up for classes on Monday nights at seven-thirty.

The faerie breathed, "You don't have to limit yourself to Monday evenings. You can come whenever you want. There are continuous salsa classes here and you can take any of them."

Suzanna felt all warm inside, as if the dance studio wanted to become her second home.

Classes were $15 a session (what a bargain!). The faerie told Suzanna to wear comfortable clothing and, if she were really serious about this, to get dance shoes. This sounded like sage advice: the faerie knitted her tiny brow when she said it. Suzanna stared mutely at her. Dance shoes. She should get dance shoes. But Suzanna had absolutely no idea what that meant.

Shoes in which I will dance, perhaps?

As Suzanna continued to ponder the mystery of dance shoes, the faerie slid a brochure toward her. Suzanna opened it. It was from a store called Dante's Dancewear, where she could buy dance shoes.

She choked when she saw the prices. There was nothing in the catalog for less than $130! Maybe she'd see about buying them later, when she was more in the swing of things.

Suzanna thanked the faerie and let her know in no uncertain terms that she would see her Monday, lest she think Suzanna a quitter. She slipped the brochure into her purse and headed toward the door, where she collided with her dance instructor.

"Oh, hi," she said. "We always seem to be running into each other."

The dance instructor blinked languidly at her.

"I'm going to start taking salsa lessons with you," she added.

He looked at her feet.

"Bring the right shoes."

Quivering from her encounter, Suzanna left the studio and the beautiful dancers behind, happy and terrified that she and her new dance shoes—which were now definitely part of the agenda—would be joining their ranks in a few short days.

Suzanna had never been much of a shoe girl. Even during the *Sex and the City* years, she couldn't imagine hobbling along the mean streets in four-inch heels. Plus, an upbringing in Napa in the eighties and early nineties didn't really lend itself to shoe lust. Napa was a big jeans-and-T-shirt kind of valley. The only place more casual than Napa, as far as Suzanna knew, was Hawaii. She had a friend from there who said he wore flip-flops and shorts every day all the way through high school. The school made the students wear long pants and closed shoes for graduation. Suzanna wondered if they had ever even heard of dance shoes in Hawaii.

It was evening and Suzanna had the bench outside the little library on Main Street to herself. She pulled out her dance shoes catalog and smoothed it open on her lap. She had stopped at Coffee Bean and Tea Leaf, ordered a Moroccan Mint Tea Latte, and poured it carefully into her bright-red travel mug. She wasn't exactly hiding the fact that she drank tea from a corporate chain, but she knew that many of her own customers would be more than a little surprised—and judgmental—if they knew she patronized such a place when she owned a tea shop herself.

One of Suzanna's little rebellions (and secrets) was that she loved the Bean. Suzanna knew there was no way to whip up those chemical-infused concoctions in her traditional space, but it was always fun to slip off to the Bean and sample whatever new, weird thing was being offered. She hadn't been in love with the Strawberry Crème tea, but, honestly, this chocolate-mint concoction was delicious . . . and the pomegranate-blueberry latte was a keeper.

Suzanna thought about her other secret. She had never kept anything from the guys before, and deciding to keep these salsa lessons on the down-low made her feel both guilt-ridden and exhilarated. Sort of like Diane Lane in *Unfaithful*, when she'd slept with Olivier Martinez and was horrified and proud of herself at the same time. Suzanna flushed. She knew just how Diane Lane's character felt. Powerful, for the first time in ages. Alive. Taking a chance, no matter what anybody thought. Ready for a change.

But too chicken to say it.

Taking a long, soothing sip, she thumbed through the dance shoes catalog, already feeling as if she'd been accepted into a secret club.

I am one with the dance world . . . or I will be when I settle on some shoes.

There was much to absorb. There were ballroom shoes, jazz shoes, tap shoes, and various rounded-toe versions of athletic shoes. Suzanna immediately discarded the jazz and tap shoes as they were footwear for avenues she was sure she was not (at this time) prepared to dance down. She was drawn to the athletic shoes, but something told her that these were not going to fly in the steamy world of Latin dancing. She didn't think athletic shoes were what the instructor had in mind when he sneered at her feet. Next, Suzanna rejected the ballroom shoes. They were too fancy, too high, too Beyoncé.

And then she saw them. A whole category called "character shoes." These were the perfect shoes for a woman in her thirties. A woman—grounded and with modest goals.

Well, if you called wanting to nail your new dance instructor a modest goal.

Made in the USA
San Bernardino, CA
19 April 2014